SHIVER

a novel

GRACE BOGAERT

Cover design by Danny F. Santos

Printed in Canada

ISBN 978-0-9936086-1-2 (pbk)

In memory of my parents,
free of winter at last.

Soon comes the cold, and the night that never ends.
George R.R. Martin

Prologue

Anna could step into the shoes of her clients and see their journeys. She could replay the events that led them to being on the wrong side of the law. Like this person here. Anna knew everything about her. The tumultuous upbringing. The lack of steady parenting. Her problems with drugs, alcohol, and money. Her vices and dangerous appetites. The ruinous decisions that undid her best intentions. The misguided quests for things and people she should have avoided.

Anna saw it as though she were living it herself.

Exactly like the defendant who stared wide-eyed, her long black hair dishevelled, her clothing unkempt and smelling like a few nights in jail. She could feel the glare of the judge, the jury, and the visitors. She could sense the frustration of the prosecutor who struggled to grasp how things had come to this. Anna knew that they didn't understand. As far as she was concerned there really was no such thing as the presumption of innocence.

But Anna could make the other side come around. She could make them understand. That was why she was one of the best criminal defense attorneys in town.

CHAPTER ONE
Trial and Error

Anna wore a slate-coloured suit with mother of pearl buttons. The tunic style jacket came down to the top of her hips. It was a simple, slender cut. It gave her an air of strength and authority. The grey tones set off her dark eyes and glossy black hair that trailed over her shoulders like long silk tassels. In her manicured fingers she held a graphite stylus pen that she used to point at details in exhibits, tapping insistently on certain elements for emphasis. Like a magician's wand, the pointer directed the eyes of the jury to places she wanted their minds to go. Almost controlling their thoughts. It added an air of drama and kept her audience alert and attentive to the ideas she wanted to convey.

Her wedding ring was never left at home, certainly not during a trial. The simple gold band sent a subconscious message to the twelve jurors that Anna Docstedder was loyal and trustworthy, that she took her vows seriously. She knew the jury would place more confidence in a married woman over any man. She used that to her advantage.

She could be dramatic and today she felt like she was in her element. She gestured toward her client, Lance Munson, who was on trial for murder. She had convinced him to shave his scruffy beard and trim his eyebrows. She made sure his long greying locks were shorn, replaced by a more corporate hairstyle. She coached Lance to improve his posture, sit up straight, and keep his shoulders back. She trained him to meditate to keep his thoughts mellow while antagonistic witnesses gave testimony. The last thing the jury should see were any outbursts of anger or dagger eyes that emerged when his temper flared.

He had played along for the most part. He wore out his one good suit that his sister, Tawny, had bought for him. He alternated between two dress shirts. Neither very crisp or neat after the 11 days in court.

"Lance Munson is a thief and he has a record a mile long. He had a tough childhood that led him to make mistakes. But Lance Munson is a good son. He's been a kind brother to his two sisters. You heard Tawny and Rose tell of his gentleness—his thoughtfulness.”

Despite her speech, Anna wondered to herself about Lance's sisters. Did Lance ever threaten them? And Lance's mom—did she feel guilty about the drunkards she brought home who beat her son?

“Lance has been enrolled in a carpentry program and he's proven himself to be a good worker.”

In fact, Anna's own father, Perry, was mentoring Lance. The elder was impressed with Lance's natural ability with wood. According to her dad, Lance had the makings of a master carpenter.

As Anna pivoted back to Lance, gesturing to him as though introducing him at a debutant's ball, she was caught off-guard for a second. Her eyes met up with those of Dale Corbeau, the lead investigator. Dale scowled at her, and she faltered briefly. *If looks could kill*, Anna thought. She took a deep breath and flung off his imaginary daggers.

He had a right to be angry, she admitted. She bird-dogged all his attempts to bring other cases into the mix—rapes, assaults, unsolved murders and even missing persons. He wanted to turn Lance Munson into some kind of criminal garburator, responsible for a swath of misdeeds over the past two decades. But it was not going to happen on her watch, so she fought everything with a series of motions and objections.

Right back at you, Dale.

It did not help that the Glace Bay PD had bungled the collection of evidence. After the body of Candace Louk had been found, they had failed to secure the area, thinking at first her death was an accident. By the time they had decided Candy had died of foul play, it was too late to go back and get tire track mouldings or other evidence.

Finally, Anna had been able to bring in Candace's boyfriend, Terrence Johnston, as a potential suspect. The former football player had been in and out of Miss Louk's life and their relationship had not always been trouble-free. She had once taken a restraining order against him. The steroids he abused added intensity to his jealousy. The former athlete went to great lengths to keep Candace from moving on without him, including blocking her with his 280-pound bulk.

All in all, there was only circumstantial evidence against Lance Munson. There was just not enough to convict him. But Candace's death had been gruesome, and so Anna worried that the jury would want someone—anyone—to pay for this. Demonstrating reasonable doubt might not be enough to keep Munson in the clear.

She spoke directly to the jury, appealing to them with her heartfelt words: "You don't want to send Lance to prison. You want to keep Lance on the path to rehabilitation. You want Lance to get out there and be a productive member of society, building homes for people and keeping them safe."

She studied the faces of the twelve jurors. Throughout the three-week trial, she had made a point of looking their way often, making direct eye contact to build trust and to gauge their understanding of the proceedings. The Glace Bay locals who made up the jury consisted of four women and eight men, mostly blue-collar types: a miner, a logger, a retired mechanic, but also a teacher and two homemakers. The eight white and two First Nation jurors were rounded off with two immigrants, one a Pakistani woman who ran a motel, the other a 50ish Lebanese man who had long given up hope of resuming his career as a dentist and now plied the gritty streets of his new northern Ontario hometown in an orange and green taxi cab.

Anna felt she had gotten to know them very well by now and sensed her words were having an impact. She thought she could see them turning. They gave her open gazes and even slight nods. Her closing statement was completed. The defense rested. Justice Tanner, gave the jury instructions and they were led out.

*   *   *

There was no news on the first day. Nor on the second. On the third day of jury deliberations, Anna had trouble concentrating on work. She had other cases to prepare so it was not like she could take the time off. She found it helped to pump music. She tucked ear-buds in and attempted to tackle some mundane paperwork.

There was a call just before eleven. The jury wanted to see the list of cell phone calls to and from Candace's phone. Anna thought it was a good sign. Rather than return to the office at lunch Anna withdrew to The Willow, a quiet, dimly lit bar, with an upstairs area that offered a glimpse of Lake Superior. No one was likely to bother her at this out-of-the-way place. She ordered a sparkling soda with lunch. She could not drink because she was pregnant, and oh, yes—she had once been an out-of-control barfly. But that was so long ago she hardly thought about it anymore.

3

She loved the feeling of being pregnant. The warm glow in the small of her belly. This pregnancy was going well, unlike the several others that had ended in miscarriage.

Anna was picking away at a goat cheese and pear salad when the call came to return. The jury had made a decision. At last. Her heart thumped, and her breathing became shallow and rapid. She fumbled in her purse for cash. She didn't want to waste the extra moments trying to pay by credit card. She grabbed her bag and hurried down the narrow hallway to the exterior door and pushed through.

Outside, the winter sun hit her eyes like a laser beam, temporarily blinding her. While reaching for her sunglasses, she heard a scraping sound behind her. Suddenly a woman in a ripped ski jacket with soiled cuffs appeared at her side, standing far too close for Anna's liking. The woman had stained teeth and sallow skin. Her long grey hair loosely knotted in a braid.

Anna wanted to hurry past but the stranger blocked her.

"You know your carpenter guy—the only thing he's good for is to make coffins. You're going to need a lot more of them if he gets out."

The shock of being accosted in the street unnerved Anna. Who was that woman? And what the hell did she know about Lance Munson?

The interloper with the ripped jacket vanished almost as quickly as she had appeared. Anna tried to put the incident out of her mind as she returned to the courtroom, hurrying into the oak panelled chamber. The pink granite floors clattered with the rush of feet as a crowd gathered to hear the verdict.

Suddenly Anna felt compelled to turn and glance up. She caught the glare of 'Ripped Jacket,' who at that moment was leaning over the railing in the upper gallery like a hostile gargoyle. Anna's heart leapt to her throat.

"All rise," came the deputy's voice.

With relief, Anna turned away again. She hauled herself to her feet unsteadily, palpitations rising. Perhaps it was the second heartbeat within her that stole her energy or perhaps the hostile look from behind her, but most likely it was that this was Anna's moment of judgement. When she would learn whether she had won or lost. She forced her hands to her sides, palms pressed inward. She darted Lance a warning look, as if to say: "keep cool."

As the jury was called back in, Anna scrutinized the expressions of each of the twelve members. The eight men and four women always entered in the same order. Midst their serious expression were a few tears. Anna took it as a promising sign that they averted their eyes from the victim's family and the prosecutor.

Judge Tanner cleared his throat. "Do you have a verdict on the charges of rape, forcible confinement and murder?"

Anna held her breath. She gazed as the jury foreman unfolded a piece of paper and shifted his body, holding himself with feet apart as though expecting to be tackled for what he was about to say. After each count, he read: "Not guilty." Then again, "Not guilty." And "Not guilty." It was like a slot machine win—three lucky sevens in a row. A wave of relief swept over Anna.

Munson clenched his left fist and pulled it tight to his side. "Yesss!" he hissed.

Anna smiled inwardly, feeling a weight lift from her. Even though she felt that the prosecution had failed to provide enough evidence, she hadn't been sure the jury would have seen it that way.

While Anna shook Munson's hand, a roar of protest erupted from behind them. A woman shouted "Murderer!"

Anna avoided looking for the source of the outburst. She had an idea who it was anyway—most likely Ripped Jacket making herself known. Anna quickly gathered up her papers and quietly asked Munson to meet her at the office.

*   *   *

"Maggie, you mind, when he comes in, just keep the door open and, uh—your ears tuned," said Anna to the pleasant-faced woman who helmed the front desk.

"Will do," said the receptionist. "Panama," she added winking. The country name was their safe word. Anna also used it at home.

Margaret Swann, or Maggie, was Cochrane McKay Docstedder's sixty-something receptionist and 'superwoman.' As the firm's mainstay, she had been begged away from retirement several times. Maggie could be relied on in any sort of emergency. Before becoming a legal assistant, she had worked as a parole officer and youth counsellor, so Maggie knew the system. On many occasions, Anna had sent Maggie in to talk to a teen in custody or calm a parent down after their kid had been charged with some misdemeanour. The woman had a good sense of whether a young person was destined for hell or would straighten up and eventually fly right. You could not buy wisdom or experience like Maggie had.

Anna just felt more comfortable and safer with Maggie around. But apart from the reassuring presence of their elderly receptionist, the law firm had instituted other safety precautions. Emergency alarms in each of the offices; locking doors; the police on speed dial; CCTV cameras and various recording devices. It was normal at this firm whose business was two-thirds criminal law.

Her phone buzzed and Anna grabbed it.

"Mr. Munson to see you," came Maggie's voice.

"Send him in."

Within seconds Munson strode into the room, jaunty, still revelling in his newly freed status. Anna noticed he had already loosened his tie. He pulled the blue silk accessory off and dumped it unceremoniously on her desk.

"Won't need this noose anymore!" Munson laughed.

Anna chuckled. "There are men who wear those day in and day out."

"Suckers. Can't see it myself."

"Guess, it's not who you are, eh."

"Damn straight."

"You thirsty?" she asked, getting up.

He grunted something that sounded like a yes. No matter. She was antsy and nervous and had to keep moving. She went to a small refrigerator tucked into a wall unit and got him a can of Sprite. When she handed him the soft drink, he looked slightly disappointed.

"Don't suppose you've got something to throw in here?" He understood by her frown that she did not have the Jack Daniels he was hoping for. "And you should be popping the bubblies. Come on. That was some performance."

"It was, even if I say so myself. Thank you."

"Man, Corbeau was pissed. You get a look at him? He had steam coming out of his ears. Anna, you got him good."

She felt a tinge of guilt. But why should she? *What was the matter with her—was she going soft? Hormones perhaps.*

"If any of those gals heard you, they'd be sure I's innocent too—Guess they're not gonna get the chance."

Anna froze. The statement hit her like a pail of ice water thrown in her face. Callous and chilling, the words sullied her honest work. Had he really just said that?

"I'm just kidding," Munson added quickly, noting Anna's pale expression. He flashed her a reassuring grin.

She nodded and forced herself to smile. Was she naïve enough to believe that just because he was found not guilty, that it meant he was actually innocent? She had been so focussed on finding the flaws in the investigation that she chose to ignore what it meant if she were to win the legal battle. It was a win for justice as a whole—*but was it?*

Anna told herself that the rumours that swirled around Munson were only that. Besides, you can't convict on gossip and anecdotes. You need hard evidence, which the prosecution had failed to provide. Anna was just doing her job. A job she did well.

Munson quietly slid a small parcel across her desk. Surprised yet intrigued by the gesture, Anna reached for it. Munson watched while she opened it, waiting expectantly—like a child anxious to please a parent with a gift purchased with his entire piggy bank savings. As Anna peeled apart the tissue wrapping, she felt sharp edges protruding, already tearing the delicate paper. Inside was a small carving, beautifully made, with fine detail, fashioned into an unusual design, almost like a Celtic knot.

"What is it?" Anna asked.

Munson shrugged. "It's just something I came up with."

"It's very special," she whispered, her admiration sincere.

"Thanks," he said, touched that she appreciated his gift.

"Where do you get your ideas?"

"Just comes into my head," he said, uncomfortable with the flattery.

"Wow, that's very sharp," said Anna, testing the edges with her fingertips.

"That could kill someone if you used it the right way," Munson added.

Anna's heart skipped a beat. She paused before speaking, "You mean *the wrong way.*"

"Whatever."

*　*　*

Later as Anna drove home, she thought about Munson's take on art. His tiny sculpture that was decorative but also lethal. Beauty with a deadly purpose. It was an insight in how he viewed the world. She wondered what could Munson have become had his life been different. Would he have created things that were pure art and not weaponry that happened to be artistic?

Lost in thought, Anna was unaware that her speed had crept up. When her car started to slide, her mind refocused, suddenly in survival mode. She braked and the car slid, everything within it catapulting forward. Her monogrammed leather briefcase slid off the seat, opening and disgorging papers. Fortunately, she was alone on the road, and she quickly regained control, moving back into her lane. It occurred to her that had she spun out into the ditch, there would have been no way for her to call for help. On this remote stretch of the highway, there was no cell service.

It was with considerable weariness, that Anna finally arrived home. Once in the driveway, she leaned over the front seat and took a few minutes to gather up her papers from the floor of the car. There among the debris of her briefcase contents, she found Munson's carving—his gift to her from that afternoon. His token of gratitude, with the jagged edges. She placed the object in her pocket.

The path to the side door was uneven from the lack of regular shovelling so Anna stepped gingerly. Her husband Xavier was preoccupied with the huge addition project that he had undertaken and had little time left for small maintenance chores. The smell of chicken and celery greeted her as she entered. A half-eaten casserole along with greasy dinner dishes sat on the table. From the far interior of the house came the grinding whir of a saw.

Passing through a series of dust-covered sheets of plastic, staggered like an entrance to a quarantine, Anna arrived in view of Xavier. He did not notice her right away, his peripheral vision obstructed by the safety goggles covering his eyes; and the sound of her voice blocked by the loud buzzing of the saw.

"Xav!—Hey!"

When he finally became aware of her, he turned off the machine. He smiled and lifted his glasses. As they kissed, tiny particles of sawdust transferred from his sweatshirt to her coat like pollen carried from one flower to another.

Their son René, who had been tinkering with a small hammer and nails in a corner of the room, jumped up when he saw his mother. He was a lithe little boy with glossy black hair and deep brown eyes. He had his mom's olive skin colour and almond-shaped eyes. The five-year-old joined in on the hug, squeezing in between his parents.

"René sandwich," teased his father.

CHAPTER TWO
La Famille

A horn blasted from somewhere outside. Anna peered out onto the driveway noticing a newer model black SUV.

"The PQs have arrived," Anna said. PQs was code for Xavier's parents, Sophie and Charles Durand who came from Montreal. The PQs were here for a belated Thanksgiving celebration.

Ever since René was a baby, Xavier and Anna had hosted the Durand and Docstedder clans for Thanksgiving dinner. But this year the celebration was delayed for several weeks because Anna was preoccupied with Munson's trial. Also, she was in the early stages of her pregnancy. Given her history of miscarriages, they had agreed to wait until she had safely passed the first three months.

Anna preferred Thanksgiving to Christmas because she didn't have to fuss with gifts and decorations. There were no stressful shopping trips and late-night wrapping sessions. She could focus entirely on food and fun.

She laid out the table in rustic fashion, arranging circular slabs of pine on a sheath of rough linen. Xavier had taken a router to the discs and gouged out holes to fit small votive candleholders. Anna wove boughs of evergreen with oak leaves and acorns around the pine disks creating an indoor forest effect.

She hoped no one would mind that she was using plain white Corelle dinnerware rather than *grand-mère* Eloise's old china. The delicate porcelain required washing by hand to preserve the gold edging and Anna had no energy for that extra work, not with all that had been going on.

Sophie and Charles had decided to book a hotel in Glace Bay instead of staying with Anna and Xavier. Xavier groused to Anna: "Is our home not good enough for them?" Xavier interpreted—and Anna could not disagree—that his parents were once more making a point about Xavier's choices. His decision to be a carpenter rather than follow in his father's footsteps as an architect; his choice of wife, a First Nation's woman who spoke no French; and his home in a remote northern community, so far from Montreal, and in another province as well.

Charles and Sophie weren't overtly hostile but certainly Anna always detected a slight coolness toward her, although since René was born their treatment of her had improved—but just a bit.

Anna cringed as Charles unpacked a case of wine. The heavy glass clanging, bottles butting up against each other. She hated that they drank so much and assumed that everyone else must as well. He began to unload rounds of goat cheese, Oka, and red pepper jelly. *Specialités de la belle province*. Subtle hints to Xavier of the sacrifices he was making by living in this backwater. Glace Bay offered none of the same gourmet offerings. Pickled trout, fry bread or pemmican just did not compare.

During pre-dinner preparations, Sophie took Anna aside and whispered that she wanted to show her daughter-in-law something. They exited the house and crunched carefully along the path toward the rental vehicle. Sophie popped the trunk. Stashed inside were shiny green and red wrapped parcels protruding from several shopping bags—Christmas gifts, almost entirely for René. There was no doubt the elder Durands loved René and were determined to spoil him. It would be good, Anna thought, to have another grandchild in the picture to balance out the attention.

As they stood in the driveway, a cold wind ruffled the lush fox fur collar of Sophie's elegant winter coat. With her large matching hat, she looked like a Russian tsarina. Anna leaned into the car to grab the presents. As she did, the crisp plastic crackled from the cold. Sophie made a feeble effort to take the bags from Anna, gesturing with her calf-skinned gloves, "You should not! Let me!"

"I'm fine," Anna lied. Nevertheless, the handles of the heavy bags bit into her palms. Needles of pain snaked through her shoulder, but she couldn't let her elderly mother-in-law take the parcels.

While they trod back to the house, their feet cautiously navigating the icy walkway, Sophie told Anna that she and Charles would be on a cruise over the holidays and would miss Christmas with them—again. Anna knew Xavier would be disappointed. She could safely predict he would grumble about not seeing his parents for the holidays, while in the same breath he would complain that they were spending his inheritance on extravagant vacations.

"Where are you going?" Anna asked. She wondered if there could be any place in the world they had not already seen. They had been on so many tours. Surely there was little left unexplored by them.

"For two months we voyage to Argentine, Uruguay, and Brazil," said Sophie, her accent lending an extra exoticism to the South American destinations. "We have four weeks by ocean, and then by the land we travel to the shoots of Iguazu."

"Oh!" said Anna, puzzled at first, but then she understood, that by *chutes* Sophie meant waterfalls. "Iguazu Falls."

"A *merveille* of the world," Sophie said.

"That sounds amazing. They say you have to try the *cuy al horno*. It's roast guinea pig."

"Non, non!" protested Sophie with a sweep of her fine gloved hand. "I do not eat Fido, even if my plane is falling to the Andes. I would prefer to starve."

Yeah, I bet, thought Anna.

* * *

The turkey came out glistening and golden. Xavier carved it up into juicy slabs that they slathered in gravy. Aunt Flo contributed a spicy pumpkin pie with a buttery crust, and Perry a wild rice dish with mushrooms and nuts. Anna had double servings of everything—her excuse was she was eating for two.

There were lots of questions about her condition. Her history of miscarriages had firmly planted the idea that it was unlikely that Xavier and Anna would ever have more than the one child, so the fact that Anna was now safely into the second trimester was a miracle.

Once the wine was flowing, Xavier's parents relaxed that slight air of snobbishness they always tended to show when around Anna's relatives and they began to engage in genuine conversation with Perry and Flo. Charles, was a renowned Montreal architect, who had designed an art gallery in the Gaspé, mansions in Westmount, and a prison outside of Ottawa. Knowing that Perry had been volunteering with a group of ex-cons at a halfway house for several years now, he asked Perry about his work. And soon the two got into a discussion about how prison spaces affected the chances for the rehabilitation of convicts. Anna listened with half an ear to the men while also tracking the conversations between Flo and Sophie. René sat contentedly on his *grand-maman's* lap, allowing her to run her fingers through his silky black hair as though he were some well-behaved pet.

Anna exchanged a look with her husband. He raised his eyebrows and smirked, as though to say, *"Can you believe this?"* He was likely just as pleased and surprised at the congenial atmosphere of their family gathering as she was.

As dinner wound down, Perry got up to show the guests some of the handicrafts of the former prisoners he worked with at the shop. "It's quite something, the stuff these guys make," said Anna's father as he hefted a cardboard box onto his empty chair and unfurled a crumpled newspaper, pulling out several carved wooden pieces.

Perry would often pick the best of the ex-cons' work to share with the family. Decorative and functional items he nick-named "ConCraft." He paid a nominal amount to buy the samples, but the money went to a worthy cause. As Anna had learned months before, her dad had also mentored Munson. It was a family business, she mused, the care and guidance of wayward men.

René's eyes lit up as he took in one of the pieces, a woodsman with a movable arm. At the end of the limb was a silver axe that swung up and down onto a tree stump. The creation was clever and skilful. It was the next best thing to a Transformer.

They had already started to drift away from the table when Xavier proposed they all sit by the fire. The guests moved slowly, their bellies laden with food, and their legs stiff from sitting so long. They gathered in the den where Xavier opened the fire screen and threw on another log. Embers scattered in the hearth like panicked fireflies.

Perry slid the coffee table to one side to make room for charades. They began by taking turns, Anna, then Charles, followed by Flo, choosing politicians and everyday objects, as well as movie and book titles as topics. For his turn, René did a cryptic robotic mime that Anna quickly guessed was a Transformer. Knowing he relished being in the spotlight of his adoring grandparents, Anna let him go on for a few minutes before shouting out her answer.

"How did you get that?" Xavier queried, eyeing his wife with mock suspicion.

"How did you not!" laughed Anna. "You don't know your own kid!"

Xavier scoffed.

Sophie rose next, rolling an imaginary movie camera and gesturing with her fingers to indicate a four-word title. She began to act out the second word when suddenly she became agitated. It was baffling. Shouting "*incendie*," she pointed above their heads.

Charles immediately protested, *"Il ne faut pas parler, cherie!"* he said, reminding her that talking was against the rules of charades.

"Mais, non! Il y a une incendie!" she insisted.

"Quoi?"

While her in-laws still argued, Anna turned around to look behind her. She gasped to see a mass of flames. The dining room table was ablaze. The rustic wood centrepiece had caught fire. The melting candles must have connected with the very combustible garlands of pine boughs.

"Shit!"

Anna dashed to the table, grabbing glasses of water and dumping them on the flames. Xavier was right behind her and slammed a pot lid overtop the candles, squelching the fire's source of oxygen. Perry soon followed with more water and doused what remained of the fire. Within seconds the fire was out. The table glistened like a newly misted vegetable display at the supermarket.

Whhheeeet! Whhheeeet!

Only then did the fire alarm respond to the trace of smoke.

René who had hopped onto the coffee table for a better view, stomped his little feet in excitement. He put his fingers in his ears to block the shrill sound. Flo took hold of his waist to make sure he did not fall, but a bowl of potato chips was not so lucky. The container toppled, scattering its contents. Peals of laughter broke out midst the cacophony and ensuing chaos. The irony of the alarm's belated timing was not lost on them.

"That's just great," said Xavier as he hauled a stool underneath the shrieking alarm. He stood up and fussed with the ivory plastic disk, cursing in French as he struggled to find the reset button. At last, the alarm was silenced.

Xavier hopped off the chair. Perry was chuckling. Charles shook his head.

"I feel so safe," Anna quipped.

"Yeah," grunted Xavier. "Well that's what happens when you have high ceilings."

"Well," said Charles. "Maybe you should give the tour of the house now—before it all burns away."

Everyone laughed, including Xavier but Anna could tell he was miffed.

As Xavier exited with the charred disks of pine and singed tablecloth, a blast of cold air flooded the room. With it came a low rumbling sound. It was the droning of distant snowmobiles, louder at times then fading like waves on a shoreline.

Their voices died down and the family was drawn toward the windows, curious to glimpse the source of the noise. Here and there they could see small cones of light criss-crossing the lake.

"There they go again," said Anna, "'tis the season."

"That shouldn't be allowed," grumbled Flo.

"How come?" René asked.

"Well, honey, because it's late at night and people expect some peace and quiet," Anna replied, brushing her son's shoulders. "Besides, it's so dark. It's dangerous. You wouldn't know if there is wire fence there or how thick the ice is."

"What are you going to do?" the boy asked.

"I don't know that I would, or could, do anything," she shrugged.

"She will sue them, take them to the court," said Charles, laughing.

Anna ignored her father-in-law. She found a pair of binoculars and hung them around René's neck.

"I can't see—" René's small hands clasped the black rings.

Anna leaned in and adjusted the focus for him. "That better?" she asked.

"Oh! There's one! Cool!" René cried. "Can we get one?"

"A snowmobile!" Anna replied.

"Yes!"

"It's not as fun as it looks," she said.

"Maybe when you're older," Xavier added, putting his arm on Anna's shoulder.

"Awww. How old?"

"Then he can whiz by the trailer park and keep those folks awake," Perry chuckled.

Long after the adults had grown bored of watching the distant lights from the snowmobilers, Anna noticed René still gazing out the window, adjusting the binoculars on his own. She wondered if he would ever be like these night marauders, blasting around the snow dunes, machine-gunning nature in its dormant season, when creatures just wanted to hibernate in peace.

*   *   *

"Okay, let's do the tour. Maman and Papa want to leave soon," Xavier said.

The Durands however seemed to want to skip the tour altogether. "It's late and I'm tired from the *voyage*," said Charles.

14

This annoyed Anna. *Tired from the trip, really? More like pissed to the gills.* Did anyone else notice how much they drank? *Vini, vidi, vino.*

"You folks can stay here," she offered, a part of her was thinking about the legal implications of allowing a drunken guest to get behind the wheel of a car. In her head she went over the many winding turns on the road back to town.

"All our things are at the hotel," Sophie demurred.

"We can drive you back too," suggested Perry. "It's on our way."

"But then the *véhicule* is here," said Sophie.

"*Merci*, but I think tomorrow, it's not so obscure, we can see better, so we will depart now," said Charles.

If it was too dark to have a house tour, then it was too dark to drive, Anna thought, but she saw the futility in trying to argue with her in-laws. Xavier made a grunting sound, as though this was as firm as he could get with his parents.

"Somehow I have the idea it will not have changed much by the time we return," chortled Charles.

Anna made a face. She did not like the teasing at Xavier's expense. The Durands' only son had been eager to show off the progress of the 'west wing.' The overly ambitious addition, Xavier's pet project, had been undertaken in a time of unfettered optimism. When plans made up on paper—with Charles's assistance it should be noted—were deemed easily transferable to reality. But the sheer scale was overwhelming at times. And Xavier mostly had to toil away on the addition alone.

She knew he must be disappointed his parents were lukewarm about seeing the work. So after Sophie and Charles left, she encouraged Xavier to show Perry and Flo around anyway. Even though Flo, herself, was not a big fan of the project. Before they had broken ground more than a year ago, Flo had been vociferous in getting Xavier and Anna to abandon the idea.

"You'll never get to enjoy it," she had said. "You'll always regret it."

And they were loath to admit it, but already the cavernous monstrosity was draining them of energy and money. The cosiness of their original home was sucked out through the gaping hole that was their dream space. The sky had once been the limit but now it was bounded by the inaccessible and uninsulated rafters.

As the guided tour got underway, Xavier led the group through a hallway sealed off by wide sheets of plastic. The thin opaque film whooshed as bodies moved past. Displaced air hissed and particles of dust wafted up like a thousand miniscule ghosts. The cold travelled quickly, inserting itself in their clothing like prying fingers. The warmth was all gone in an instant. Flo gave a shiver.

"Must be costing a lot to keep your house heated," Perry said, stating the obvious.

"Yeah," Xavier said. "But I should have the insulation up soon.

They discussed hiring someone to help enclose the space and keep out the cold. "I might know a few guys who could help," Perry offered.

"Dad, if you're thinking of any of your clients," Anna piped up, "I'd really like to keep work away from home." She met his eyes, knowing he would understand that her home would not—could not—be an extension of his halfway house.

Flo was mumbling something now.

"What's that?" said Anna.

Flo hesitated, then spoke up. "You can burn all the sage you want, but you can never burn enough to clear out the bad spirits."

Xavier and Anna shared a look. They had heard this from Flo before but never with such insistence. She was usually more circumspect, more diplomatic. Tonight she was adamant that they sell the house immediately and move. As though they could just snap their fingers and make it happen, assuming that is even if they wanted to. Xavier tried to humour Anna's aunt.

"Come on, Flo, it can't be that bad."

"It is that bad, Xavier. This house is cursed, and the land you've built on."

Anna sidled up to Xavier and rubbed the small of his back, as though with this gesture she could brush away Flo's negativity.

Perry hinted to Flo that it was time to head back to town and the old woman seemed more than eager to comply. "I'm going to go with the Flo," Perry said, "because it doesn't seem like any of you are."

Anna laughed half-heartedly while Xavier remained silent. "It's not like we're really against the Flo," Anna teased.

Flo bristled at the good-natured ribbing. "It's no joking matter. Swear to God, you'll come crying to me," Anna's aunt said as a final statement. She huffed as she exited with Perry.

After Xavier closed the door behind them, he turned to Anna with a forced smile, "You think Flo hates our house?" he said.

"Naw, what gave you that impression?" Anna shook her head, laughing.

"Something about the ground opening up underneath us and our falling into a pit of poisonous snakes."

"I'm okay with snakes," Anna giggled.

CHAPTER THREE

Goodnight Fish

"Not a whole ton, sweetie. Count them out in your palm first. Think of each of these grains as a whole slice of bread." Anna hovered over René as he dropped fish pellets into a wide aquarium perched in one corner of his bedroom.

"You wouldn't want a loaf of bread for dinner, just a few of slices, right?"

The blue and black creatures seemed startled by the food cascading down. The tiny swimmers darted back and forth near the water's surface and then after the pellets were consumed, slipped away to the safety of the fake rock castle and plastic ferns.

Following the feeding of the fish, the brushing of teeth, and the other bedtime rituals, Anna tucked René under the layers of moose print flannel sheets and soft duvet. He had to be toasty and warm. Whatever the state of the rest of the house, his room was a well-appointed boy-cave.

"Mom, are there snakes under the house?"

"Geez, nooo!" Anna could kick Xavier for joking about a reptile invasion while René was listening, all ears.

"Why did Aunt Flo say that?"

"Did she?"

"Uh-huh."

Anna sighed. "You know she just wants us to move to town."

"How come?"

"Because she's lonely and she misses having us close by."

"Why don't we?"

"What? Move to town?"

René nodded. His solemn black eyes drove straight to her heart.

"Well, we like it here. Don't you like living by the lake? Soon we can go ska—"

"Is the table still burning?"

Anna winced. Here was yet another anxiety of his revealing itself. "What? No, sweetie. No! We put the fire out. You saw us."

"Yeah but sometimes it burns on the inside."

Anna was surprised at René's fear. She didn't want to simply dismiss his worry and thought over how to reassure him that they were safe. "I'll get Daddy to check it one more time," Anna said. She moved to the doorway and called out. "Xavier!"

Seconds later, footfalls could be heard, and then Xavier appeared in the doorway, slightly out of breath.

"What's up?" He squinted at Anna, taking in her look of concern, and René sitting upright in the bed with a worried expression.

"Honey, René is thinking that the table might be burning—*on the inside*—can you put some more water on it?"

Xavier nodded. "Yeah, I've heard of that happening. Good thinking." Xavier gave René a thumbs-up. "Better to be safe than crispy."

Anna rolled her eyes at Xavier's attempt at humour.

To encourage calm, Anna moved slowly to René's side and stroked his face and let her hands softly brush his shoulders. After a moment, she tiptoed to the side of the room and eyed the bookcase. She picked through the boy's vast collection of books, stuffed on several shelves. There should certainly be something here to distract him from his anxieties.

There were compelling yarns about animals and heroes, but René's preference often ran to catalogues of machines. Anna wanted to avoid that tonight. She was not keen on lists of excavators and their functions. They compromised and settled on a popular classic about a steam shovel that got stuck in the basement of a building it helped construct. The saga ended happily with the steam shovel being repurposed as a furnace for the new building.

As René listened intently, Anna thought about the book's underlying message—the self-sacrifice of the steam shovel, it's rehabilitation and transformation—or entrapment— for the good of others. She wondered what her little boy got out of the story.

Xavier came in at this point, gripping his guitar. He took the pick between his fingers and began to strum a little lullaby as Anna listened, snuggling with René.

After a few moments, Xavier put down the guitar and came toward the bed. He leaned down to kiss them both, mother and son. To Anna he whispered, "What do you say, you ditch the kid and come over to my place?"

Anna smiled. "I'll be there soon," she promised.

Anna stayed a little longer, ensuring René was fast asleep. Then she also took leave. She was quietly inching out of bed and reaching to turn out the light on the bedside table, when she noticed something beside the lamp. It was the statue of the woodsman.

She reached for it and brought it in for closer examination. She felt she already knew the craftsman just based on the pattern of the many tiny divets and gouges. She had seen the energy of this carver's knife before. As Anna turned over the woodsman figurine, and read the initials on the bottom, she was not at all surprised.

L.M.—Lance Munson. Here was the proof. He was an art-ist—not a killer.

CHAPTER FOUR
Xavier and Anna in Love

Anna felt dead tired as she scraped the turkey bones and blobs of cranberry off the plates. The stack of dishes was daunting. She jammed as much as possible into the dishwasher and set the machine on start, waiting for the much-appreciated hum—the signal that the machine had promised to take it from there. *You can go rest now*, it seemed to say.

She lifted a large platter into the sink and covered it in suds using one of those dual sided sponges. She did not hear him come up from behind her, what with the dishwasher running and the tap streaming. He locked in behind her and grabbed her, squeezing her breasts. A signature Xavier move. He was not the most adept of lovers, she thought to herself ruefully. He had obviously not remembered from the last time that she had been pregnant that her nipples could be sensitive. Still, she felt flattered that he desired her, despite her protruding belly and her moodiness.

He led her out of the kitchen and up to their bedroom. She let him peel off her clothes until she was naked. He was always ready to go in ten seconds flat, like a rodeo bull knocking at the gate. It was good to have him back inside. The warmth of his body and his musky scent restored her. She rode with him to the outer reaches of bliss. When they were done, she lay back on the large fur rug and exhilarated in the afterglow, the ripples of pleasure continuing to vibrate.

"I think you got me pregnant," she said teasing him.

His long fingers slid over her belly and inched lower. She exhaled in the expectation of more. "It's going to be twins then. Or maybe triplets." He eased back into her and they were off again.

Afterwards they showered together, sharing the hot water and the steam, like scalloped shells bumping against each other on a beach as waves pulsed.

As Anna dried her hair, Xavier retreated to the living room. When she turned off the blow dryer, she caught the strumming of his guitar and his voice tentative as it tested a new song.

21

She shuffled downstairs and found him next to the fireplace, pencilling notes on a scrap of paper. He was writing a song he planned to dedicate to the baby. "What do you think?" he asked.

It was so sweet, thought Anna. She loved that about Xavier. "I'm a fan and so is this guy," Anna said pointing to her abdomen. "I feel him kicking to the beat."

"No kidding," Xavier laughed and set aside the guitar and kneeled before Anna. He placed his head against her belly.

"You rock his world," she said. She stroked Xavier's hair as he waited for some signal from his unborn child.

Xavier stared up into Anna's eyes. Tears welling up, "I love you," he murmured.

Anna sighed contentedly. "Ditto, baby."

A distant roar snuffed out their perfect moment. It sounded like an approaching army of skidoos converging on the foreshore of the frozen lake. Xavier broke away as though released from a spell. The noise brought them out of their happy bubble.

Anna exhaled. In spite of the irritation at the intrusion on their peace, Anna could not resist going to the window to see the far-off lights of the snowmobiles. There was something exciting about the energy of the night crawlers. The zip and swing of headlights and the roar of the motors.

She could not see her son but upstairs, René tossed in his sleep, the noise penetrating his dreams.

When Anna turned back from the window, Xavier was placing his guitar in its case and leaning it against the wall. He was done with the music for now.

CHAPTER FIVE

Flo's Medicine

As Anna pulled René off his booster seat, she felt a little twinge in her back. She must stop doing this, she thought. René can unbuckle himself. Just because he was a tiny kid didn't mean he wasn't capable. Although, for safety reasons, they had drilled into him that he could not just undo his seatbelt without his mom or dad's permission.

Anna grabbed her purse, tucking a crisp white drugstore bag inside. This was a meds run for Aunt Flo. The receipt was stapled to the top: Flora Docstedder.

Anna tapped on the door of the 1950s' bungalow in Morse code fashion, then used her own key to open up. The smell of baking wafted from the warm kitchen. Flo was a raging diabetic but that didn't stop her from repackaging sugar in various forms like a hard-core dealer.

When they came in, Bitty the cat bounded off the top of the lounger and tiptoed toward them. Bitty was an ironic name for the black and white feline who was by no means 'itty-bitty' at all but quite massive, perhaps because she emulated Flo's bad eating habits. Because of her colouring, she resembled a miniature Holstein, which led Anna and Xavier to refer to her as the 'Cow Cat.'

René found his way to his great aunt and they exchanged a hug. Flo stooped over the little boy and playfully swatted his bum twice, "That's for not visiting me more."

"Hey!" Anna said, giving Flo a mildly angry look. "We don't do that in our family."

René was unperturbed. He knew Flo was 110 per cent love. He made a beeline for the countertop where a tray of oatmeal chocolate chip cookies was cooling. René was crazy about Auntie Flo's cookies.

As Anna was about to scold him for being forward—she thought he was going to grab a cookie without asking—he turned to his great-aunt and asked in a sweet voice: "May I have one, please?"

"Ya sure can, kiddo! Take a fistful for all I care."

"Thank you!" said René eagerly.

"I don't eat that stuff myself."

Anna scoffed.

"And you," Flo said, pointing at Anna, "better have three, you look starved."

Anna pressed a fist against her stomach. "I'm still feeling queasy. My appetite's not great."

"I wish I could give you some of mine."

Anna got up to make tea. While she waited for the water to boil, she glanced around Flo's kitchen. It was a tiny open concept affair with an island dividing the cooking area from a small dining room on the other side. It was piled high with dishes, jars, bags of wool and beads.

Flo was crafty and artistic. She always had some project on the go. She carded wool and made weavings, incorporating interesting found objects. Anna admired her aunt for keeping up the traditions and making up some of her own along the way.

"How's the house going? Almost finished?"

"Hah!"

"How many more weeks?

"It'll get done when René graduates from high school—if we're lucky."

"Why don't you sell it and move to town?"

Anna sighed. She knew where this was going. Flo would talk about the bad roads, Anna having to drive back and forth, René having to be on a school bus, the lake, and the crazies out in the woods.

"There's a nice house for sale, three blocks from here. All fixed up."

Anna rolled her eyes.

"It has a hot tub on the back deck. You could give birth to your next one in that."

"Flo, geez."

"Oh yeah, it doesn't have a view of the lake—but hell, all your view's good for is to see the swarm of black flies coming at you from a mile away."

Anna sunk lower into the floral loveseat opposite Flo.

"And the work you're gonna have, trying to scrape the dead bugs off those damn big windows."

Everything Flo said was true. Anna hadn't wanted to think about the logistics of cleaning those giant panes, getting a ladder tall enough to wash the huge windows. Notwithstanding the spectacular vistas of Lake Mikwam, it would be a challenge to try to get the cobwebs out of the arching ceilings and the fly spots off the glass.

"Even if we wanted to, we couldn't sell the place the way it is now."

Flo shrugged. "I dunno about that."

"We're stuck. We've sunk everything we have into it." Sadly, that was no lie.

Anna could tell that Flo was truly worried about her and the family.

The water kettle was whistling now. A shrill non-stop shriek. Flo started to get up but Anna patted her aunt on the leg. "I'll get it," she said, making her way to the kitchen. She lifted the kettle off the burner and poured water in a brown chipped teapot. She covered it with a boiled-wool cosy, decorated with colourful embroidered flowers.

Anna brought the teapot to the low table at Flo's side. She noticed her aunt's heavy legs. A while back there had been talk of amputation, stern warnings to Flo about changing her diet and trying new drugs. That reminded Anna to give her aunt the package from the pharmacy. She retrieved the bag from her purse and handed it to Flo.

Flo scowled at the drugstore bag. "I don't need that poison. I have this," she said, burrowing into a basket and pulling out a necklace of dark green and black Serpentine stones. She thrust it at her niece. And although Anna had seen the necklace several times before, she still felt compelled to take it from Flo. She fingered the intricately carved strand of sea creatures and serpents. As the cold beads slipped across her palm, the fleeting impression of a writhing snake passed through her mind. She shivered involuntarily.

"It's really nice, Flo, but I'm betting it won't do anything for your blood sugar."

"How about this for a deal: You sell your house on the lake and I'll stop eating sugar."

Anna gave the idea two seconds of consideration. It was a bargain that neither party had any chance of upholding. She gave her aunt a wry smile and made a chuffing sound. She turned to her son. "Come on, snookums."

Flo would not let up. "How 'bout I call the real estate lady?"

"Not gonna happen. Just give it a rest."

Flo shook her head. As Anna and René made a move to leave, it prompted Flo to rise as well, which she did with great difficulty, gripping the sides of her armchair to propel herself up. She shuffled behind Anna and René toward the door. She draped her wrinkly hands over Anna's arms and then stooped to give René a hug.

Anna felt pity for the old woman. Gazing upon her scalp, the thin greying hair, she was struck anew with the extent of Flo's vulnerability. Anna wondered if she had come off as too curt, too dismissive of her elderly aunt.

"Don't get me wrong, Flo. I don't mind this town, but we like where we are because it's private. There's no chance I'm going to run into any of my clients."

"Oh, sure."

"I appreciate your advice."

Flo sucked in her cheeks. "Don't doubt it."

Anna narrowed her eyes at her aunt. She was trying to read her mood, but Flo was not making it easy on her. Anna thought she detected an extra edge to her complaints.

"Tough times ahead, Annie. You'll always be my family," she said cryptically.

Anna gave Flo a quizzical look, and then turned to go, taking René by the hand.

*   *   *

The next day, Anna stopped by the halfway house on River Crest. There she found her father replacing a blade on a table saw. She showed Perry the woodsman carving.

"L.M? That'd be from Leonard—no Lance," Perry said. "The B&E guy, Lance Munson."

"What was he like?"

"Seemed alright. Polite enough and keen on the work." Anna's father gave her a puzzled look. "You got my reports already."

Anna nodded. "Ever notice anything go missing?"

Perry shook his head. "Nope," he said. "Because everything's numbered and I do a check when the workshop's over. Perry frowned. "Didn't you get him off the charges?"

"Yeah," Anna said, taking the carving and wrapping it back up.

"So, why are you still asking questions about him?"

*   *   *

Anna swung into the Glace Bay P.D. parking lot and found her usual spot vacant. From many other visits, she was well familiar with the place. The officer on the desk waved her through and she found her way to Detective Dale Corbeau's office. Dale had grown out of his hair. A shiny chrome dome replaced the crew cut he once sported as a beat cop. Since becoming a detective, he also lost some of the muscle tone but he was still too wide for the off-the rack suits he tried to squeeze into. He spotted Anna and gestured for her to sit down.

"What's up? I wasn't aware you were on any of my cases." He was still peeved at Anna, not bothering with hello or how are you, but he seemed to soften a little when he noticed the slight protrusion of her abdomen.

"It's about Munson."

"Lance Munson—?" Corbeau seemed surprised, as though wondering why Anna did not leave that sleeping dog lie.

"Yeah."

Corbeau waited, holding his breath.

"I was wondering what you thought."

"About what?"

"The trial."

Corbeau leaned back in his chair, frowning. "You want me to congratulate you. Is that it? You come here to rub salt in my wounds?"

"No." Anna shook her head. She folded her hands together and waited while Corbeau blew off steam.

"I don't know what to say. You got the guy off. You did your job. We didn't do ours so well. But—it happens."

Corbeau slapped his hands on the desk hinting that her time was up. "I'm kind of busy, there are lots of other Lance Munsons out there." He stood up as though wanting to show her the door.

"Are there?"

"Are there what?"

"Lots of Munsons?"

Corbeau paused. He sighed as he sank back down. "No. Actually, there's just one like him."

Anna dug into her briefcase and pulled out the small ornament Munson had given her. She placed it on Corbeau's desk. "He's good with knives—quite a carver."

"Munson do this?"

Anna nodded. "Early Christmas present."

Corbeau spun the object in his hand.

"He's an artist and a designer," added Anna.

"Yeah, he created most of his tattoos," said the detective. "The other prisoners used to ask him to sketch their ideas."

"No kidding."

"Do you mind if I hang onto this?" Corbeau asked.

"It was a gift," Anna said, realizing too late how strange that must have sounded, like she would treasure something from the creepy felon.

"I'm not going to keep it forever."

Anna waved her arm, "Go ahead," she said by way of approval.

"Be right back." Corbeau exited with the ornament and returned a few moments later giving her a photocopy of it as a receipt.

He paused next to his desk, leaning toward Anna, giving her a probing look. "Anna, what exactly are you after? To tell me that Munson is good with knives?" He waited but she gave no reply. "I got that. You saw the crime scene photos. You know his work—artistic and otherwise." He spun the ornament in his hand.

"There was no proof it was Munson"

"But you came in to see me!" Corbeau growled. "Does your client have things he wants to get off his chest? Is this about making a deal on other cases?"

"What other cases?"

Corbeau shook his head and sighed. "You know very well. The rapes, the other murders we tried to introduce."

"You can't throw in just anything when there were no charges, no convictions. You're lucky there was no mistrial." Anna shuddered inwardly, remembering the photos from the discovery materials.

"The similarities were amazing," countered Corbeau.

Anna felt a sharp pain in her side. She adjusted her position in the chair. Corbeau was studying her, gauging her reaction.

"In Morneau in January of 2012, and Lamont two years later. Both places that Munson could have travelled to."

A wave of nausea hit her as Corbeau filled in the details of the killings. "Same M.O., a nurse driving home off a late shift. Looks like some vehicle cut her off. Possibly a snowmobile."

Anna was only half-listening. The memory of snowmobiles roaring around her home the past weekend wended its way through her brain, rattling her thoughts.

"How far along are you in the investigation?"

Corbeau's face took on a hard look. His voice got very low. "He's going to do it again, Anna."

She found herself speaking as though outside of her own body. The words came out automatically, "I think you're mistaken about him." In truth, she no longer believed in Munson's innocence. It was like walking on a tightrope, being a defense attorney, advocating for the right to a fair trial, yet wondering about helping a killer walk free.

Corbeau inhaled deeply. His complexion became mottled with red patches. She could sense him bursting with anger.

"My dad mentored Munson at the halfway house," Anna said weakly.

"Yeah, I know!" Corbeau sputtered.

"He taught Munson joinery and carpenter's basics, and he was—"

"Anna. I was there at the trial. I heard Perry's report. I respect your dad's work. He's a good man—but he's not a cop."

Corbeau shifted closer to Anna, giving her a look that seemed to reach into her soul. Despite his arrogance, his rude posturing, and his sulkiness at her win at trial, she wanted to help. So she threw him a bone. Why, exactly she did this, she wasn't sure.

"I asked Dad if they were ever missing any knives or chisels at the workshop and he said no. You know, they inventory all the tools at the end of every shift. And I imagine you guys had all the blades tested, right?"

From Corbeau's somewhat astonished expression, Anna could see this had never occurred to him.

CHAPTER SIX
The Helper Man

"We'll throw a bulb in there to see if it works."

The instruction came from Armel Busey, owner and founder of Busey Electric. The seasoned electrician watched as Lance Munson hung up a pendant light fixture— an unusual lopsided contraption with metal tubing and mesh. Busey wondered why one would go through all the trouble of building a beautiful addition and then stick something ugly-as–all-get-out up there.

Busey had asked Xavier where he got the light, planning to badmouth the vendor, but Xavier said the piece was a special order from an artist out of Montreal. When Xavier had told him how much he had paid, Busey made a mental note not to give Xavier and his lawyer wife any discounts.

Busey, who was in his late seventies now and semi-retired, was helping with Xavier's electrical work. He told Xavier that there was no way in hell he was getting up on a sixteen-foot ladder and so he found a casual labourer through a service from Glace Bay.

The electrician wasn't bothered too much that the fellow had once been in jail. A lot of the day labourers got into trouble when they drank, but Busey didn't care what they did on weekends as long as they came to work sober. Munson was more than qualified and showed up when he was supposed to, which was more than you can say for most workers these days.

They made good progress over the next few days. They strung hundreds of feet of Romex electrical cabling, put in more than a dozen outlets, installed a new 200-amp breaker panel and a separate one for the furnace and the sauna they planned to get.

When it was all done, Busey felt well justified in handing Xavier a bill for a few grand. Xavier raised his eyebrows slightly, saying nothing at first. Then he mumbled something about it being higher than the original quote.

But Busey did not back down. If the guy who made the crooked wind chimes that passed for a light fixture was getting a

30

few grand, surely he could expect a little extra for coming all the way out to this god-forsaken place.

"We had a lot of travel time and I had to hire a helper to do the ladder work," Busey said.

* * *

Although Xavier was shocked by the steep bill, it wasn't anything that he and Anna couldn't afford. It would go on their line of credit anyway. The good thing was Xavier could move ahead now with the next stages, insulation, vapour barrier and drywall. Finishing the work before the baby arrived was now a realistic possibility.

He was grateful to Busey because getting an electrician to come all the way out to the property from town had been nearly impossible. Just for somebody to give a quote involved over an hour of driving, so almost no one he called would even bother.

The silver lining from all of this was that Xavier convinced Munson to come back and work for him. Initially unaware of the connection to Anna and Perry, Xavier hired Munson simply because of his construction skills.

Xavier decided not to share this fact with Anna. He reasoned she didn't need to know all the details for now. He hoped to surprise her in a few weeks with a finished addition.

* * *

Peals of laughter reverberated through the near-empty room. The Boberge light with its two bulbs shone over a game of tag. Anna chased René around a maze of bundled insulation and stacks of drywall. She tagged René and he veered quickly toward Xavier, who leapt over the sawhorse and then jumped on top of a bundle of insulation.

René squealed, "That's cheating!" He reached for his father's foot, but Xavier pulled up his long legs just in time. Then Anna lifted René up, assisting her son so he could tap his father's leg.

"Hey, that's two against one," said Xavier. He drew back suddenly, toppling over and landing on the floor with a thud. "Ow, ow," he yelped. He sprawled in the sawdust, cradling his right wrist. His face twisted in pain.

René stopped short, "What's the matter, Daddy?"

Xavier moaned, "I think I broke it."

Full of concern, René hurried toward his father. Just as René was within reach, Xavier lunged for the boy and tagged him. "Gotcha!" he chortled.

René sputtered with laughter.

"Oh my God," said Anna, "that was sneaky!"

The little family was so wrapped up in their fun that none of them heard a faint pop as one of the two light bulbs in the ceiling fixture above went dark.

CHAPTER SEVEN

Room to Grow

Thunk! Thunk! Ppphhtunk! A hand gripped a nail gun. It swung wildly, firing again and again. The soft pliable material shuddered as metal shot through the surface. A beat-up compressor bumped along in zigzag fashion, occasionally butting up against the walls, following the bearer of the nail gun like a drunken sidekick.

The man stood tall, his back cast in shadow. The weapon-shaped tool an extension of his arm, taking aim and then blasting randomly as though unable to find the right target, just taking it out on the wall. In the waning light, the man loomed like a spectre. It was hard to tell who he was. A builder? Or a destroyer?

Outside, an orange school bus paused at the end of the driveway. A little boy hopped down the stairs and ran over the stained snow. "Daddy!" he shrieked.

At the sound of his son's cries, Xavier, wearing a torn down vest and stained jeans, emerged from the house. He grinned as he scooped up René and carried the squealing boy under one arm. Xavier waved to the driver and the bus moved on.

Inside the house, René shed his backpack, coat, and his boots, dropping them all to the floor. Xavier snapped his fingers at his son and pointed to the gaping door. "What did I say about that?"

René sauntered to the door, a bit of sulk in his body posture, as though rebelling at being scolded. He slammed it hard, but the door popped back and opened wide again.

Xavier frowned. He went to the door to demonstrate how to close it.

"You gotta give it a little push and make sure it clicks. Like this."

"I can fix that," came a voice from behind them.

Xavier and René turned to see Munson. He had been watching the father-son exchange, as though unaccustomed to seeing such tenderness between a parent and child. It was almost too much to believe. That would have been the day his own dad would have put up with any sass from him or his siblings.

"Yeah, it's been something I've been meaning to get to," said Xavier.

"It's never-ending," said Munson. "Taking care of a house is non-stop, ain't it." In truth the apprentice had never owned a home and had no idea how much upkeep was required for a place like this. His current home was a trailer borrowed from his sister's ex. The place sorely needed sprucing up, but once Munson got home at night, his energy for domestic chores extended only as far as peeling off the wrapping from a microwave dinner and running it for five minutes. Even taking out the garbage was too much trouble.

Munson had found it a strange turn of events that he had ended up here—of all places—working at Anna Docstedder's house. He had learned that this was her home only after the first day by noting the mail on the kitchen counter, the family photos on the bedroom dresser, and, oh yeah, the slender high-heeled boots he remembered from several of their meetings.

Munson made note of the few nice pieces around the house: paintings, silver, and soapstone sculptures. He planned to nick them at some point but was smart enough by now to realize he should come back for them later. The timing was wrong just now. How does the saying go? *Don't shit where you eat.* Besides this was a pretty sweet gig. The pay was good, the Frenchie was reasonable and the commute across the lake was great.

Munson grabbed a wood plane and a screwdriver to remove the latch and doorknob. Then he set himself up near the side door, kneeling at the opening. The shock of cold hitting him in the chest prompted him to get his jacket.

He determined that he wouldn't need to take the door off the hinges. He could get away with just shaving off a few millimetres of excess paint. If that didn't do the trick, he would unscrew the locking mechanism to tighten it up so the door would shut property. Easy peasy. A job he could pull off in twenty minutes, half an hour tops.

And he would have finished it, had he not heard the crunch of tires in the driveway. He peered out and felt a jolt as he recognized Anna's vehicle. "Well this blows," he muttered to himself.

He didn't spend a lot of time wondering how she might react to finding him at her house. He just grabbed his gear and bolted out the door, heading for the snowmobile.

By the time Anna had parked, collected her purse and briefcase, Munson had already mounted the skidoo. He shoved in the key and twisted it. The blue Polaris roared to life and with a vroom, shot out of the Durand-Docstedder yard, gunning snowy mounds with a spray of crystals on its way down the incline, toward the lake. The beast would proceed from there, across the frozen water to Norris Road, and then to the Pines trailer park where Munson lived for the time being.

*   *   *

All that Anna could see when she got closer to the top of the driveway were the tail lights of the retreating machine. She paused briefly and then turned to enter her home. She pulled up short, stepping over the tools scattered near the doorway but thought nothing more of their presence.

"Xavier! René!" she called out cheerily.

Then she spotted her son at the window. She came up to him, and slid her arm over his shoulder, pulling him in for a hug. She noticed he had been watching the departing snowmobile.

"Who was that?" she asked, planting a kiss on top of his head.

"The helper man."

"Hmm."

Xavier appeared in the kitchen and greeted Anna with a peck on the lips. If Munson's rapid departure puzzled Xavier he said nothing about it to Anna.

"How was work? A lot of slashings and robberies today?" Xavier asked.

Anna grimaced. "Slight uptick in business. They're still counting the corpses."

"Good to hear."

"What's a corpse?" René asked.

Anna and Xavier froze. They had forgotten their son was in the room. He had turned away from the window and was watching his parents. Xavier smirked while Anna, somewhat flustered, tried to explain. "Mommy was just being silly. She was making a joke about something that's not really funny."

This was exactly what she had always wanted to avoid: shop talk following her home to little René. She would have to be more careful from now on.

"But you never told me—what's a corpse?" René asked again.

CHAPTER EIGHT
Perry Pitches In

Munson noticed the old man's hip had gotten a lot worse since he'd seen him last. Perry insisted it was not that bad, but it was obvious he slowed down over the course of the day. The 'helper man' observed Perry attempt to deal with the discomfort by popping pain pills with every coffee he drank—six or seven not including whatever he might have had over breakfast.

Lance really felt for the old guy. He briefly considered hooking him up with some Oxycontin but then thought better of it. Once more, the former prisoner was using his head and experience to stay out of prison. He often thought about the things he should have done differently. Ways he could have avoided getting caught.

After lunch he went out for a cigarette, strolling around the property, taking in the warmth of the afternoon sun but also having a good look around, scanning for entry points. He observed the windows, the doors, and even located the rock that covered the spare key. He made a plan to return in the spring when the ground was firmer and the snow, which revealed tracks so easily, was gone.

* * *

Meanwhile inside the house, Perry was reclining on a bale of insulation. The pain in his hip and down his leg had become unbearable. It felt worse when they stopped for a break and work no longer distracted him from the gnawing ache. Damn getting old.

He squinted up at the ridiculous light fixture that the kids had ordered somewhere off the internet. *Damned if there wasn't already a burnt-out bulb. How the hell do you change a light bulb every time on something like that?* He would have liked to talk some sense into this daughter and son-in-law, but he really didn't have the energy anymore.

As Perry continued to stare up at the vaulted ceiling, his thoughts communing with the higher spirits caught up in the cobwebs above him, Xavier's face appeared.

"Hey, Pop, got your java juice, here."

"Set it on the ground there, Xav. I'll get it in a minute, soon as I finish my nap."

As Perry studied the meeting of the joists and the trusses at the ceiling's peak, he thought how much this was like the bottom of a ship. A Viking vessel turned upside down. The oarsmen had fallen out and were stranded somewhere—adrift at sea. He was pulled out of the stream of consciousness by a rustling sound. He could hear Xavier pulling out a packet of gum, popping the aluminum skin and extricating a pellet from the noisy plastic shell. Perry couldn't chew gum himself, given how bad his teeth were.

"Does Anna know?" Perry asked.

Xavier abruptly stopped the gum smacking. Perry could tell he was thinking.

"About what?" he said the words slowly, warily.

"About him?" Perry pointed in the direction of the outside, indicating Munson.

"Oh!" Xavier exhaled deep from within.

"Yeah—not yet," he admitted somewhat embarrassed. "I got him through the electrician. I didn't really know at first."

Perry made a face, his eyebrow arching in disbelief.

Xavier dragged a tub of drywall compound toward his father-in-law's makeshift lounger. He plopped down on the low plastic seat, leaned forward and folded his hands together, almost prayer-like.

He has a history," Perry continued, tilting his head sideways to look at Xavier full-on. "Police come talk to me the other day, asking about him."

"Yeah?"

"If it's true, he's pulled some real serious shit."

"Like what?"

Perry grunted. "You gotta ask Anna."

"Well, what do you think of him?"

"A guy can seem alright but sometimes you just don't—" Perry suddenly stopped and frowned. He felt the hair stand up in his neck. It was an instinctual and ancient reaction of the hunter—or the hunted—that freezing in place, becoming very still.

Anna's father brought his finger to his lips in warning. Then he pointed toward the doorway, beyond the barrier created by the pink R-40 insulation bats. Xavier turned his head in the direction of the unseen doorway. He cocked his ears. The room was quiet—too quiet.

Xavier rose up slowly from his seat, his gaze fixed as it ascended over the stacked insulation. As his eyes met Munson's stony look, Xavier shuddered imperceptibly. The ex-con stood rigid and fierce, like a warrior ready for battle.

"Hey, you're back," said Xavier, trying to come off as nonchalant. But the deep gulp he took—the Adam's apple wobbling in his throat—gave away his fear. There could be no more pretending anything anymore. Xavier couldn't ignore what he knew, Perry's warnings, the danger he felt coming from those unreadable reptilian eyes.

I gotta fire this creep, thought Xavier. But when? Today or by the end of the week? Whatever—Munson would have to go—and hopefully before Anna got back and found out he had ever been in their home.

CHAPTER NINE
China Eyes

She saw her name on the agenda. As she often did, Anna would be providing the First Nations perspective as a law conference panellist, this time on "Civilian Oversight of Law Enforcement." Ever since her student days, her scholarship and mentorship by the federation of First Nations Councils, she had been on a list somewhere. She was the go-to person for comments on anything controversial regarding First Nations victims or perpetrators. Whenever the press wanted a quote or two they would track her down and stick a mic in her face.

Hah, the stories she could tell. But she would have to keep it polite and informative, neutral and educational. She was after all the poster girl.

Earlier in her career the speaking engagements had helped her gain profile and garner a few new clients. It was a perk that she decided was worth cultivating. Even though it took her away from her family, it provided her with a nice break from work, and a chance to travel all expenses paid. She realized as the plane touched down at Pearson International Airport that once the baby was born she would likely have to scale back her involvement in these out-of-town symposiums and meetings. It was hard enough to leave five-year-old René—even though she knew he was in good hands—but with a newborn she realized the jet-setting—such as it was, with pretzels and cramped seats—could not continue.

* * *

The floor of the conference centre was awash in blue, grey and black. Men and women in suits milled about the registration table, dressed like overgrown private school students, unable to give up the pinstriped armature even on days off. She had forgotten about this vibe, the cool, competitive aura that she had never gotten used to. As soon as she was registered, Anna fled upstairs to her room.

It was on the 34th floor of the same luxury hotel that was host to the conference. Between the towers of glass and concrete, she glimpsed a sliver of Lake Ontario, rippling gently, unfrozen. A

39

miniature ferryboat traversed the water toward a series of small islands. Compared to Glace Bay, the temperature here was almost tropical.

The suite was like an oasis. Done up in white and grey tones, it boasted sleek furniture and polished marble. Just to walk on clean floors without seeing her footprints in sawdust or grinding her soles in food debris was a treat. Pristine 400 thread count sheets, ironed to smooth perfection, covered the king size bed. Like a cloud held taut by angels, thought Anna. She was sorely tempted to take a nap before the evening meet and greet. In the days before coming to the conference she had burnt the midnight oil in order to clear her desk of last-minute matters, and to brief her colleague, Brent McKay, to handle any emergency that might arise while she was out of town.

Five minutes, she thought to herself. A five-minute power snooze, that's all. Had she been honest with herself, she would have set her phone alarm to wake her up. She unzipped her long leather boots and threw her coat on a chair. She pulled back the duvet and slid into the bed fully dressed.

When she awoke, she realized her nap had taken up the rest of the afternoon. It was already time for the "Welcome Dinner" according to the conference program. She hurried to join the other attendees downstairs.

At dinner she picked at her meal. The fellow next to her turned out to be a defense attorney originally from eastern Ontario, Phil Di Nardo, whom she remembered from the bar admission course. They had graduated the same year from Osgoode Hall. She could barely recognize him from the younger version of himself.

Years ago, he would have best been described as a skinny version of a Sasquatch. He had allowed his facial hair to completely overtake his face and neck. She guessed it was his severe acne problem that had led him to hide his skin behind the moustache and beard that were now gone, revealing mostly smooth olive skin with only a few faded pock marks remaining of that pubescent scourge. Now that he had sheared back the layers of his former Neanderthal look, he was very handsome, but he was—oh so arrogant.

They discussed developments in genetic genealogy and incorporating that as evidence. He had that aggressive, always-got-to-win air about him. Anna had no doubt he would make a good representative in court. They agreed to keep in touch and Anna tapped his contact information into her phone, and he took one of her cards.

"Glace Bay," he mused.

He expressed surprise that she had chosen to settle there, after all, she had lived in Toronto and had had a taste of the big city life. Anna did not want to delve into the year after graduation—how her life had taken a near self-destructive dive and how she had barely recovered in time to salvage her career.

"It's a lifestyle. We love nature and we have a large property on Lake Mikwam," Anna asserted, almost apologetically.

"Sure. But don't you miss civilization?"

Anna winced inside. This was an often-heard objection to her home community. It irritated her that she had to defend where she lived.

"Civilization is sometimes very uncivilized," she replied. "Aren't you tired of the big city crime and gangs?"

"That's why I live in the suburbs," Phil said, seemingly unconcerned.

"Then you've got those crazy long commutes." Anna felt a little hypocritical making that statement. Monday to Friday she was clocking nearly a hundred kilometres a day.

"I've a condo downtown," he smiled. "Not too far from here actually. A penthouse suite. Like a bedroom in the sky. It's got a killer view."

He didn't come right out and say it but he seemed to hint that they could escape to his pad with the 'killer view' should Anna wish. She didn't know whether to be flattered or offended. She pretended not to get his drift until it became all too obvious.

"I noticed your boots earlier. Quite something," he said meaningfully, staring her up and down. "Snow must get awfully high up in Glace Bay."

Thankfully, the conversation and the innuendos came to a halt when the after-dinner speeches began. Before dessert was served, Anna made her escape. She phoned home and caught Xavier just as he was putting René to bed. They exchanged a few words and then she air-kissed them both, making smacking sounds on the phone. Geez, she had only been gone a day and was so homesick already. She sensed the rest of the conference would really drag by.

In the morning as she headed to a talk entitled "Working with Juvenile Witnesses and Childhood Memory," she spotted a familiar figure, an old law school classmate, Deirdre Paquette, or Dee as she preferred to be known. Dee burst into a smile when Anna stopped her in the hallway.

"Oh, my God, Anna!" exclaimed Dee. "Look at you!"

Dee was a short dumpling of a woman with a bubbly personality. Her razor-sharp wit had kept Anna not just awake but in stitches during many a dull lecture.

"You can't believe how happy I am to see you," gushed Anna.

"Me too, girlfriend." Dee waved her hand in a circle, "Whenever I eat raspberry torte I think of you."

Raspberry torte was an inside joke. Dee used to make raspberry faces during their excruciating 'Torts and Defences 201' class with Professor Underhill, a.k.a. 'Professor Over-the-Hill.' Following his retirement from an active law career, Leonard Underhill had decided to bestow his knowledge on up-and-coming lawyers. But the sage had a gravelly, difficult-to-hear voice that might have been better suited to putting insomniacs to sleep. His bright rosacea cheeks helped the professor earn his "Raspberry Torte" moniker.

Despite her cheery, jocular demeanour, Dee had been a serious student. She graduated cum laude with several job offers already in hand as she stepped onto the stage to receive her diploma. She was now working at a top Toronto law firm.

"Hey, let's say we skip the rubber chicken at lunch and head out for some dim sum," Dee said.

"You know, that would be awesome. That's something I really miss up north," said Anna.

The restaurant selections in Glace Bay were indeed pitiful. While there were a few South Asian eating establishments that had popped up recently to add variety to the local restaurant choices, the only Chinese places still dated back to the 70s when the highlights of the menu were westernized dishes like pineapple pork or sweet and sour chicken balls coated in a neon red sauce.

* * *

As they tromped down Spadina Avenue, Dee pointed to Anna's boots accusingly. "How come you tall people feel the need to make us shorties feel even more height-challenged?"

Anna groaned. "The truth is I just didn't pack very well." Between making sure that the household and the firm would survive without her, Anna had neglected to ensure she had comfortable walking shoes. No matter, it was only a three-day trip.

The former law school friends found themselves at Ling Ho's, a hole-in-the-wall place tucked in between a wholesale store selling imported clothes and plastic toys, and the Wicker Emporium. Short on time, they agreed to be seated with strangers at a large circular table covered in layers of white plastic sheets. When one meal was finished, the plastic would be lifted and thrown out. It was not fancy, but the food was authentic and delicious.

Dee smiled as the waiter started speaking to her in Cantonese. She nodded, feigning understanding. She fired back at him with a few words in Cree.

"The black bear is hungry for fish," said Dee.

Anna could barely restrain herself from bursting into laughter. She admired Dee's ability to keep a straight face. The waiter gave Dee a blank look, then plonked down a pot of tea and a stack of small porcelain dishes and left.

Once he was out of earshot, Anna and Dee erupted into giggles. This was a familiar occurrence. How often had they eaten at a Chinese restaurant only to be spoken to in Mandarin or Cantonese.

After they debated which and how many of the small plates to order—stuffed eggplant, sticky rice, steamed shrimp dumplings—they tried to get caught up on their lives.

Dee had been unlucky in love, or as Anna thought—but held back from saying out loud—had made some bad decisions, not just once but time and again. It was a frustrating aspect of knowing someone who had been abused and was instinctively drawn to abusive partners, never realizing their part, the subconscious signals they emitted to attract dangerous lovers. It was like watching a slow train wreck.

"I live in a condo now with top-notch security," Dee whispered. "I carry mace, and an alarm."

Worry lines formed across Anna's forehead.

"I used to carry around switchblades, but then I would forget I had them in my purse and they would get confiscated every time I went to the courthouse."

Anna couldn't help but laugh at this. "Oh my God, Dee," she said, shaking her head.

"Kind of made me look pretty badass, lemme tell you. But when it happened I'd have to explain that I'd received death threats and had a couple of active restraining orders," said Dee. "Trying to carry a concealed weapon into a court of law—not exactly great for one's reputation."

They were silent for a moment. Anna refilled her plate with short ribs and scraped the rice off the banana leaves. She lifted off the lids of the round wicker steamers and looked for more.

"Hey, I've been counting dumplings, Anna, and I think you've had more than your fair share."

Anna laughed. "I know," she admitted guiltily, "the food's so good here. Baby keeps saying, 'I want more.'"

"How old's the other one?"

"René is five, almost six. His birthday is January 3rd. He's a winter baby."

Anna sighed contentedly. She was sated after the full lunch. The easy laughter had warmed her. Nothing was spoken between them for a moment. The din of the crowded restaurant covered their silence.

After a time, Dee said: "How do you do it, Anna? How do you manage to get such an idyllic life after all the shit you've lived through?"

Anna stared at her long-lost friend. She was a little taken aback. Was her life really so enviable? That's certainly how it appeared to Dee. But what did Dee really know of Anna's situation? Her small-town law office with clients who often couldn't pay. The years she and Xavier spent building a cabin that they were now struggling to make into their dream home. The fact that Xav was only employed some of the time. Dee only saw what she wanted to see. Yet Anna had to admit things were pretty good at that moment.

But still Anna wanted to tell Dee that sometimes you just couldn't tell by appearances. That the truth was waiting to be discovered—just below the surface.

* * *

Anna slept poorly that night. Whether it was the heavy meal or the swirl of thoughts that ran through her mind, she did not know. Was it lawyer's guilt, PTSD on behalf of all of the victims, or her own personal struggles? Toronto was certainly a trigger for Anna. The memories of Dee's ordeals also criss-crossed Anna's brain, intermingling with moments in her own life. For the first time in years, Anna cried for her mother's death. It had happened, not at the hands of any man who had struck her, but through suicide.

Her father had waited to tell her until after her exams were finished, not wanting to throw Anna off. She had been doing so well. Anna remembered now, his arrival at the airport. The strangeness of him coming to see her. His serious demeanour should have been a give-away.

It was such a rarity to have a visitor from the north. No one had ever come to help her get settled in school or to celebrate a graduation—no one had ever been there for the difficult mo-

44

ments—but now her father was here to bring her the equivalent of a suitcase filled with dynamite.

"Surprise! Your mother killed herself." It was a nasty trick.

Perry and her mother, Louise, had long divorced by then but Perry kept in touch with his ex-wife, for Anna's sake, as best he could. After Perry had delivered the news, Anna's reaction was immediate. Her legs carried her on adrenaline and she flew through the night streets, getting lost in the taverns on Parliament, letting herself melt onto the sticky beer-coated counters, her joints becoming loosened of the will that held her body together.

It was her father who had to make her excuses the next day to Banner, Larch and Hahn, the firm where she had managed to get a permanent position after receiving her law degree. Perry would not have been wrong to think how similar this was to his picking up after Louise's mistakes.

Adversity did not make Anna stronger. Rather it left small chips in her granite facade. Hairline fractures, where afterwards dark seams appeared. She looked strong, so few people realized that if you pushed her too hard, she would come apart. The mighty statue on a pedestal might someday lose her head.

Anna retreated to a world where she felt safer. Where life was more familiar. Where she had company in her loss. She slunk away to Glace Bay and burrowed in the layers at her aunt Flo's place.

After months of hiding out there, she re-emerged, prodded into action by her impatient aunt. Flo had given Anna an ultimatum. She set a deadline of six weeks. She got Anna to make one small change every day. Offer kindnesses, Flo suggested. Ride a bike, walk through a forest, pick up litter, sit with an elder, make stew for her dad.

"Why," Anna screamed in her head. "Why do I have to keep giving, when all the world has ever done is take from me?"

A little bit of Flo's advice did sink in finally. Flo got more than she bargained for when Anna signed up for a tree-planting gig. The crew was to meet up in Edmonton and from there travel west in a convoy of vans.

Flo held her breath for the first few weeks, half-expecting Anna, whom she had mistaken for a 'softie,' to come crawling back to her place. But no, Anna took to the trees just like she did to the paper that they produced.

And then there was another unexpected turn. In that hinterland, Anna met Xavier, a ruggedly handsome French-Canadian, who became her lover by the end of the summer and 70,000 spindly saplings later. Nothing else matters when you are at the top of a clear-cut and you fight the rocky uneven soil day after day to accept those new shoots of life that years from now will be towering forests.

Their love was stripped away of facades and dating rituals. Absent the urban setting, there was no possibility of evenings out in bars, movies or fancy restaurants. It was bare bones. No distractions. They got to know each other at their worst and at their best. It came down to their very essence, like Adam and Eve in a northern wilderness garden. The apple was a pinecone, and the devil was a grizzly bear.

By summer's end, Anna had acquired muscles in her arms and body, and most of all, the strength and discipline to cope with the roughest of situations. The frosty mornings, late snowfalls, blisters, and excruciating physical fatigue had also built up her mental endurance. She had become tough. She had the ability to power through her obstacles.

When she flew home to Glace Bay, a few months later, her skin had tinted like the colour of red ochre due in part to the time spent in the sun and the rest from the Alberta soil that still clung to her. After her first long soak in the big tub at Flo's, she left a pattern of debris that made the bath look like a dry creek bed, with the finest silt channelling toward the drain in undulating lines.

Flo, in a rare display of anger, told Anna to rinse out the tub and "scrub it good, and then scrub it some more."

Anna had not only brought back a bucket of dirt on her person and in her clothes, but she also brought with her a few seedlings: a Jack Pine, a spruce, and a hemlock—and the tallest tree of all—Xavier Durand.

Flo let them hang around and she watched her niece, happy for the first time in years. The couple continued to prefer sleeping out in the tent for the next while, possibly because it was the one place where they could have some privacy. Finally, as the crisp fall nights set in, it occurred to Anna and Xavier that they could no longer camp out. Winter would come eventually. They would have to find another place to live.

Anna put together an interview suit and made the rounds at the local law firms—the few that eked out an existence in the small town. She brought coffee and doughnuts to the lawyers' receptionists while dropping off her resume, touting her Osgoode credentials and history of scholarships. It begged the question, if she were so qualified, what was she doing settling for Glace Bay? Perhaps it was because of this that she got no response at all from her many cold calls and her efforts at beating the pavement.

The reality of her situation hit Anna like a cold wind blowing in from the arctic. But rather than give up and head for the big city, she stuck it out. She signed on with Legal Aid Ontario and finally got her first client, Rosalie DeMesurier, a Kenora woman who was caught writing bad cheques. In Rosalie, Anna saw reminders of her own mother: a tendency to be drawn into unhealthy situations.

Anna was part counsellor and part social worker to 'Rosie.' Anna tried to argue in court that Rosie's actions were a result of her trying to escape an abusive situation. The battered woman's attempt to get police help on previous occasions had only resulted in more severe beatings from her common law husband, so Rosie had stopped expecting real help when she called 911. Rosie had to feed her baby and was left with little alternative than to kite cheques to buy food.

Xavier went back to Montreal but within weeks had returned to Glace Bay, announcing to Anna that he was abandoning his degree in architecture. Anna did not try to talk him out of this foolishness. They were in love and they wanted to be together. That was all that mattered. Finally she had someone who truly adored her and was devoted to her.

He looked for work in construction. He got his certificate as a forklift operator, which led to a part-time gig in a lumberyard. He joked to Anna that he was coming full circle from planting trees to selling wooden planks to installing them in houses. Their tree-planting savings helped tide them over when Xavier's small income and Anna's legal aid monies did not cover their expenses.

Within months Anna had been noticed in court for several wins as well as her impassioned pleas on behalf of her mostly penniless clients. For the jaded courthouse lawyer who was bored and had some time to kill between trials, watching Anna perform provided welcome entertainment. She began to acquire some fans: older guys in suits who hung around, smirking and sometimes chuckling at her over-the-top performances. *What a green-horn*, they might have whispered to each other, while marvelling that she was damn cocky and didn't hesitate to put herself out there.

Her reputation was growing, her star ascending. But the bar was low in Glace Bay. You could only get so far on beginner's luck. She could bust her butt trying to win these legal aid cases but no matter how many hours she put in, the pay rates were still abysmal. She was treading water. What she really needed was a break.

It finally came in the form of an off-hand suggestion from another lawyer, Brent McKay, a young man only a few years out of law school, but who was already established in that he had a firm place in a local law firm. Brent, a shy yet competent thirty-something local guy, had worked with his father Arthur McKay but following his father's death was left alone to run the firm. Brent was struggling to cope with cases that were outside his comfort zone. He saw in Anna someone who was gutsy enough to deal with the thornier issues, the tough criminal law matters that had once occupied a third of the elder McKay's practice.

When Anna toured the fusty McKay offices she was secretly heartsick, but outwardly displayed enthusiasm, giving Brent smiles and nods. Hell, what else did she have to fall back on? She wondered if this was it? Was this as good as it would get? Second fiddle to a quiet, uninspired paper-pushing introvert who only became a lawyer because his dad had been one.

When she confided her misgivings to her aunt, Flo appeared understanding at first but when Anna continued to be depressed, Flo prodded her back to reality. Flo had little patience for moping and shot down all of Anna's objections saying that she could turn this situation into the perfect set-up.

"There's no room in there for my desk," Anna whined. "He insists on keeping all of his dad's files going back to the 50s."

Flo scoffed. "Well, then you find a new space that suits the both of you."

"With what money?"

"You still got some of your tree-planting cash, don't you?"

Anna was reluctant to consider this option. She had really hoped to use her nest egg to buy a house some day. "Prime office space doesn't come cheap," she griped.

"How about you get something that needs a little work. And get your Frenchie boyfriend to do the renovations," said Flo.

Anna pondered what that would mean for her relationship with Xavier—this sudden demand on his time and perhaps his savings as well. That would be a big commitment and sacrifice. Were they even at that stage in their relationship?

"And while you're doing all this, you might as well get a third lawyer in there to balance it all out."

Anna squinted at her aunt. That was not a bad idea. She wondered where Flo had gotten all this business acumen. Why had

Flo never used it for her own benefit? She could have been a CEO somewhere, definitely something more than a mere peddler of baskets and homemade soap.

Following Flo's suggestions—*going with the Flo,* so to speak—Anna agreed to partner with Brent McKay, but when she brought up including a third partner in the mix, Brent took some convincing. Finally, they came up with several names of sole practitioners and finally narrowed it to Alice Cochrane. Alice specialized in family law—divorce, pre-nups and mediation. She readily agreed to join Brent and Anna.

The former McKay & McKay office space was too cramped for Cochrane McKay Docstedder so they had to look for a new location. They settled on a mothballed manufacturing building, the former Welland Glass Factory on Railway Street. To save money, but also keep some of the original charm, they left the faded lettering across the red brick exterior.

While Anna and Xavier camped upstairs, Xavier spent the next two months refitting and modernizing the main floor. Some of the old plank floors were polished but the cement work surfaces were re-poured and smoothened out, then sealed with a glaze.

When Cochrane McKay Docstedder opened its doors six weeks later, the smell of varnish and raw cedar still lingered in the building. Heavily in debt and nerves on edge, the trio of attorneys hung out their new shingle and began the hard slog of making a living as honest lawyers.

CHAPTER TEN

A Feeling in the Pit

Even before the light of dawn crept through the edges of the thick hotel curtains, Anna had been awake, searching online for alternate flight options.

She had decided by four that morning that she would skip the rest of the conference. For whatever reason she had to get home. Her body was urgently telling her to leave, to just get away from this place.

Accompanying her pounding headache was an overwhelming sense of dread. Not only that but baby—or 'Little Peanut'—had been making herself known that night, kicking up a storm. Pressing high into Anna's lungs and jabbing her sensitive organs. Baby was reminding Anna that she was long past that hideous period where she had wanted to give up on herself. The times she had wondered about the point of it all. Those memories kept bubbling up, especially here in Toronto.

Baby was trying to tell her not to lose sight of the future. Now there was a reason for living. There were people who depended on Anna. And soon a new person would be welcomed into that circle. She or he would be loved and cherished. Anna vowed to protect her baby from evil from as long as she could and as best she could.

*   *   *

Anna's wheelie bag bumped across the threshold and onto the train. She found a seat near the luggage hold and settled in for the ride to the airport. She felt a sense of urgency as the airport-bound train whooshed out of Union Station. She could not get home fast enough.

The alternative to her originally scheduled trip was a patchwork of regional flights with a stopover in Whaling Station. Anna was not a fan of the smaller planes on this route, even less so while pregnant. The plane had fewer than forty seats and the overhead bins were so small her carry-on bag had to be checked in. As the crew prepared for lift-off, a wave of nausea hit Anna. She could not

50

get sick now. If she were vomiting even before take-off, they might make her stay on the ground and she could not risk that.

Anna tried to think calming thoughts. She searched her purse for a mint and found instead a homemade balm, courtesy of Flo. She uncapped the small tin and dipped her index finger into the concoction and smeared a dab under her nose and on her forehead. She adjusted the seatbelt over her tummy bump and buckled it. It reminded her of the waist chains worn by the worst of prisoners.

As the engine moved into full throttle, Anna closed her eyes feeling the plane shudder. The flaps closed on the wings and then the plane was alight, buffeted by wind and bouncing on drafts hurled by the gods of winter. Anna placed her hand on her belly as though coaxing her baby to stay calm down. Come on, Little Peanut, she channelled silently to her unborn child.

Before the tinny aircraft veered north, the sun projected its strong rays. Anna blinked, feeling tears wash over her stinging eyes. She willed herself to look at the expanse of the city she was leaving behind, the never-ending line of civilization that stretched along the lake. From the air, it all looked so tidy and efficient. Farewell Toronto, thought Anna, inexplicably tearful. She had an irrational thought that this would be her last visit to the city.

Anna tried to preoccupy herself with work. She had agreed to look into the conviction of Dennis Brisebois, a 61-year-old from Atikokan, for the murder of his wife some 18 years earlier. Brisebois claimed he had found the mutilated body of his spouse, Eleanor George, when he came home from trapping. Eleanor had been raped and stabbed several times. She had been alone with the couple's young son, a two-year-old at the time. Brisebois, a semi-illiterate man, who only spoke rudimentary English, had been unable to prove that he was out on a trap-line while his wife was killed. With only the help of duty counsel, Brisebois ended up being sentenced to life for first-degree murder.

Anna had only recently met with Brisebois for the first time, even though he had been sending her childishly-scrawled letters for several years now, begging for help. Anna had finally given in. Looking over her notes and the old police reports from the time, something about the case niggled at her.

Absorbed in the Brisebois file, Anna failed to notice that they were starting to descend into Whaling Station, a community whose origins dated back to the hunt and processing of whales. The rattle of the plane caused her to glance out the window. She stared below at the white snowy landscape. Strings of trees, and the occasional rock protruding from the snow. So barren and sparsely populated. A rare dwelling or road, becoming even rarer as they travelled north. It was a world away from Toronto.

They swung wide over the frozen bay and circled around for landing. They flew over a small figure below. A man on a snowmobile pulling a sled packed with boxes.

Anna marvelled at the desolation of this area. What did these people do in an emergency, she wondered.

*　*　*

It was a half hour before boarding time and Anna was stretching her legs, keeping her circulation going for the sake of her and the baby. Because of her hasty departure from Toronto, she had neglected to pack a lunch, so she had to satisfy herself with vending machine fare. She dug into a bag of Doritos, all the while studying a large map that took up nearly a whole wall in the waiting room of Northwest Regional Airport. She followed the fine blue and green lines that detailed the topography of the region. She searched for the small community of L'Ecuyer and found it. As though locating this village near Dennis Brisebois' home would help her better understand his case.

She became lost in thought as she idly gazed at the many place names that dotted the expansive territory, tiny fly-specks christened for explorers and first settlers, places where small events occurred that no longer meant much of anything: the appearance of a moose, a portage between lakes, a burnt stump. Her eyes drifted toward her destination, Glace Bay—ten more minutes to kill before they could leave—and as she followed the roads, she stopped at another familiar name: Morneau.

At first, she couldn't think why this name meant something to her. But searching her memory, it came to her finally. It was the site of another murder, one that Dale Corbeau had wanted to pin on Munson. She traced the line between L'Ecuyer, Morneau and Glace Bay, and then made another discovery. Lamont—Corbeau thought Munson was good for a suspicious death there too. Anna scrolled through her memories of the autopsy photos, the gruesome details—the similarities between all three cases.

Anna suddenly felt her weariness in full. What had she done by fighting so hard to get Munson off? She had to go to bat for Brisebois—eighteen years was too long to be behind bars for something he didn't do. She pulled out her cell phone and punched in a number. "Detective Corbeau," she said.

52

CHAPTER ELEVEN

Fire His Ass

"Look man, I won't be needing you next week," Xavier explained to Munson. Because Anna was coming home early from her conference, Xavier decided he could no longer delay giving Lance the pink slip.

The 'helper man' stiffened and turned around slowly on the scaffolding. He had been applying compound with a wide taping knife. He had the look of someone who was trying to decide how angry he ought to get. Suddenly he leapt from his perch, and landed with a thud, just inches from Xavier.

Xavier drew back slightly, suddenly fearful of the man who wielded such a sharp object. It occurred to him now that the blade of the taping knife could do some serious damage. Never reject a psychopath, he had heard Anna once say.

Merde.

Xavier regretted not having fired Munson a week ago when Perry was around and could have helped—if necessary—calm the ex-convict down.

"I really appreciate all you've done," offered Xavier, hoping that flattery would soothe the con's wounded ego. "We just don't have the money right now to keep going."

"You guys poor, that it?" said Munson, not falling for his employer's bullshit.

"Just short on cash," Xavier replied defensively.

"Suit yourself," Munson said angrily, lobbing the taping knife into the drywall tub, signalling he was not working a minute more.

Xavier pulled a bank envelope from his work pants and handed it to Munson. "I gave you a little extra."

He then accompanied the 'helper man' to the kitchen. While Munson packed up his tools, Xavier made up a snack for his son, who was intently viewing a children's show on giraffes.

Satisfied that Munson could see himself out, Xavier shook the man's hand offering a few muttered thank-yous and then left the room again, returning to the work area.

Before he left, Munson strode to the fireplace where the figure of the woodsman sat on the mantle. He picked it up and idly snapped the axe up and down. This caught René's attention.

"That's mine," the boy said, suddenly sitting upright like a watchdog becoming aware of an intruder.

"I made that."

"You did?" said René, impressed but nevertheless wary.

"So, I am going to take it back."

René was shocked by this but didn't dare say a word. He merely watched with a rising sense of anger mixed with admiration as Munson tucked the figurine into the side of his heavy jacket.

René glanced at the man's scarred rough hands—hands that had coiled into cement fists for many a fight, met the wrong side of several blades, including on occasion his own knives. With the floor creaking under the weight of his bulk, Munson strode to the door and opened it wide. He shut it, but it swung open seconds later. Even René knew you that if you didn't shut it with a push from your shoulder it would just pop back open, as it did now. Gusts of cold air blasted into the house, travelling through the corridors, around corners and up the stairs, sending forth a chill that would linger through the night, and for that matter, the rest of their lives.

René bounded towards the window. He pushed a chair against it and perched on it, trying to get a bead on Munson. Mist from René's breath fanned out from the place where his small nose pressed against the glass.

The child saw Munson trudging down the slope with an angled gait, whether it was due to the uneven ground or that one of Munson's legs was longer than the other, he did not know. The clanging metal of tools, jostling in a rough canvas bag, accompanied him like a marching band.

In fading light, René could see Munson uncovering his snowmobile, shaking off a coating of white powder. He swept his leg over the seat and mounted his steed, positioning himself forward. The engine buzzed like a chainsaw. Then with the release of the brake, the snowmobile lurched forward, its powerful treads cutting into the white powder, spitting a spray of white.

Daylight was waning, suffusing the sky with shades of pink and deep burgundy like the dregs at the bottom of a wine glass. As the snowmobile sped down the slope and reached the edge of the lake, it bounced over the stubble of frozen grass and clumps of reeds, and then found purchase on the relatively smooth surface, finding its way onto a trail made by others over the last few weeks. The snow packed down and bruised until it gave way, beaten into submission by the noisy beasts of winter.

Small red lights marked the retreat of Munson's ride, curving this way and that as he skirted the tombstone shapes of ice huts. René followed the red dots and the splayed glow of headlights. The roar dampened with distance. The sound more remote now, fading into a low drone.

The skidoo crept across the expanse. Heading for the northern shore. Moving beetle-like. Then strangely and suddenly the machine dipped and the red lights tilted upwards. Its trajectory coming to a halt. The sound blanked out just as abruptly. Fate had pulled the machine down. Taking it on another route—an underwater journey.

René blinked in astonishment. From his vantage point he saw the whole scene and sensed the man was in danger. The urgency of the situation pulled him from the window.

In his hurry to get outside he did not think to tell his father. Besides his dad was ensconced in cutting and nailing, deep in the labyrinth of the addition, behind walls of plastic sheeting. It would take too long to get to him.

In spite of the urgency, René knew at least to put his boots on but didn't bother with the fasteners. When he was found hours later, he would be missing one of the little red Sorels. It would be discovered by a volunteer searcher a few yards away. A sock tucked inside. Frozen to the shape of René's small foot.

The boy ran outside. As he came to the edge of the yard, the snow deepened. Despite the daunting height of the drifts, he paddled through as though wading through quicksand, taking large gulps of air and aspirating droplets of ice with each mouthful. His cheeks reddened and frosty breath spiralled from his small cherub lips.

The deep snow nearly swallowed René up but he leapt forward undeterred, likely not feeling the cold until later when the surge of adrenaline wore off. Such was his determination to find the snowmobiler.

By the time the boy reached the edge of the lake he was out of sight of the house. He was not looking behind him however, only ahead, trying to retrace the path of the vanished machine. Mesmerized, he was unaware of his own increasing peril.

At last he found the path the helper man had taken: evenly marked indentations in the snow. René followed the treads, calling out to Mr. Lance every few seconds. And then when his shouts went unheeded, he called less frequently, and then after a while, not at all.

It was then he noticed the cold more deeply. He clasped his arms closer to his chest. He tucked his fingers in his pant pockets and when he could find no comfort there he placed them into his mouth, sucking on the tips. He began to cry, trembling and shivering. Mucous streamed down, puddling just above his upper lip. Tears crystalized on his face. Ears and fingertips burned.

He spun about looking for the way he had come. No longer as interested in the man on the machine who had led him to this place. The formerly pristine snow was all gray now, sullied by the creeping night.

The house stood in shadow on the hill. The protruding angled windows like the blade of a hatchet pointed to the lake. Deep within was a work lamp, likely directed on the temporary table where Xavier was sawing the framing pieces for the baby's room. Sawdust spat out like a demon's fury, obscuring the clarity of the night and his thoughts. He was hell-bent on showing Anna he could do this. He could make them a home, cosy and safe and warm. And it would all be done by the time the baby arrived.

His back was turned away from the lake. He worked bent over the churning blade, entirely oblivious to the danger his only child was in. On a subconscious level he probably felt an increasing chill from the drafts of cold air sweeping through the house, rippling the plastic sheeting, but he chose to ignore the warning it gave. He was all about protecting his pride, being the man of the house, the master builder. He forgot about René.

On a normal day, René would have been playing nearby. He would have asked his dad for mac and cheese when he got hungry. He would have made tracks in the piles of sawdust or stacked up the small blocks of wood. René wanted to do all the things his dad did, that is—until he met the helper man.

Then Mr. Lance became his new focus of interest. The helper man's slanted smile, and cackling, gravelly laugh. His habit of exiting for a smoke in the driveway. The whiff of tobacco. The intricate tattoos and scars. The sense of danger and intrigue he gave off, the hints that Mr. Lance came from a forbidden life, full of secrets and adventures. The mix of disdain and admiration that Mr. Lance inspired in René's father. It made the little boy even more curious.

There had been whispering about Mr. Lance between his grandfather and dad. And just now, the brazen theft of the figurine. What was it about the helper man?

The answer to this question likely mattered less now than it had a half hour earlier when Mr. Lance was still alive. As René peered toward the dark chasm where the helper man's snowmobile had plummeted minutes earlier, he saw nothing except the emptiness that is death. The red circles of the rear lights had been extinguished. The opaque water gave away no secrets.

René now realized he had come out here for nothing. He suddenly felt his smallness, his insignificance in the face of adult fallibility. He had been misled. And now he was all alone.

The bank of ice where he was resting was already cracked from the hole created by the snowmobile. Even the slight weight of René caused the ledge to sink a little and take on water. René noticed his pants were wet from the puddle he stood in.

When he pulled back there was a dry cracking noise, a snapping where the ice weakened further. He stepped back in panic and sank even more. He leapt away unsteadily and fell into a soul-crushing face plant. Now completely discouraged, he curled unto himself, trying to gather the little warmth that was left, weeping for help. His sobs unfurled into the pitiless night along with his last breaths. The cold wet clothing hardened as the warmth left his body and he became entombed in an icy shell.

CHAPTER TWELVE

White Out

Halfway home, a blinding snow squall forced Anna to put on her wipers. Despite her impatience to get back, she slowed as she took the corners, feeling the slick surface of the pavement. By the time she had reached home, the snow had stopped, but it had left a fine layer everywhere giving the landscape a sparkling shimmer coating akin to crushed glass.

Anna lugged her bags out of the car and headed to the side door. She bristled to find it swinging wide open and wondered how long gusts of cold winter wind had been hurtling in. Glad as she was to be home, she could not help but feel irritated. Was she busting her chops just so they could heat the outside world? It had been months since Xavier had known this door had not been shutting properly. Why hadn't it been fixed already?

She rolled in her carry-on bag and set down her purse, shouting several greetings: "Hey, guys!" and a few seconds later: "I'm home!" But these were met with silence.

Without removing her boots, she strolled over to the living room where the TV was blaring a children's show, expecting René to be on the couch nestled in the pile of faux fur blankets.

"René?"

She cast the blankets aside. No kid. She glanced around, peered into the corners, and not seeing her son concluded he must be with Xavier. She strode down the hallway, until she arrived at the wall of plastic sheeting that kept the dust from rolling into the rest of the house. She pushed aside the partitions that hung from the ceiling.

"Hellooo?" she shouted. "René! Xav!"

There was no response except for a sharp grinding noise. Proceeding to the worksite, she caught sight of Xavier with his back to her, leaning over the sawhorse, severing a two-by-four. The end cut fell to the ground with a thud. Xavier turned upon seeing her in his peripheral vision.

"Hey! Where is he?" she asked abruptly.

A look of consternation crossed Xavier's face at Anna's sharp manner. Had she learned of his secret? That Munson had been working here? Xavier set down his saw and brushed off his clothing trying to buy time. "He left for the day."

Anna frowned and then shook her head in exasperation, "René!"

"René's—uh," Xavier paused, his eyes flitting sideways, searching for his son in the workroom. "He's watching TV."

"No, he's not!"

Xavier paused briefly, trying to appear nonchalant as he glanced once more around the workspace. "He was there just a minute ago," he faltered. "I made him some noodles—"

Anna turned and bolted out of the room, not waiting for any more of her husband's excuses. "And he was eating those in front of the TV…" Xavier's voice trailed off, the last syllables drowned out by the fierce staccato of Anna's boots hammering the floor. Xavier followed her, trying to catch up, but his wife was already gone. In the hallway, he found a plastic sheet torn off its fastenings, hanging loose as though a hurricane had just blown through.

"René!" Anna's voice echoed as she flew through the house. Racing into one room and then another, scanning for movement, calling out for her son, and then hurrying. "René!" she repeated into the empty rooms and hallways.

Xavier and Anna crossed paths on the stairway a few minutes later, Xavier bounding up from the main floor, just as she was coming back down. "Anything?" she asked, breathless from the exertion and the fear closing in on her.

Xavier shook his head. "He's not in the basement or the garage," he said, worry edging into his voice.

Anna realized that if René were not inside then that meant he was outside or somewhere else. Either way, he was surely in trouble. She started to run towards the side door. "Have you looked in the yard?" she said, tossing these words over her shoulder as she shot past her husband. The hairs on Xavier's skin quivered as though an arrow had just missed him.

Xavier followed Anna into the night, each hurtling in opposite directions, shouting René's name again and again, their frantic calls swallowed up in the howling wind. The ground revealed no clues, the fresh snow having covered up any footprints the boy might have made.

"Could he have been picked up by someone?" Anna blurted out, her eyes casting over the darkness beyond the driveway. She turned suddenly to Xavier who was standing behind her, "This guy you had helping—?"

Xavier tensed. His gaze darted away as though not wanting to face her probing eyes directly. She asked again about the helper man. "Who was he—?" Her words dropped like pebbles tossed at a tall window, falling away unheeded as Xavier ran back toward the house without giving her an answer.

"Call 911," Anna shouted.

Xavier nodded, "Yeah, that's what..." His words disappeared with him as he returned inside.

Anna jogged up to the road, stopping in the middle. She spun about, surveying the horizon in all directions. She called again for her son but heard only her echo bounce off the tall evergreens straddling the road. They stood like silent sentries complicit in the secret of René's whereabouts.

Then she swerved her gaze back to the property and her eyes fixed on Xavier's truck with its covered cab. She bolted towards it, sprang onto the runner board and peered inside. She shouted and pounded her fists on the windows, rattling the panes.

Pulsing with agitation, Anna dashed back into the house. She found Xavier on the phone, she assumed with the 911 dispatcher. She snapped her fingers at him and urgently whispered: "Your keys!"

He gave her a blank look and continued his conversation into the phone. "He weighs about sixty pounds—"

Impatience shot through Anna. "Gimme your fucking keys!" she hissed. Xavier drew back, startled.

"Just a sec," he said to the operator. He reached into his jean pockets and with a trembling hand withdrew a slender key fob. Anna snatched it from him. She turned to go, but then stopped, her eyes burning into her bewildered husband.

"And, he weighs 47 pounds," she spat before bolting out the door.

Once more outside, Anna flung open the door to the truck, and dove in, shoving aside boxes and tools, growing more desperate each time a possible hiding place yielded nothing.

She staggered out of the truck and flew back into the house. Seeing Xavier was still on the phone, she interrupted him. "Did you tell them about the handyman?"

Xavier nodded. Something in his look, a flicker of guilt perhaps, made Anna suspicious.

"Give me the phone," she demanded. Xavier silently handed it over.

"This is Anna Docstedder, René's mom," she blurted. "There may be people who have it in for me. I'm a defense attorney, so I have enemies." She paused. "Look, my son would just not wander off!"

While she rhymed off a list of possible suspects, she paused for a second, motioned to Xavier. "Call Dad!" she commanded. "Use my phone."

*　*　*

When the police arrived some twenty minutes later, the subject of the helper man came up again. Xavier took an officer aside and revealed the identity of the would-be carpenter explaining that Munson had been there that afternoon—and coincidentally, had just been fired. Detectives quickly jumped on the possibility that René had been kidnapped by Munson out of revenge.

Anna could not believe she was hearing his name, not directly at first, but like a badly-kept secret. Whispered and then repeated. Like an echo in a well she had fallen into. *Lance Munson? What about Lance Munson? Lance Munson, here!* She was blindsided to learn that the one-time murder defendant had been in her home for several weeks now, working near her child. Her stomach lurched, cold fear twisting her innards.

Police wasted no time in locating Munson's last-known residence, a trailer on a property on the other side of the lake. Anna learned that there was no sign of either Munson or the boy. The handyman's rusting Chevrolet pick-up was covered in snow and likely had not been used for some time. The lack of footprints in the newly fallen snow seemed to indicate that no one had come or gone from the trailer in the last few hours.

Minutes later, Anna heard the roar of motors and witnessed a stream of trucks pull into the driveway. She felt a surge of hope to see the words "Search and Rescue" on the vehicles. Men in parkas emerged and sprung into action, pulling out ropes, lights and boxes of other equipment. It was like lifting a rock and watching ants scramble in all directions. A man with a dog jogged towards Anna.

"Mrs. Durand?"

"Uh—Anna Docstedder, I'm the mother."

The man extended his hand, "Ross Poitier, and Zephyr, my tracker pooch," he said, pointing to his Malinois-German Shepherd dog.

"Oh, thank God!"

61

"We're going to need something with your son's scent. You have an item of clothing of his that has not been washed?"

"Yes!"

Anna sped to René's room, tipped over his laundry hamper, and scooped up a handful of clothes. She ran back clutching the garments in her arms, spilling most of them as she tried to give them to the trainer.

"That's great. Thank you," Poitier said, choosing a few pieces. Poitier waved a striped pajama pants at the dog's snout and Zephyr immediately jumped into action, bounding towards the side door. He then jerked away and headed on a zig-zag path toward the lake with Poitier in close pursuit. Anna started to follow the dog and its master but a muscular officer in a navy jacket intercepted her and pulled her aside.

"We're trying to keep the area clear for the searchers," he said gently

"Well, I can't just stand around," Anna pleaded, "I wanna help."

"Come with me," said the officer, nodding toward the house.

He called for Xavier and corralled him too. "Listen folks, I'd like you two to go through the house carefully. Check closets and other spaces where René could be hidden. We're going to do it room by room. It's our experience that children rarely stray from home in the winter, and that, without a careful search, certain hiding spots might be overlooked."

Anna obeyed the officer's directions, hoping that René would be discovered inside but not understanding how that could even be possible. She revisited their earlier search of each room, pulling out boxes and sweeping her arms under beds and under blankets, all the while thinking of how the search and rescue team seemed oriented towards the lake.

Whenever she crossed paths with Xavier, they merely looked at each other without exchanging a word.

When the house was cleared, Anna was once more seized with a restless desperation, unable to be contained. The vibrations of a helicopter drew her outside again. As she exited, her eyes were directed upward. She saw the chopper overhead, a strong light beaming downward like something out of a sci-fi movie. The thrumming of the bird's rotors, and the whipping of tree branches mirrored Anna's own shakiness.

* * *

When Perry arrived, he was struck by the array of rescue workers and equipment spread over the Durand-Docstedder property. A searchlight mounted from a truck, shot out a powerful beam, its trajectory moving from side to side, bouncing off trees and the house, illuminating the figures busy in their quest. That they had assembled such a large team in such a short time was somewhat remarkable. But still, they had not found the boy.

Perry came upon Anna huddled at the edge of the house, watching the activity unfold around her. She was glad to see her father. They hugged and she repeated what she knew of René's disappearance, the story spilling from her between sobs. During her vigil, she was barely aware of the cold seeping up through the soles of her feet until it had overtaken her, and she was like a leaf trembling in the wind. Alarmed by her pale complexion, Perry took her and gently led her back inside. They moved toward the windows in the living room. "You can see everything just as well from here," he said, guiding Anna to an armchair and placing a blanket around her.

"Lemme get you something warm to drink," he offered, stepping away from her and heading to the kitchen. The old man was befuddled by the fancy new coffee maker so in the end he decided to just microwave some milk. While waiting for it to heat up, Perry paced, observing Xavier in discussion with a police officer in the front foyer. The officer was probing him for information about René, and the chain of events around him going missing. Perry froze when he heard a question about how long Munson had been working there.

When he returned to Anna a moment later with a mug of hot chocolate, she ignored him, her eyes transfixed on the activity outside. He turned to see what held her gaze so intently.

Just then, on the lake, a red light sparked and leapt out. Then another seared the black night like an angry welt. The rescuers were setting off flares to mark a find.

"Oh, God!" Anna cried, rising quickly. In her rush to get outside, she collided with her father, spilling the hot chocolate all over him.

* * *

Quite understandably, given so many people had traipsed through the snow, it would have been impossible to discern René's footprints from any others, but Zephyr had been able detect the boy's scent almost immediately. The canine followed its trace to the lake.

Using powerful flashlights, the other searchers trailed the K-9 duo, methodically sweeping their flashlight beams over the snow. As soon as the group hit the shoreline they were ordered to halt until the safety of the ice could be determined. This was difficult for them all, but especially so for the dog. During the wait, Zephyr pulled at his leash and keened. It was obvious there was something out there, and he wanted to get to it real bad.

Given the condition of the ice, only one man was selected from the rescue team to accompany the trainer and the dog. Using ropes and wide aluminum sleds, they ventured forward, the reflective strips of their neon yellow vests catching the glint of flashlights.

They trod carefully, keeping the dog reined in. Within minutes Zephyr made a beeline for something and dropped down. Had the dog not signalled, the men would have easily missed the tiny lump.

Poitier brushed away the snow to reveal—a child's boot.

Then a few feet later, the hyperactive canine signalled yet another find by crouching low to the ground, its paws lined up reverentially at the outer edge of a small snow-covered mound. With a sinking feeling, Poitier recognized the prone body of a child. The dog made a pitiful whine that sent a chill through the men waiting on the shore.

Although no one announced anything out loud, the discovery seemed to ripple through the group. The tone and focus shifted immediately among the crew. Anna heard a numerical code that she did not recognize. But she sensed right away that the news was not good, simply by the change in body language and expressions among the rescue team.

"What is it?" she shouted, her voice tremulous. "Have you found him?"

She could see the streaming of the rescuers, the not so subtle converging toward the shoreline. Xavier and Perry, who had now joined her outside, also noticed it.

"René!" she howled. "Is he there? Oh, God!" Anna whirled about, appealing to the men on the shore with the radios. "How is he? Somebody—tell me! Is he alright?"

"We'll know shortly," came the vague response.

"Oh, God. Please, just tell me what's going on!"

"We're going to get him ready to transport," said one of the police officers. "I think it's best if family members wait inside."

"I have to see him!" Anna broke free and bounded toward the lake. "I'm his mother!" Her anguished voice echoed across the frozen expanse.

A man in an orange parka grabbed her arm and she teetered backwards, stumbling. "The ice is not safe. You need to keep back!" he said as he pulled her up.

"Let's get you inside." He spoke with a gentleness that betrayed his pity for her.

"No! My baby!" she wailed.

"Please, Mrs. Durand, let the rescue team do their job."

They said rescue, but Anna knew from the way the neon-coated men huddled on the shoreline, waiting, that rescue was a term used euphemistically. As she was being pulled away, Anna overheard them discussing how to remove the body. How in the process of becoming frozen the boy had adhered to the surface.

She watched in shock as they scrambled to find something to dislodge him from the ice. Someone jogged up to the truck to get a kit and an extension cord, and then another extension cord, and then moments later Anna heard the whir of a jig saw as they cut into the ice. It was as though they were severing her in half.

Words as chilling as ice drifted towards her: "He's not dead until he's warm and dead," someone carelessly commented. That was when she knew for sure.

She doubled over and dropping to her knees in the snow, she begged God for mercy, gasping between sobs.

And then the helicopter dropped a basket to the ground and they lifted a small bundle into it. The whoop-whoop of the chopper blades, the gust of wind as it passed overhead stole the last of any warmth she had.

As Anna lay slumped over, her hair hanging down over her wet face, her hands and knees pulled tight, a burly police officer stooped down next to her and gently touched her arm. "Let me take you to the hospital," he said.

"How is he?" Anna asked. Tears were frozen in thin lines down her face, like winter's claw marks.

The officer shook his head. "They'll know more at the hospital."

She let him pull her to standing. She took a few steps forward, faltering as she was led back up the slope toward the driveway.

Xavier spotted Anna and moved toward her to comfort her but she would have none of it. "You were supposed to take care of him!" she screamed, smashing her fists against his chest.

"Hey, hey there, hey, hey! Stop that!" Hands pulled her away from Xavier.

"How could you let this happen!" she wailed.

"I'm sorry," Xavier sobbed. "I screwed up, I'm sorry."

"Come on," said Perry as he led his son-in-law away. "I'll take you in."

*   *   *

Afterwards Anna could not recall how she had gotten into the cruiser for the drive to the hospital. She paid no mind to the fact that a policeman sat next to her in the back seat as if she were a flight risk. Usually so attentive to details—astutely observing the names on badges and filing them away for later reference—this night she would not have the slightest recollection of the officers, nor their physical descriptions. She was in a fog and had only one thought in her mind.

She watched the passing scenery through a blur of tears. When they arrived in Glace Bay, she had lost sense of how much time had passed.

CHAPTER THIRTEEN
Losing Hope

It was a roller coaster of hope and despair. Time and again, they thought all was doomed for René, only to be surprised by a promising development. And then, just as quickly, all hope would be lost again.

They were buoyed by stories of others who had recovered after being frozen, especially children. A Swedish seven-year-old had been revived after being plucked from the sea, her core body temperature a mere 13 degrees Celsius. They saw photos of the girl, now ten years old, smiling and red-cheeked. She had gone back to school and was taking piano lessons.

It was not just children but adults as well who were brought back after succumbing to accidental hypothermia, in one case, after having been frozen for more than twelve hours. It was not just a miracle. Science and the right medical response demonstrated that some victims could recover and start functioning again, with little or no damage.

Anna, Xavier, Perry, Flo—and Sophie and Charles who rang up from an ocean liner off South America—all clung to the promise that modern medicine provided. Its success when deliberately lowering body temperature to perform heart transplants, for example, was an indication that hypothermia did not always equate with death.

Initially, the specialists at St. Boniface Hospital were optimistic. Xavier and Anna felt blessed by the attentive nurses and doctors who eased René back from a rigid frozen condition to a living, breathing child with rosy cheeks. State-of-the-art equipment extracted his frozen blood, warmed it, removed the CO_2 and then returned it to his veins.

"Being frozen, the body goes into stasis," explained one physician, "the organs are protected simply by being kept at a low temperature."

And afterwards, there was no denying that René looked good. That just to see him, seemingly whole, his skin no longer an

67

ashen white, was a gift the family did not expect to have after the terrible night on Lake Mikwam.

But after he was brought back, his body slowly warmed to the point where his temperature was normal and his heart was beating and his lungs were pumping, René still did not awaken. To the devastation of his family, he remained in a coma: his eyes did not flicker, his body did not stir, and his brain showed almost no activity.

The statement heard on the night of René's rescue replayed in Anna's head: "You're not dead until you're warm and dead." So now that he was warm—did that mean that he was warm and dead?

It was a puzzle. Why some and not others? Separately, Anna and Xavier pondered the unfairness of it all. The two-year-old girl from a farm near Edmonton who was found frozen to death, just steps from the back door of her family home, she had wandered out one winter's night wearing only a diaper and a t-shirt. She came back to life with seemingly no ill effects from having been a human popsicle, so why not René?

The radiologist in Norway, Dr. Anna Elizabeth Bägenholm, who slipped and fell while skiing with friends, she had been trapped under ice and had already been 'dead' for eighty minutes before being cut free and airlifted to hospital, and that helicopter trip took another hour. She woke up after three weeks. Bägenholm was angry when she came to, finding herself partially paralyzed, yet in the months to follow she regained the use of her body and her mind, to the point she eventually returned to work. René might well be like the Bägenholm case, Anna prayed.

Even Bägenholm, who was a doctor, had underestimated her own ability to recuperate after dying of hypothermia. So perhaps the doctors at St. Boniface were just as much in the dark. There were so few examples of accidental hypothermia treated promptly that science had yet to understand the full extent of the human capacity to recover. As far as Anna was concerned the verdict was still out on René's case. But as time wore on, as the days passed, there were fewer and fewer people who shared her optimism.

One day, the head of the team caring for René, Dr. William Grove, broached the difficult possibility that René would not be one of the lucky ones. Gently, Grove raised the prospect that René might never reawaken. He encouraged Xavier and Anna to consider letting René go, to donate his organs and be comforted in the knowledge that his passing would help many others.

"I'd like you to think about it," he said.

His words, delivered with nauseating delicacy, were a punch to the gut. The betrayal—from a doctor who was supposedly trying to help René—was crushing to Anna. But that Xavier seemed to nod and take it all in without so much as a whimper of protest alarmed and infuriated her. After they left Grove's office she cornered her husband. "Tell me, you're not seriously thinking about it?" she hissed.

Xavier sputtered, "We may have to—eventually."

"We're never going to give up on him!"

"Anna, be reasonable—"

Anger shot through her. "Be reasonable!" she fumed. The rage mixing with the grief made a powerful concoction: she felt dizzy, her ears rang. She knew she had to get away from Xavier and the hospital before she erupted—before she did something that would hurt René's chances even further.

Perry, who was watching a hockey game in the visitor's lounge, saw the look of distress on Anna's face. She explained the conversation with Grove and he nodded soberly. "I've got to get out of here," she said. Perry offered to take her home and she agreed.

On the drive back to the house, she called Alice Cochrane, one of the partners at the law firm. After Anna explained the new developments, they discussed strategies to prevent Xavier from acting unilaterally to remove René from life support. There was no way Anna would give up her boy without a fight.

Perry listened to Anna's conversation. He remained quiet, occasionally sighing. The other tragedy in all of this was that if René didn't pull through, there was no hope for Anna and Xavier's relationship either. He mused at how quickly love had turned to hate. They could barely stand to be in the same room together anymore to the point they now took turns keeping vigil at René's bedside.

* * *

When Anna arrived home, she found the house dark and cold. The first thing she did was light a fire.

"Do you want me to stay, hon?" Perry said, putting his arms around his daughter.

"No, Dad," she murmured through tears, "It's alright." She wanted to be alone. She wanted the space to mourn. To grieve the death that deep within her she knew might come. Anna gave her dad a long hug and then accompanied him to the door. She watched as his truck pulled out of the driveway then she hurried inside.

She found herself drawn toward René's bedroom. Her body moved up the stairs with a leaden heaviness. She let herself sink onto her son's bed, her head falling onto the pillow that still smelled of him. She stared up at the airplane light fixture and her son's array of stuffed animals. She scooped up a floppy-eared dog and held it in her arms as she sobbed, crying herself to sleep. Days of napping on hospital waiting room couches and the stress of not knowing René's fate had taken its toll on her.

She woke up some time later, feeling chilled to the bone. She shivered and pulled a small fleecy blanket around her shoulders. As she swept up the blanket, it caught the edge of a lamp on the nightstand. Anna grabbed it just before it toppled over. It was then she noticed—once more—the carving of the woodsman. Lance Munson's work. The man whose name was whispered the night René wandered outside. The man she should have helped send to jail forever.

She was suddenly seized with an overwhelming anger. She grabbed the carved figure and ran downstairs with it, hurling it into the fireplace. The hearth spat and sizzled as the carving disappeared in a knot of blue flames. She watched it burn until it was nothing more than a bit of charred wood.

She added more logs to the fire and curled up on the couch. She had no desire to sleep alone in the master bedroom. Before she fell asleep she texted Xavier. Not surprisingly, there was no news. Not so much as a flicker of an eyelid, nothing at all. When would the nightmare end?

The fire crackled and lulled her into a drowsy state. Her head felt heavy. She must have dozed off for several hours because when she opened her eyes the fire was out. She lay there for a while, reluctant to leave the warmth of the blankets.

Then she remembered her nightmare—she sat upright, texting Xavier again to ask about René. "Sorry. Nothing to report," he replied.

Her heart sank.

"You think some more about what Grove said?" Xavier continued a few seconds later.

Anna sighed. She was dying inside. This could not be happening. Why was Xavier so insistent? How could he give up on René so soon? Xavier was clearly thinking about letting the hospital just pull the plug on their boy, but she could not consider it. There had to be something else. They could still get a miracle. Anna decided to make a call.

"Hey, Auntie," Anna spoke softly.

"You calling with good news?" Flo replied.

Anna's chest tightened. "No," her voice faltered. Flo made comforting noises while Anna cried. "They want to take him off the ventilator. Can you believe it?" Anna said through tears.

Flo moaned. "You know what—" she said, trying to break in through Anna's bawling. "Let me say something for a second—"

"How could this happen?" Anna wailed.

"Listen, honey! Listen!" Flo insisted. And when the crying continued, "Damn it! Can you just let me a get a word in!"

Anna took a deep breath, trying to contain her sobs.

"Tell you what we're gonna do," Flo began quickly before Anna could get the chance to launch into another crying jag.

Anna felt a prick of hope as she listened to Flo.

"I want you to get some of his toys, his stuffies, all of his favourite things. Then I'm gonna need you to get a bunch of lake water—"

"What? Lake water? From out here?" Anna shivered recalling the desolate place where René had lain.

"That's right, honey," Flo said calmly and firmly.

"I dunno." The thought of going back out on the lake where her son had died filled her with dread.

"You want to try this, or what?"

"Yeah, yeah," said Anna with resignation. What else was there to do?

"And bring it all to the hospital for tonight," Flo commanded.

When Anna hung up, her heart was racing. She got up off the couch with renewed energy. She had a purpose, and for the first time in a long while—hope.

* * *

Anna strode gingerly over the ice. The detritus of a desperate nocturnal search was evident along the route to the location: tangled police tape and used flares; footprints now frozen into the formerly smooth surface; spray paint staining the snow. It triggered memories of that night. Her body could almost feel the thunderous vibrations of the helicopter swooping down to pick up René like a nighthawk capturing a mouse.

She slipped as she trod the uneven and icy path. In one hand she held a bucket for scooping water and a bundle of rope, and in the other hand, a long pole. It was insane. If anyone were to ask her what she was doing, she knew she would struggle to come up with a plausible cover story. It was madness to go back on the ice where her son had died—rather, had almost died.

As it had been explained to her, when the search and rescue team had found René's body, he was facing the shoreline as though he might have been heading back to the house. Had he just kept going for a little longer he might have made it home safely. Why had he stopped? Had he become disoriented from the onset of hypothermia? Had he not been able to see the house?

As she replayed the events of that night she remembered now those brief panicky moments as she drove home and the sudden white-out that had blinded her. Had that same weather mass swept down on her son as he staggered across the lake, confusing him, blocking the view of the house?

And what had drawn him here in the first place? One theory was that René had seen Munson leave and had tried to follow the handyman. Maybe someday René would be able to tell them what had happened. They could only hope he would.

Anna found the hollow in the ice where René had slowly become frozen before his rescue. She set down her bucket and pole at the slight depression on the surface. Rather than pull René off the ice the rescuers had cut around him and lifted everything up, ice block and all.

Anna kneeled at the edge of the small hole, now crusted over. She tapped the surface letting water bubble up. She dipped her bucket in and scooped up a small amount. Instinctively she clasped her hands together in prayer.

Oh, unholy water, she thought. *Undo your evil.*

As Anna crouched on the lake, she noticed, not far beyond the site of René's recovery, a dark patch. She guessed it must have once been a hole in the ice. As she got up, she decided, quite foolishly, to investigate this area. Without understanding her compulsion, she made her way there, her heart leaping at every groan from the ice as it yielded to her weight.

When she arrived at the spot, she could tell that something heavy had caused the ice to break here. In the intervening weeks, as winter progressed and night temperatures remained below freezing, the edges had been filling in with a near-transparent skin, almost like a wound being healed.

Every lake typically froze from the outside in, with the shallower water hardening first. The local ice fishermen knew this and would not set up their huts before February. It was not unusual for the middle of the lake to freeze over last but this gap was different. It was as though something had broken through here.

She squinted through the near transparent layer of ice, down into the watery abyss, and immediately felt a chill from deep within.

The sun shone down at that very moment giving the underwater scene an unmistakeable clarity. Appearing before her was the vague outline of a machine, the blue and silver body, the elongated runner and the oblong treads.

She had seen this snowmobile before.

She gasped suddenly as the ice began to give way. A section broke apart and she sank a few inches. It was like standing on a flimsy raft. Water raced up and pooled at her feet. She froze, gripping the long pole that, if need be, she would use to keep from falling all the way through.

As the lake opened up, a terrible stench hit her nostrils. That smell, she thought, it was familiar. And repulsive. Her memory finally revealed the source: a decaying body.

*   *   *

Anna stood in her son's hospital room and debated whether to make the call. Finally, she pulled out her cell phone and punched in a number.

"Dale, it's Anna Docstedder."

"Anna." Corbeau answered. He faltered, "How—How's your son?"

She paused, searching deep within herself for some reserve of strength. "Well, it's complicated. I'd rather not get into that right now—I'm calling because of Munson."

The mysterious disappearance of Munson had only been briefly investigated by police. The evening René went missing, they had checked Munson's trailer home and had talked to relatives of the ex-con but the matter was dropped after René was found. In the days and weeks that followed, no one had even bothered to file a missing person's report for the man.

When René was examined in the hospital, there was no sign that there had been any foul play. It was assumed his going out onto the lake was nothing more than a tragic accident.

"Munson?" repeated Corbeau, his surprise evident.

"Yeah, I think I know where you might find him."

When Anna finished the call with the detective, she turned to the boy in the bed. There he lay, statue-like. During the whole time she was on the phone he had not stirred. He had not moved since she had come in the room earlier. Not so much as a flicker of an eyelid or a twitching of his hand. Nothing.

*   *   *

Xavier stood gazing out the living room window as police crisscrossed the ice.

He held a phone to his ear.

"They are going to come back tomorrow and tow it out."

"Really?" Anna replied, showing less surprise than Xavier would have expected.

"All this time, he's been out there."

Anna remained silent. She now knew that he had secretly hired Munson to work on the addition, despite Xavier knowing full well that Munson was an ex-con and a serial burglar—and perhaps far worse.

So what if Munson were dead, lying at the bottom of Lake Mikwam. No longer able to harm them. The point was that Xavier had put them in danger. She still wondered if Munson might have lured René outside.

The betrayal was not something Anna could easily forgive. She remained bitter about the thoughtless way Xavier had kept Munson around, even after learning who he was. She shivered to think how vulnerable they were living there in such a remote loca-tion. Not a neighbour in sight. Munson would have had the perfect opportunity to case their home, to observe their routines, and later return to rob or attack them.

Xavier broke the silence. "Alright, well, I've just got some stuff to do here and then I'll be back after dinner."

Anna's mind raced. She did not want him back at the hospi-tal that evening. "Why don't you take the night off?" she suggest-ed. "I'll call you if anything happens. Besides, there's no point in both of us being there."

Xavier paused. Perhaps he wondered if this was a trick ques-tion because he asked, "You sure?"

"Uh huh." She tried to sound as casual as possible. The last thing that Anna wanted was for Xavier to show up in René's room that night of all nights. She had not shared with him the plans that she and her aunt had concocted. She was certain that had she asked Xavier's permission, he would never have agreed.

"But we still have that meeting with Dr. Grove tomorrow."

Anna stiffened. "I know, I know," she answered tersely. Hopefully, she could meet Dr. Grove in the morning with good news; that by some miracle René would have started to 'live' again.

74

"Anna, we've got to make a decision." Xavier's voice was pleading.

Her anger flared. She was tired of him pushing her like this. They didn't have to fucking decide anything. It was far too soon. With the tap of her finger, she ended the call. Within seconds her phone was ringing again. It was Xavier, but she ignored him and put her phone on silent.

CHAPTER FOURTEEN
The Ritual

The light was fading from the sky and the sun disappearing in a shroud of muted pink haze. As planned, Perry and Flo arrived at the hospital as darkness fell. Flo had a shopping trolley filled to the brim with her voodoo paraphernalia. In a moment of wisdom, Perry had thrown a blanket overtop so other than the rattle and tinkle of metal and stone no one would have any inkling of the old lady's magic kit hidden underneath.

The nurses had done their rounds and Anna asked them for some quiet family time. They seemed to understand. They were aware of the pressure to end the life support and perhaps assumed the relatives had come to say goodbye one last time.

As soon as they were assured of privacy from the hospital staff, Flo was all business. She started bossing Perry and Anna around, ordering them to distribute René's stuffies and toys in a semi-circle on his bed, with a few next to him on the side tables.

Flo took the mason jar of lake water from Anna and unscrewed the cap. The old woman dipped in her wiry hands and scooped out some, sprinkling it on the blankets and daubing it on René's face and hair.

It reminded Anna of a priest's ritualistic use of holy water. Doubt crept into her about Flo's abilities if they drew on Catholicism, a religion they had all come to reject. Time and again they had heard of the horrors of residential schools and the abuse suffered by children there.

But Anna began to feel more reassured once Flo got into her groove—so to speak. The little old lady who played bingo and watched too many soap operas was suddenly imbued with her native powers, calling upon the spirits to bring René back.

Even more strange was that Flo had Anna and Perry fasten a rope to René's wrists and this in turn was looped around themselves forming a circle. They sat on either side of René with Flo at the foot of the bed, directing the shamanic ritual.

Ancient chants came easily to Flo's lips like advertising jingles branded subconsciously. For the first time in weeks Anna felt encouraged. She felt herself relax, daring to hope in a way she had not allowed herself to do for some time.

Flo's steady voice wafted over them. "Bring the spirit of René back to his body. We welcome his spirit to return to the living world. We ask René to return. Return, René, Return. Be reborn. The Mighty Gitchimanitou so willing."

The repetitive chanting lulled them into a drowsy state. It was calming and soothing, if anything. Only once did Anna glance up and notice her father staring at her, his face lined with concern. If she could read his mind she would have guessed he was worried that she was setting herself up for it all to come crashing down on her—again. Anna gave him a reassuring smile.

"It's okay," she mouthed. She was willing to accept the outcome, or so she thought.

In her mind Anna echoed Flo's prayers. "Come back René. Come back among the living." Anna was all in. She realized there was nothing left to lose. And besides she really believed in Flo's powers.

Hadn't Flo stopped her from taking the school bus the day it crashed en route to a hockey tournament. No one died, but a couple of kids were badly injured. She had helped Anna get pregnant when fertility doctors had long given up. Some poultices and prayers said over Anna's abdomen and nine months later René had arrived. Flo had also warned them about the house by the lake. How Anna regretted not listening to her auntie. But the property had beguiled them. The glistening lake with the leaning trees, the land so sheltered and private, far away from big city crime.

Their first house had gone up so easily. Xavier and Perry blazed through the framing and even Anna helped on weekends and holidays. It was their paradise, their little oasis. Their together project.

Was it just Anna's imagination or was Flo's chanting louder now? A humming reverberated in the room, melding with the noise of the machines and the hospital ventilation. Everything was turned up to high volume. Anna's head throbbed as though packed with tightly coiled wires, zinging and pulsing. With a feverish intensity, electric energy ripped through her veins, zapped her spine.

She wanted to get up and get something cold to drink but strangely felt fixed to the spot. As though drawn by a magnetic force, her chair slid closer to the bed until her knees were locked against the frame.

She glanced at her aunt just then and the sight of Flo's wild eyes caused Anna's heart to lurch, sensing that the ceremony had been ramped up far beyond the old woman's expectations. It was either wildly successful or completely out of control. But to her credit, Flo kept the incantations going, as though letting the spirits know she was still in charge.

Perry had the look of someone who had stepped onto a Ferris wheel and realized too late he was afraid of heights. He hung on for dear life as the air in the room swirled around him, and his chair tilted and rocked.

In all the chaos, Anna kept one eye on her son as well, but he seemed like an island of calm midst the storm. She watched as one of his stuffed animals became engorged and burst at the seams. But René himself was quiet and still.

Then she saw the strangest thing. A black thunderbird burst from René's chest and flew over them, hovering in the tiny room, bouncing from wall to wall. It was all so absurd but at the same time perfectly normal.

Flo began to weep and moan, no longer able to utter comprehensible speech, she sputtered and babbled guttural noises. It was as though the bird was in charge now and Flo had lost control.

Anna was terrified yet fascinated at the same time. She felt time shrink to nothing and suddenly she was among her dead relatives. Her mother and brother sat with them in the room, all taking part in this event to bring back René.

Her little boy was coming back to her, she could feel it. A presence, a happy joyous spirit enveloped her. She could hear him laughing, she could feel him squeezing her hand. He was here! René was back! Anna exhilarated in his aura. She felt her heart swell to bursting.

But turning to look at the embodiment of the boy, she saw him as still as ever. A statue. Frozen. It was incomprehensible.

A gurgling sound compelled Anna to turn away from her son toward her aunt. She was astonished to see Flo's necklace come alive, each bead manifested as a glistening serpent. One overlapped the other, forming a thick coil around Flo's neck.

Auntie was choking but Anna could do nothing to help her. She was riveted in place, unable to reach over to Flo and untie the serpents. Anna could only watch in helpless terror as the reptiles slowly strangled her aunt.

The atmosphere in the room vibrated, every nail, screw, fastener shook from the movement of air. The electric pulsing sent all the machines haywire, until they screeched and beeped and shrieked multiple alarms. Then suddenly the rope that held them all together tightened even more and pressed them hard against the bed.

Just then René opened his eyes, but only for a second. He loosened his grip on a tiny figurine that Anna glimpsed for the first time at that moment. She stared in shock as the carving of the woodsman—the same carving that she had thrown into the fireplace the night before—moved all on its own. The little man brought down his axe.

Snap!

The taut rope holding them together ripped apart and Flo and Perry went flying backwards. Anna flailed before catching hold of the bed railing. The serpent coil around Flo's neck disentangled and each snake dropped away, shrinking and shifting into shiny green and black beads once more.

The thunderbird that circled overhead, spun backwards and dipped toward René's chest. In an awful movement, the malevolent force dove into the child's torso. And still René seemed asleep, unaware of the abuse, the terrible invasion of his being.

* * *

Deep within Lake Mikwam, a body stirred. A man trapped under his machine unfurled his tangled arms for an instant, opened his eyes and looked upward, to the surface. His gaze held hope—of a rescue, perhaps.

* * *

Hours later there came a small knock at the door. A woman peered inside. It was a nurse. Her brass nametag read Kelly Kinsey, RN. Kelly whispered apologetically as she tiptoed inside.

"Sorry, I just need to check the machines. Everyone's having a little snooze, I see." Or so it seemed.

Flo was slumped over in her chair, while Perry leaned back in his, mouth open and snoring. Anna had her head buried in the blanket on René's bed, an arm extended toward her son. She stirred as Kelly moved around the room.

"How is he?" Anna asked the nurse.

Kelly paused, somewhat uncomfortable with the question. René's case was well known on the floor and there had been instructions not to divulge too much when discussing his prognosis.

"I can get Dr. Grove or Dr. Wilkes to see you when they do rounds this morning."

The non-committal words floored Anna. The nightmare was back. She bit her lip. Tears began to well in her eyes. She understood that the nurse's reticence meant there was no good news.

As she retreated, Kelly stumbled over something on the floor. Her foot had made contact with a bead from the broken necklace. It was still rolling away when she picked it up and scrutinized it.

"What do we have here?" The nurse held up the bead for Anna to see.

"Oh, that's ours," said Anna. "My aunt's necklace must have broken." She took the bead from Kelly and pocketed it.

Rather than confront her aunt and father with a face full of tears, Anna bent over and picked up the remaining beads scattered over the floor. She fought an overwhelming desire to sink to the linoleum and remain there, flat and crumpled, like an animal run over by a truck.

She wondered now what was to come of her little boy, who as far as the hospital and others were concerned was clinically dead. She was challenged with her worst fear, that despite all their efforts—their prayers, the medical interventions and the shamanic ritual—they had failed to bring René back to life, and he was dead, and gone forever. And there was nothing to do.

CHAPTER FIFTEEN
The Edge of Despair

Anna tried to be brave as she accompanied Flo and Perry to the elevator. They too were devastated, not to mention physically crushed from the exertions of the night before. Anna wanted the continued comfort of their presence, so she asked when they would return.

"Hon, I can't do this again. I said my goodbyes to him," Perry said, holding his daughter close.

"But what if it isn't the end? What if..." Anna whimpered.

"I hate to say it, Annie, but it's over."

Anna sobbed, hugging her father. "Dad, no! I can't let him go."

"I'm sorry." He patted her arms.

Flo offered no predictions, neither hopeful nor dire but her grim expression seemed to say it all. When Anna hugged her goodbye, Flo kept silent. Her eyes dark and closed off. The elderly pair retreated into the elevator. As the door closed behind them, Anna felt desperately alone.

* * *

From the large hospital windows, Anna could see the city was waking up and moving. The twinkling lights of fast food restaurants and gas stations were eclipsed by a bright morning sun. Cars were travelling hurriedly. Everyone had somewhere to go. For them, it was another normal day. But for René it would be the end, she thought. The day when his earthly body would no longer exist. The day his heart would stop beating. The day his dreams would die. And the day her hopes would also die.

She was absorbed by these depressing thoughts and did not hear Xavier enter the room. When she turned away from the window, she saw her husband taking René's hand.

As he stood gazing at his boy, he addressed Anna. "How did it go last night?"

She searched her husband's face. "What do you mean?" she said, worried that there was something left behind in the room that gave away the secret ritual.

81

Xavier seemed perplexed by her question. "Well, René's vital signs—"

Anna spoke in an anguished voice, "There was nothing. Nothing happened! But that doesn't mean—"

"Anna, how many weeks has it been like this! We can't go hanging on forever."

"Xav, please, Xav. Just a little bit longer."

"This is killing us."

"I'm not ready—"

"We're going to have another baby—"

"It's not René—"

"René's dead. Anna. He's a vegetable—"

It was the wrong thing for him to have said. He realized it as soon as it came out of his mouth. His words set her off like a match to gasoline.

She flew at him like an ancient mythical bird, all claw and venom. Stabbing his face and dragging her fingernails across his skin, she shrieked all the vengeful thoughts that had been stewing inside of her for weeks now.

"You killed him! You let him go and die and freeze! You want to kill him again! Murderer!"

Xavier lifted his arms protectively, fending off Anna as best he could. She was deep in the grips of rage when an orderly pulled her away. When Xavier let his arms down away from his upper body, it revealed several scratches to his face.

The orderly called security and soon the room was abuzz. A nurse tended to Xavier's wounds while another tried to calm Anna, even suggesting she take a sedative.

"I'm pregnant. What do you think!"

When two heavy-set guards prepared to escort Anna away, Xavier tried to stop them. "It's okay, man. It's alright. It's no big deal."

"Don't you fucking touch me!" Anna screamed.

And when the guards still proceeded, Xavier asked, "Where are you taking her? She needs to be here for our son."

* * *

Anna's mouth felt dry. When she tried to stand her legs were unsteady. Her stomach churned. A wave of humiliating memories washed over as she recalled her outburst. The horrified looks, the shocked reactions of the hospital staff came back to her now.

Nevertheless, they had been quite forgiving of her. They put it down to stress from the loss of her son and the hormonal upset from her pregnancy. Xavier agreed not to press charges. Anna would be allowed to go home but had to report back to the hospital for outpatient counselling.

Before she could leave she had to meet with Dr. Grove and Dr. Wilkes to discuss René's status—whether or not to keep him on life support.

If she had been in her best lawyer mode, she would have said that they were making her decide under duress, but Anna had decided to give up fighting. She would sign the consent form. She feared many more things than René's passing. Most importantly, she feared that she might lose her baby once it was born.

Her attack on Xavier had put her and her family under further scrutiny. Social services had legitimate reason to check in on her and the Durand-Docstedder family situation—the several alarming incidents in their household: a child wandering out on a lake and freezing to death; a mother nearly scratching her husband's eyes out; the unsupervised presence of an ex-con and one-time murder suspect in the home with their young son. Ample evidence of neglect. All major strikes against them. Anna realized she could not push her luck.

*   *   *

Later in the conference room, she could not look at Xavier's face as he slid the consent forms toward her. The scratches under his eyes were puckered and crusted over. She felt everyone watch her with probing looks. As she picked up the pen, she could not keep her hand from trembling. It was the sleepless night and the stress, and the still-bubbling anger. She signed knowing that with it she gave away a power that had already been stolen from her. Fate was an indiscriminate thief.

Xavier and Anna would be allowed back in René's room once the machines had been disconnected. It would only take a few minutes they were told. They sat alone for a while in silence.

Then Xavier spoke: "We're doing the right thing—"

"Don't fucking talk to me," she said under her breath. And so they became silent again.

It seemed like barely a minute had gone by when a nurse hurried into the conference room and insisted they come right away. It was very odd, Anna thought. Had René died already? Without even a chance for a last goodbye?

She and Xavier jogged behind the nurse, dodging stretchers and slow-moving patients in their rush to get back to René's room. When they got to the doorway, they found it clotted with people.

News had travelled fast and apparently everyone from the meal service to the cleaner had converged on the room. If they couldn't get inside they craned their necks in the doorway to get a glimpse of what all the fuss was about.

"Excuse me!" Anna said with alarm. "Let us through!"

Inside they found a wall of medical staff surrounding their son's bed. There was murmured excitement, gentle laughter, and exclamations of surprise. Anna pressed through the crowd. At last several people shuffled out of the way to allow Xavier and Anna passage. When she got to René's side, she was startled to see him sitting up, looking as normal as can be.

"*Bon dieu!*" Xavier gasped.

"Oh, baby!" Anna whimpered, disbelieving her eyes.

At the sound of her voice, René turned to her and smiled as though relieved to see a familiar face. Anna was overwhelmed and surprised that he even recognized her.

"Oh, dear God!" Anna said, her voice choking.

"Mommy, I'm thirsty," was the first thing the miracle boy said.

If she could have melted from love, she would have. She was not aware of the hands that caught her as she slumped, falling over from the shock.

CHAPTER SIXTEEN

Back Home

Anna trailed René as he wandered through the house. It was as though he was a kid coming back after a month-long summer camp, refamiliarizing himself with home after weeks spent in a bunkhouse with strange kids. He did the things that she would have expected him to do, and that he had always done, but still his behaviour seemed strange and novel to her. A back-flip on the couch, jumping on the bed, putting too much fish food in the tank.

"Hey, these are different," he said spotting the new fish that Anna and Xavier had snuck in to replace the dead ones. Killed from lack of care during Xavier and Anna's long hospital vigils.

"Yeah, the other ones missed you when you were away, so they…" her voice trailed off.

"Died?" René gave her a mildly irritated look. Anna felt a sting of guilt. Here was another instance of her being a negligent mother.

"Sorry." Why was she apologizing for a couple of dead fish when she should have been seeking forgiveness for a whole lot more? That conversation would happen later. Not today.

While in René's room, Anna caught sight of the workmen through the window. They were dragging panels of black metal fencing from a truck and setting it up around the yard. It was a temporary solution that came too late. It was something they should have done as soon as René was born.

"Is that supposed to keep me out of the lake?"

Anna turned around sharply. René was also watching the fence construction.

"You know, I can just walk around from the front yard and get in that way," he chuckled.

Anna gave him a troubled look but he simply scoffed. "It's not like I would do something so stupid—again."

Anna moved to hug her son, tears filling her eyes. "Sweetie, it wasn't your fault," she murmured, burying her face in his hair.

*   *   *

Anna spun through the rest of the day. Hyper-alert to whatever René was doing. If she could not see him, she would find him. Each time overcome by relief and flowing with tears of happiness as though the discovery of a child doing something terribly ordinary, like playing with Lego or running a car up a wall was a miracle. His dark eyes would stare back at her, puzzled, and sometimes with a trace of annoyance even, as though tiring of her hysteria.

Anna could not relax unless she had René in her sights. At one point she slid the couch across the doorway and told him to stay in the living room, within view. She put the TV on for him and began to prepare dinner for their celebration that night. They had missed his sixth birthday and Christmas so this was a multi-purpose event.

It was only going to be a small gathering with her Dad, Flo, and a few close friends. Although Xavier and Anna wanted to do something to mark this amazing event, this gift from heaven, Anna could not shake a vague feeling of unease. That somehow it was too good to be true. Medically there was no explanation. René was supposed to have died, not just once, but twice. Why was he spared?

When her aunt arrived, Anna pulled her aside and in a hushed voice asked her not to speak of the ritual. Flo nodded.

"It didn't work anyway, right?" Anna said. "He didn't start breathing on his own until they pulled off the ventilator." Anna was hoping for some reassurance from Flo, some confirmation that this was indeed the case, but Flo was noncommittal.

"Please don't mention it to anyone," Anna begged.

"Of course not," Flo whispered, her voice hoarse.

Anna studied her aunt, suddenly taking note of the bulky scarf around Flo's neck. "What's this?" Anna asked as she reached toward Flo, gently pulling down the scarf. She gasped. Encircling Flo's neck was a chain of deep red marks.

"Oh, my God!"

The old woman drew back slightly, repositioning the scarf below her chin. "It's nothing," she said, shaking her head. She took Anna's hands in her own and squeezed them. "It's you I'm worried about."

Flo gave a furtive glance to either side to confirm that they were alone. "You're not safe here."

Anna's heart sank. She was tired of Flo undermining their choices. "Believe me, Auntie Flo, you don't know how happy I am." But there was something weary in Anna's tone that suggested otherwise. Flo held onto Anna's hands as long as she could, not in the least bit convinced by her niece's reassurances. The old woman felt the malevolence in every corner of the house, stronger than ever.

*   *   *

Although he had been given a clean bill of health, Xavier and Anna were reluctant to let René go back to school right away. But keeping him home presented a logistical challenge. Anna and Xavier badly needed money, and both would have to work hard to catch up on the accumulating bills. The medical expenses, the lack of income from the long absence from work, and the interest on the line of credit was destroying them financially.

And then there were other unanticipated outlays. Surprise repairs from problems due to the cold: the furnace failing on the worst day of winter, ice jamming the eaves, followed by a pipe bursting.

*   *   *

"What caused it?" Anna asked the plumber as he was writing up his invoice for the emergency call.

The plumber shrugged. "Extreme weather conditions. On really bad days, you want to keep the water flowing so it doesn't freeze in the pipes."

Great, Anna thought, keep the water running all winter. That wouldn't be cheap either. She sighed as she took the invoice from the plumber and wrote him out a cheque.

"Also, you gotta beef up the insulation," the plumber added as an afterthought. "It's awful cold in here. In fact, I don't think I've ever been so cold on a job *inside* a house."

Anna raised her eyebrows. She wanted to protest, remembering spending hours with Xavier tucking bats of itchy pink insulation in the rafters of the attic and between the joists of the basement ceiling. It was not like they had neglected that part of the construction. Still Anna she had to agree with the plumber that it was "awful cold" in here. She too felt the constant numbing chill while inside.

*   *   *

"This house is a money pit," declared Anna. "It's freezing all of the time. The dollars are just getting sucked out of here through that hole," she said, jabbing her finger in the direction of the addition.

"Inside voice, Anna," said Xavier, teasing.

87

Fuck you, she thought to herself. While their home was freezing, he was strumming away on his guitar. He just didn't get it.

"Tell you what, I'm just going to close off that section. Wall it all off until the weather improves," Xavier declared.

"Fine," she huffed.

"Come on, Anna. Things are rough. We've been through a lot. But look on the bright side. We got René back. We're going to have another baby. We're all healthy. Life's good."

He opened his arms as though to welcome a conciliatory hug—one of those 'we're good' type embraces but instead Anna stood still, staring coolly, unmoved by his grand speech.

Xavier regarded her with pity. She was a wreck, so pale and worn. It was likely the stress and pregnancy taking its toll. Her nose was red from a bad cold, one that had plagued her for several weeks now. She clutched her arms together for warmth, huddling in a thick sweater. On her hands she wore those ridiculous Fagan gloves with the fingertips cut off. She kept those on all the time now. And the giant oversized down boots. Where was the sexy beautiful Anna he had once fallen in love with?

* * *

It was just one of those days where she was tired and feeling cold and crummy. She should have stayed in bed. Instead she let her irritation get the better of her. She and Xavier had been squabbling all morning.

"You know, I would have finished the baby's room at least but my helper just went AWOL."

Anna could not believe her ears. The liar, she thought. "Your helper, he went into the lake."

"What?" Xavier seemed truly surprised.

"Munson—your helper—drowned! His skidoo broke through the ice."

"Shit, Anna. I didn't know. I mean I didn't know that was— that he was that same guy. I just thought…" He spoke earnestly, but she was having none of it. She didn't believe it for a minute.

"Oh, yeah," she seethed, furious at him for pretending he had not hired Munson. It was such a bald-faced lie.

"Look, by the time I found out who he was, he had already been here for weeks."

She gave her husband an icy stare. It was always there—her anger at him. Just below the surface. Would she ever be able to forgive him?

88

CHAPTER SEVENTEEN
Tamryn's Day

The plan was for Xavier to put himself out there for carpentry work, and for Anna to keep up her law practice at least until the baby came. And then they would take it from there. Maybe sell the house if they had to. But this new plan also required hiring a babysitter to stay with René during the day initially and later when he had returned to school, to meet him coming off the bus.

Tamryn Spettigue had finished a degree in sociology and was thinking of doing a master's. Her mom knew Anna from spin class and heard they needed a temporary babysitter. Tamryn had little experience with children but she knew everything there was about people given her 3.6 GPA in Sociology.

It wasn't too bad a drive as Tamryn lived less than ten miles away. True it was a winding route skirting the lake, so she was grateful her dad had put snow tires on her car.

* * *

As Anna showed the 23-year-old around the house, the young woman decided right away there was no reason to go into what she called 'the beyond'—the messy construction zone: a dusty and cold section being added to the house. It turned out Anna wanted her to keep out of there as well.

"My husband's going to close that part off," Anna said with an edge to her voice. "One of these days. Please keep René out of there."

Tamryn began on a cold Monday in early March. She breezed through Anna's detailed instructions and laughed when reading the steps she gave for making macaroni and cheese the way René liked it—with a pinch of paprika and bacon bits. Anna also itemized what television shows were appropriate. Tamryn was impressed with Anna's attention to detail. Tamryn had heard Anna was a successful criminal defense attorney and wondered if this was why she was so good at what she did.

Tamryn saw the babysitting job as a stop-gap thing until she could figure out her life. She knew it was short term anyway because Anna would be going on maternity leave soon. Tamryn didn't care. She didn't expect to be there long. But after the first few hours, she wasn't even sure she could stick it out for the rest of week. By noon of that Monday, Anna had called her twice. It was kind of annoying. Did Anna think she was incompetent?

When Tamryn phoned her mom to talk about it, her mother said it was normal for Anna, who had almost lost her son, to have these 'jitters.' "Don't take it personally," her mother advised.

Anna's hovering and micro-managing was one problem, but the kid was another. Tamryn had expected to be molly-coddling a frail child with possible brain damage but there seemed to be nothing wrong with the boy's mind—except a bad attitude. That was his real problem, Tamryn decided. One thing for sure, he had his parents wrapped around his little finger. She guessed he was using his hospital stay to get whatever he bloody hell wanted.

Tamryn spent hours trying to cajole René into doing a little homework. But the little boy stared at the exercise sheets before him, giving Tamryn an odd look. Almost like he was seeing through her. It made her uncomfortable. He twirled the pencil in his hand for a few minutes, while his babysitter waited.

"You need some help to get started?" she offered. She grabbed a blank sheet of paper and was about to draw ten circles.

"Uh-uh," he said with a bored sigh. Finally, he grabbed the fat pencil and bent his head over the paper. Noticing his stubbly hair with the patches of bare skin where the monitors had been gave Tamryn a twinge of pity. He had been revived after dying. That had to be rough, she conceded. Maybe she was being too hard on the kid. He had been through a lot.

She was surprised to see René whizzing through the addition and subtraction problems without hesitation. Then he went on to the word exercises and sped through those questions as well. Not bad for a six-year-old, thought Tamryn. When he was done he gave her an insolent look, then put his palms on the pages and shot them toward her. The papers spun across the table, overshooting the edge, and falling and scattering all over the floor.

How annoying, thought Tamryn. She was tempted to ask him to pick the papers up but thought better of it. She didn't have the energy to negotiate with the little monster. She got off her chair and stooped to the floor to grab the pages. Then as she got up, she saw the kid smirking at her. She fumed inwardly. What a spoiled brat.

It was only 10:30 in the morning. It was going to be a long day.

She tried to read a story to him, but he started to chime in every few words, saying the word she was about to read just seconds before she read it. It was very annoying. She gave up, slamming the book shut.

There were more school exercises that René could have done but Tamryn had her fill of teaching him. Besides she was not getting paid enough to be this boy's tutor as well.

"Look, I'm going to make some lunch. You want to watch TV?"

René shrugged.

Tamryn flipped through several stations before settling on a children's program: *Max and Ruby*. She caught René rolling his eyes at her choice. He may not like the show, Tamryn thought, but that was just tough for him. She left him in the living room and went to the kitchen.

She pulled out a pot to boil water for the macaroni and filled it halfway. There was something wrong with the stove, she felt. The water was taking too long to heat up. Thinking it was because she was 'watching the pot' that things were dragging, she left the kitchen and went to the living room to check on René. Everything seemed fine, so she popped back in the kitchen. Within seconds, she noticed the boy flipping channels. From what she could tell, he had switched to a true crime show. *The little bugger.*

"René, put it back! That's not suitable."

He ignored her and kept at it. It did not matter what Tamryn said. Or that she would come back into the living room and return the station to the original one. As soon as she left he would click it back. Rinse and repeat. Then she wised up and took the clicker and placed it on a high shelf. First he rebelled by turning on the volume super loud. Then he must have found a way to reach the remote control, because the next thing she knew, he was back to changing the channels again.

He was watching whatever he wanted. Tamryn sighed. She made a note to herself: Do not become a teacher. Kids today are way too entitled.

*   *   *

At lunch, René ate heartily. He packed away several servings, plus a ham and cheese sandwich.

"You still hungry?" Tamryn asked, astounded at his voracious appetite. She wondered if it was the long stay in hospital with little more than a saline drip to nourish him that had spurred this intense feeding frenzy.

While Tamryn was washing up the lunch dishes, René went to the window and stared out at the lake. She would have liked to take him out to play in the snow, but Anna had strictly forbidden it. There it was in Anna's notes: "No outdoor activity. If bored, try board games!"

That seemed overly protective. At some point, René would have to go out in the real world. In this country, you could not avoid winter. It was just a matter of dressing properly for the cold and—not staying out too long.

In the afternoon, Tamryn set up paints and playdough on the big harvest table. This would be a little less stressful than those homework sheets. As far as Tamryn was concerned, René could miss the rest of the school year and still not have trouble keeping up when he returned in the fall.

René dove into the fingerpaints with relish. He jabbed with his index, swirling the tips of his fingers into strange and exotic patterns. Dogs and birds. Not that Tamryn really paid close attention. She was glad for some downtime. She was feeling tired and sluggish, so got out her tablet, eager to get back into an absorbing novel that she had almost finished.

But damn, it was hard to get comfortable in that draughty room. She threw some logs in the fireplace, but it was a losing game. She wore her coat and scarf inside, yet still felt the chill.

When she was not stoking the fire or brewing some more hot tea to keep warm, Tamryn was thinking of ways to get out of this babysitting gig. What excuses could she come up with to bail on this job without causing a rift between Anna and her mom?

Had Tamryn known that she would not live out the day, she might not have fretted so much over her little white lie—one she would never get a chance to try on anyone. She hadn't yet decided on the exact words when Xavier returned just after five o'clock to relieve her. He seemed happy to see his son. Tamryn didn't want to bum him out by telling him she was quitting because his son was weird and their house was freezing. She resolved to handle it later.

She planned to call Anna after discussing the matter with her mother. But Tamryn would never get to make that call. No one would ever know the inner turmoil she suffered over her day with that weird kid.

*　*　*

What a relief, thought Tamryn, getting into her car and driving away from the Durand-Docstedder house. How could it be that it was warmer outside than inside? After she got the motor going and scraped the windows, she hopped into her 2008 Nissan with the brand-new snow tires, and headed home via Lake View Road.

She popped her ear buds in and began to relax, dreaming of the hot bath she would have when she got home. She was bopping to Ariana Grande's One Last Time, following the curve in the road where it hugged the edge of Lake Mikwam, when just then a snowmobile came up onto the road from out of nowhere, it seemed. It was bizarre, Tamryn thought. The machine was all frosted over, like it had been sitting in an ice cube. The driver too was all glazed with icicles and particles of shimmering snow. In her headlights the wintry apparition glistened like an ethereal other worldly traveller.

She was braking all the while knowing the snowmobiler was doomed. It had come up so suddenly, there had not been enough time to stop or veer out of the way. When her Nissan hit it, she thought it was odd that there was no crunching or crashing sounds, but only a sharp low whistle like the hiss of wind over a frozen lake.

In that instant, she felt the cold engulf her, freeze her lungs before she got out a single scream, her hands locked in icy rigidity to the steering wheel, keeping her from redirecting the car out of the spin like she had been taught in driver's ed.

Her mind was fully aware as the vehicle spun, and yet she was frozen in terror, unable to stop the car from being pulled to the edge of the road, where it ground along the guardrail, sparks flying, the vehicle never slowing. Tamryn's foot was like an ice block pressing heavily on the gas, until the car became airborne, and catapulted over the cliff toward the lake. The trajectory would later baffle the accident specialists. All of it occurred with as little effort as it took for René to topple one of his little matchbox cars.

Just like the one that he was gleefully running over the arm of the couch at that very moment. His small hands releasing the toy and letting it tumble and crash onto the wide plank floor.

"Boom," his little voice giggled.

The windshield smashed into the shape of an angry snowflake, with Tamryn's bloody head at the centre. In her rush to get home, sadly she had not fastened her seatbelt and was propelled forward with deadly force.

Soft sticky snow began to fall. It soon covered the skid marks and broken tree branches in a thick blanket of white. You could not blame anyone peering down the embankment toward the lake for not seeing the mangled car. It was now obscured in downy layers. And until the snow melted, it would not be found.

It was nearly ten o'clock when Anna's cell phone rang. It was a few seconds before she could grab it. She had fallen asleep on the couch, a sheaf of documents on her lap. Her eyes caught sight of the matchbox car as she reached for her cell. She was disoriented but came awake quickly at the urgent tone of her friend's voice.

"Is Tammy still there?"

Janice Spettigue was forgetting that her daughter no longer liked people calling her by that version of her name. She wasn't a baby anymore. In fact, she wasn't anything anymore.

"Tammy?" Anna repeated the name, confused at first.

"I'm sorry to be calling this late. Is Tamryn at your place?"

Anna thought back to the evening. "No. No. Tamryn left when Xavier got home. At least that's what he told me. She's not here now." A knot formed in the pit of Anna's stomach.

"Did she say if she was going anywhere on her way home?"

"Not that I know of. But I wasn't here. Did you try her boyfriend? Her other friends?"

"Yes, everyone I could think of."

Anna wanted to suggest calling the hospitals and the police but she hesitated. "Lemme ask Xavier." Anna got up gingerly. She was stiff and cold. She gasped as she almost tripped over the small car René had been playing with earlier. She kicked it out of the way.

"What's that?" Janice's voice was back, pitiful and frightened.

"Nothing." Anna turned on a light, ambling toward the stairway. "I'll call you back, Jan, okay?"

*   *   *

She touched Xavier on the shoulder and he awoke with a start. He sat up halfway, peering at Anna through his tousled hair.

"Xavier, did the babysitter say anything about what she was doing after work?"

"Nope. She had her coat on and was ready to fly out of here the second I got in the door. It was odd, she couldn't get out fast enough."

Anna called Janice back and reported on her conversation with Xavier. "She didn't say much. He had a feeling she was in a hurry to get somewhere. If she was probably going to meet someone after work, she never said who or what."

Janice sighed. "I don't know what to do, Anna."

"Has she stayed out late before? I mean, she's probably not used to living with her parents anymore. Not used to having to check in with anyone."

"No, no, she's very responsible."

Anna imagined every parent thought that about their kids until they learned the truth. She tried to reassure Janice, even though she felt uneasy herself. "It's only just after ten now."

"Yes, I know. That's why I haven't called the police yet," Janice said with resignation. "I just don't have a good feeling about this."

Ditto, thought Anna. Though she kept that to herself. Anna didn't like that Tamryn disappeared after leaving their house—with the implication that they were somehow involved.

CHAPTER EIGHTEEN
Tamryn is Gone

When Tamryn didn't show up for work in the morning, Anna realized with dread that she had to let Janice know. Anna guessed even before she spoke to her friend that Tamryn probably hadn't returned home the night before.

Anna offered to call the police and use her sway to have them bypass the 48-hour waiting period before beginning a missing persons investigation. Janice had already called hospitals and checked with the roads department for accidents.

Tamryn's stepfather Neil had gone up and down the route their daughter would have driven home the night before and had seen nothing. He would go back in the light of day and search some more. They had a message in to the cell phone company to see where Tammy's phone had last pinged. The girl's parents were covering all the bases.

Meanwhile Anna had to get to work. She felt the heaviness of her advanced pregnancy, her fitful sleep, her cold and aching body, and the strange uneasiness that enveloped her, particularly relating to the mystery of their missing babysitter.

Just as Anna was about to call Flo, her aunt's number showed up on her screen as an incoming call.

"Auntie!"

"Are you alright?" Flo asked by way of greeting.

"We're fine. Why?" Anna knew what was coming but bit her tongue.

Flo sighed. "Oh, these dreams I've been having!"

"Uhuh." Anna waited for more elaboration. She was not sure she wanted to tell Flo about the missing babysitter.

"You're in danger. You've got to get out before it's too late."

Anna was a lawyer. She would need more proof before up-rooting the whole family.

Flo continued with a marked reluctance in her voice. "You're going to think I'm half whacked."

Or 100 per cent whacked, thought Anna. "Tell me, Flo, why you think we have to move?"

"I keep seeing you being followed by a bad man. He is living in the house. In the addition. He watches you at night."

Flo was so stubborn, even in her dreams. She would not let go of the idea of the addition being a mistake. The reno was definitely haunting them but not in the way that Flo thought. "Who is this man?" Anna asked, more out of politeness than a real concern that there was someone uninvited in the house.

"I want to say Manson—?" Flo replied tentatively. "I'm not sure. Charles Manson? Does that ring a bell?"

Anna wanted to burst out laughing. "Auntie Flo, Charles Manson definitely is a bad man but he's on death row in California. He couldn't possibly be all the way up here."

"Hmmm. No, no, you're right. It's a different Manson. I could have the first name wrong. It's his cousin. It's the whole family. They're all up to no good. A cousin, or a brother. Someone just as bad or worse."

* * *

After she hung up, Anna called her dad and asked him to bring Flo out to their house. He readily agreed. Anna explained that their babysitter hadn't shown up that day and Flo would be filling in.

"And just so you know, Flo thinks Charles Manson is living in our addition."

"She does, does she?" Perry laughed heartily.

"I wanted to let you know before you started driving, so you wouldn't go off the road when she told you," Anna smiled to herself, thankful for a little humour.

"You gotta wonder, Annie, what's going through her head sometimes."

Anna murmured in agreement. "Okay, Dad. I'll let you go, so you can go with the Flo."

"Will do," Perry said, chuckling.

* * *

The courthouse was busy that morning. Anna applied for several motions and was pleased that they were all granted. This bought her some more time on a few of her cases.

She was feeling good somehow, not as cramped and cold, even though she was on the street walking between the courthouse and her office with her coat unbuttoned.

From across the street she spotted a familiar figure: Dale Corbeau. She called out to him, trying to catch him before he scooted off. She sensed his hesitation at seeing her. She crossed the road and caught up with him. They exchanged some small talk, which led to how René was doing and what a miracle it was. Then Anna launched into a question that was foremost in her mind.

"Anything on Tamryn Spettigue?"

Dale shook his head. "We expect she'll turn up. She's probably sleeping it off at a friend's house."

Anna winced inside. She knew how college students were perceived by the police, but Anna was sure Tamryn was not that irresponsible.

"Not this girl, Dale. There's no way she would do that to her family."

"The truth is, Anna, we don't have anything to go on."

"So what's next?"

"Maybe we'll come by your house and look around, if you don't mind. I mean she was last seen at your place."

If you don't mind, my ass. It did not matter whether she minded or not. "Sure," said Anna, inwardly shrinking. Even though they had nothing to hide, it would be uncomfortable having the police scrutinize their life. Again.

Before letting Dale go, she thought to ask him one more thing. "Oh, by the way, does Charles Manson have any relatives up here? Cousins or brothers?"

Corbeau tilted his head, squinting his eyes at Anna. "*Manson?*—don't you mean Munson?"

Anna's jaw dropped. It hit her just then that Flo had been dreaming about Munson. Of course! Lance Munson who had worked on their addition.

"I don't think Munson has any more family out here. His sisters moved out west." Corbeau said. "You okay, Anna?"

No, she definitely was not.

CHAPTER NINETEEN

Magic Beads

Flo's pinched face greeted Anna as soon as she got home. Flo had been watching the side door like a puppy dog waiting for its master to return. The old woman huddled on a short painted footstool that Anna had often used to seat René when tying up his laces. Flo already had her coat on, so as not to waste any time.

"I'll wait for you in the car," she said briskly as she pushed past Anna. Flo did not even say goodbye to her nephew or to Xavier, who were watching TV in the living room. That's weird, Anna thought.

She had been hoping Flo would spend the next few nights, to save the return trip each next day, at least until Tamryn turned up again or they could arrange for another babysitter. Flo's excuse was that she did not want Bitty, her cat, to be alone for too long.

"Hey, guys," Anna called out to her husband and son who were watching a show about truckers up north. At her greeting, they hardly stirred from the couch. "I'm gonna drive Flo home," Anna said as though into a vacuum.

She exited and opened the car for her aunt. Flo couldn't get into Anna's car quick enough. Had Anna known, she would have left the motor running. "What time did Xavier get home?" Anna asked once she was seated. She stretched the seat belt over her wide belly.

"About an hour ago." Flo sighed. "He offered to drive me but I said I would wait for you."

"Sure," Anna secretly griped, it would have been nice if he had taken Flo home. Anna was dog-tired.

"To tell you the truth, I didn't want to be in the car with him."

Anna was startled. "With Xavier?"

Flo did not reply right away. "With René," she admitted finally.

"Oh, no." Anna felt a pang for her elderly aunt. "What happened today?" She glanced at Flo but the old woman just stared straight ahead. "Did he misbehave?"

"I'll tell you all about it sometime, but not now while you're driving," Flo said firmly.

"Alright," Anna agreed reluctantly. It was probably a wise decision on Flo's part not to get into a heavy discussion while Anna was navigating the treacherous winter roads in the dark. Still Anna was anxious to hear what had prompted her aunt to make such an extreme statement about her son. Not be in the car with him? Why not?

The mood from then on was uncomfortable. They travelled the twenty miles along the forest roads in silence. There was only the humming of the car heater and an occasional raspy breath from Flo. It sounded like she was coming down with a cold or something.

"Did you get your flu shot this year?" Anna asked, trying to remember if she had already discussed this with her aunt.

"Phhht," Flo scoffed.

"I guess that means no," Anna said, sighing.

Anna felt some of the tightness in her chest disappear when they reached the outskirts of town. The tall gaudy totems of fast food restaurants and gas stations meant they were back in civilization, and however trashy and unwholesome, they were welcome signs.

Anna told Flo they were stopping at Mother's Kitchen, one of those so-called homespun eateries where they were sure to have chicken soup on the menu. Anna didn't like the heavy catch in Flo's breathing or her aunt's chattering teeth. Anna herself was feeling chilled—and starved. She tried to think back on her long day at work and whether she'd even stopped to have lunch.

The main reason for going to the restaurant however was so Anna could get Flo to spill the beans. If she took her straight home, Flo might avoid explaining what had put her in such a bad mood. If Anna faced Flo in a restaurant booth, it would be harder for her to avoid Anna's questions, especially if she resorted to her courtroom style grilling.

*   *   *

"How are you all doing?" asked Beverly, the waitress, for the umpteenth time. Why did restaurant staff have to appear just when you were deep in conversation?

"What are you thinking about, dessert? Any more coffee?" Beverly continued.

I am thinking, we want to be left alone. "We're good, thanks," Anna said, smiling through gritted teeth.

The interruption made Flo lose her train of thought. Anna was sure she had been on the verge of something revealing. Until then it had been like pulling teeth.

When the waitress left, Anna tried again. "Auntie Flo, you can tell me anything. I am not going to judge you." Not realizing that within five minutes, she would contradict herself.

"There's something going on in that house." Flo whispered at last. "You know I've said that before."

Anna nodded, careful not to overreact. "It's not a very zen space, for sure. But it's a temporary problem."

Flo shook her head. "You're blocking the truth, Anna. You want me to talk, but I can talk all I want, till I'm blue in the face." Flo pointed a gnarled finger at Anna. "But you don't listen. You don't want to hear what I have to say."

Anna's eyes flitted to the last remaining french fry on her plate. She grabbed it and brought it to her mouth, chewing it slowly.

"I just want to go home and get to bed," Flo said with genuine weariness.

"But," Anna started, suddenly panicking. As far as she was concerned they weren't done talking. "Auntie, what went on today? Why aren't you telling me?"

Flo stared at her niece. "It was a mistake."

"What was?" Anna struggled to follow Flo's train of thought.

"He was dead and that's the way we should have left it."

"Oh, that!" said Anna, reluctantly remembering.

"That!" Flo spat.

"That or it—the ritual—that's what we're talking about, right?" said Anna.

Flo nodded.

"Sorry to break it to you, Auntie, but that voodoo thing didn't work! It was worth a shot but as it happened René started breathing all by himself. The doctors will tell you as much."

Flo's eyes flashed. She shook her head. "So blind!" she muttered.

"Oh, please!" Anna said.

"I will regret it for the rest of my life." Flo cried. "I did you in, Anna. I doomed you all. No good will come of this."

"For Chrissakes, nothing happened! He came back on his own," said Anna. Her aunt could be so stubborn and exasperating.

"René did not return—*someone else did*," Flo said. "Your son is dead!"

It seemed that at that moment, all the restaurant's cacophony: the clattering dishes; the friendly wait staff cajoling customers into ordering cheesecake or pie; the hum of the ventilation system—suddenly all of it went silent. Anna's head spun.

She took a sip of water and looked around the room. Now, where was that annoying waitress when they really needed her? Anna just wanted to pay and go.

CHAPTER TWENTY
Drawing Conclusions

Anna held René's hand and quietly led him past the receptionist. Maggie smiled at the boy.

"Hello there, little guy! No school today?"

"Just junior law school," Anna quipped.

"You gonna help your mom?" Maggie offered cheerfully.

"Couldn't get a sitter," said Anna by way of explanation.

* * *

Anna set up her son at the coffee table with empty legal pads and a stack of blank paper. She had a pile of work to get through and she hoped René would keep himself busy.

After lunch, Maggie came into Anna's office to bring her the mail. She smiled at René who was quietly occupied, sketching happily as Anna worked. Drawings spilled onto the floor all around him.

Maggie paused trying to get Anna's attention. "Anna, do you mind if I leave a little early today?"

"Sure, no problem."

"They're expecting a bad storm starting late this afternoon."

Anna frowned. "I hadn't heard." She glanced out the window at the clear sky. It was hard to believe that such a sunny day could turn nasty.

"You might think about cutting out early too. It's supposed to be a lot worse out your way."

"I'll be alright, Maggie," said Anna distractedly. She had so much work to do and all before her maternity leave began.

"I'm worried about the little one." Maggie tilted her head in René's direction. Anna felt a pang of guilt. Of course she could not endanger her child by risking being stuck on a remote road in the middle of a snowstorm.

After Maggie left, Anna was no longer able to concentrate. She fretted about the weather. Glancing out the window from time to time, she saw changes in the sky. In the distance, flint-coloured clouds scudded across the horizon. The air was changing.

She decided at that point to cut her workday short, making a few quick phone calls before piling her things into her briefcase. She turned to where René was still drawing intently and froze in her tracks. The images that she saw depicted on the sketch sheets made her heart go cold. The familiarity of the peculiar scrolling lines, the details echoed other artwork—René's ink scribbles were eerily like the designs created by Lance Munson.

Anna stood there speechless for a moment, and then finally she asked her son: "Where'd you get the idea to do that, sweetie?"

"I dunno. Just came into my head," René replied.

Then as she stooped to gather the artwork, Anna noticed the photocopy Corbeau had taken of Munson's ornament, the gift the ex-con had given her following the successful trial. Anna felt overwhelming relief. It appeared her son had simply traced Munson's art using the photocopy.

"Oh, I see," she said, breathing easier now. That the photocopy offered a reasonable explanation for René's elaborate sketch still did not completely alleviate the gnawing worry in Anna's mind. She could not tune out Flo's warning from the background track that ran on an endless loop through her brain.

Finally in a weak voice, Anna asked René to put his coat on. The boy grabbed his jacket and slid into it part way. Anna kneeled to zip him up, and spontaneously pecked him on the cheek. Then she glanced into his eyes, suddenly stopping short. His cold remote stare took her breath away.

"Mommy, will you love the baby more than me?" Even though his tone was slightly mocking she took him at his word.

Anna hurried to reassure him. "No, sweetie. Of course, not. We have lots of love for both of you." She swept him into a hug. "Always and forever." She wondered if that explained his coolness: a fear of rejection or fear of being replaced. She thought she understood him better now.

"But you don't love Daddy forever."

Anna paused, keeping her face averted. Like most children, René was always watching. She realized how perceptive he was. She had tried so hard to keep her anger toward Xavier hidden from René. Xavier and she were still a 'team,' so to speak. They still had the mutual goal of creating a happy home for their child, but obviously René had picked up on the cold war between his parents.

Anna stared sadly at him. "Daddy and I were so worried about you that we blamed each other. But you—René—you didn't do anything wrong. You know that, right?"

René nodded, his eyes narrowing into slits, like the entrance to an impenetrable cave. "You hate Daddy, don't you?"

Anna sucked in her breath. God, this kid really knew how to push her buttons. He was zeroing in on all her lies. "Sometimes forgiveness just takes time." Yeah, right, she thought to herself. Even if hell froze over she might never forgive Xavier.

* * *

When they finally got to the car, a light snow was coming down. If she had been smart, she would have headed directly home, but Anna felt compelled to stop in on Flo. She felt bad about their last conversation at the restaurant. She regretted being so unkind to her aunt.

Anna went to Flo's door alone, leaving René in the car with the motor running. After knocking for several minutes, Flo answered, clearly the worse for wear. The woman was stooped over. Every other breath was accompanied by a cough.

"Auntie, you look awful!"

"Yeah, well. Everything hits you hard at this age. A little cold is not so little." In spite of her illness, Flo was still hospitable. "Come in, have a coffee—"

"I can't stay. I just wanted to give you this drawing René made for you."

Flo tensed slightly at the offered artwork. "You seen the outside of my fridge? It's already crammed full."

Anna pretended not to hear Flo and left the drawing on the counter. "Can I get you anything? Some cough syrup—"

"I still have all that poison from last time—" A barrage of deep coughs interrupted Flo's speech. She leaned forward, her body shaking with every bark and wheeze.

"Oh, Auntie. Let me take you to the hospital," Anna pleaded.

Flo shook her head. "Nothing makes me feel better," she said between breaths. "I am going to die knowing I didn't do enough—" Flo suddenly stared down the driveway, her face taking on a ghostly pallor. "You brought him here, didn't you?"

"René? Yeah, he's in the car. In fact, I should probably head out."

Flo stiffened in fear. As Anna went to comfort her, Flo pushed Anna back, as though repelled by something but too embarrassed to admit it.

"You should go—" Flo said.

Anna had barely left the threshold when Flo slammed the door shut.

* * *

The snow had gotten worse. Anna had to clear the roof and windshield before they could back out of Flo's place. It was slow going. Cars were spinning in the street and it was fifteen minutes before they got to the edge of town.

Thinking back on her conversation with Flo, Annie's mind spun. At the heart of it was Flo's apparent rejection of René—she didn't want his drawing and even the idea of him being in a car in her driveway was too much. Or was Anna just imagining it? Anna had wanted to ask if René could come in but Flo wasn't welcoming. Or could it be simply that Flo was too sick and didn't want to pass on her cold?

Anna noticed the warning light on her fuel gauge and decided to make a quick stop at the Petro Plus station on the way out of town. She brought René into the store and asked him if he wanted a snack but he shook his head. She bought a couple of chocolate bars, just in case.

Leaving the service station, Anna waited behind a station wagon, also trying to get onto the highway. Vapour billowed from its exhaust pipe like a genie from a bottle. The exit lane was slick with ice. Tires spun, spitting fragments of tainted snow, sand and road salt. Using the lull, Anna dug out her two cell phones, the one from work and her personal phone, and plugged both in.

Once on the road, she kept a steady pace. The conditions were not too bad after all, she thought. She marvelled at winter's unexpected beauty: the branches of the evergreens bending under the weight of the snow, the soft, pillowy appearance of the landscape. The way all sounds were muffled. The volume of life turned down a notch. It was nothing short of magnificent.

"Mommy, I have to pee."

"Huh?" Anna glanced in the rear-view mirror. She groaned inwardly. "Can't it wait till we get home, sweetie?"

"No," came René's firm reply.

"Are you sure?" They couldn't be too far from the house. Anna estimated another ten minutes, perhaps?

"Uh-uh," said the boy stubbornly.

"I wish you had said something before we left town—we could have gone at the gas station. Remember I asked you?" She knew it served no purpose to chastise him. Had she not been in such a hurry, she would have taken him to the bathroom and sat him down on the toilet. Then he would have been good for the entire trip home.

Damn it, anyways. There was nowhere to stop here on this narrow winding road. The shoulder width could be deceiving too. You might think you had space at the side to pull over safely, only to find yourself sinking into the ditch.

In typical Anna style, she decided to ignore the problem for as long as possible. But René would not let up.

"Momeeee!" he wailed. "I have to go!"

Anna looked back at the boy. His face was contorted in discomfort. She felt herself giving in against her better judgement. She braked and slowed down. She eased the car to a stop and flicked on her hazard lights. She put the car in park, but kept it running while she hopped out and circled around the back. She came up to the far side of the car and reached the handle to open the door but was surprised it was locked. She signalled for René to open the door but he didn't budge.

"René, lift the button!" Still there was no reaction, only a blank look. It didn't make sense but Anna didn't dwell on it. She ran back to the driver's side, prepared to unlock the doors from there but as soon as she tried that door, she found it locked as well.

Panic swept over her. The ramifications of her carelessness hit her now. Her purse, both of her cell phones, and her keys were all locked inside—with René.

She returned once more to René's door and tried to get his attention. She tapped and gestured. "René! Unlock the door! The little button! Can you see it?"

He didn't even turn to look at her, but just stared ahead as though in a trance. Anna rapped on the door with both hands, her fists hurting now. She cupped her face and stared inside at her uncommunicative son.

She riffled through her pockets and found the two chocolate bars she had purchased at the gas station. These would surely tempt him, she thought. She pressed them against the glass and pointed to them.

"One for me and one for you—*if* you open the door!"

He didn't even look in the direction of the candy.

"René! Come on! RENE!"

"You can have both of them! Just reach over and flip the button!" His lack of response bewildered her.

She ran back to the driver's side door on the off chance she had pulled the handle wrong. It was still locked. She circled the car like a whirling dervish, trying all the other door handles as well. But none gave way. Could it be the cold freezing the mechanisms?

But that didn't explain why René was so quiet and still. Was he having a flashback? Was this whole thing traumatizing him?

Anna went back to pounding on the windows. Minutes rolled by. She even contemplated smashing the glass, but worried that shards of glass would land in his eyes. But what alternative was there? And then it was no longer just a crazy thought. It became a plan. She would get a rock and smash open the window. She began to look for one but in the snow-covered landscape this was a near impossible task.

Stepping into the ditch and running her hands through the drifts she searched until at last she thought she had uncovered something. She brushed away the snow and indeed she had found a rock. But it was firmly frozen to the ground. She picked at it, struggling to pry it free. She was cursing a blue streak, when a sound caught her attention. Suddenly, the car was moving, *it was reversing toward her!*

"René!" she screamed before diving into the ditch to get away, swallowing a mouthful of snow. The car was close enough she could smell the exhaust and feel the threatening vibration of the motor. Seconds later, she gulped as the rear tires spun above her.

With no time to spare, she rolled away as the car plunged into the exact spot where she had just lain. Still gasping from the close call, Anna scrambled up the embankment in the opposite direction, grasping saplings to keep from sliding back. Confused and frightened, she wondered if René had unbuckled himself and climbed into the front seat? Did René try to drive the car and accidentally put it in reverse?

She wanted to go to the car window and check on him, but something made her hesitate. Before she could get up the courage, the sound of another vehicle reached her. She slipped as she climbed up the side of the ditch. She bounded onto the road, waving furiously.

It was nearly dark, but Anna could see a tow truck approach, the orange flashing lights signalling hope.

"Heeeelp!" she screamed, darting towards the truck. "Please!" The rumble of the truck's motor wound down and the driver's window came down a few inches. "I'm so glad to see you!" Anna shouted.

"Sorry ma'am, I'm on my way to another job. I can call someone—"

"Oh, God! Please, please, can you just help me out—my kid's locked inside and I can't get to him. We've been stuck out here and I don't have my phone."

The man glanced toward Anna's pregnant belly and sighed. He reversed his truck toward her car which now hung over the ditch. Then Chuck—according to the name stitched on his down vest—got down out of his vehicle and peered through the fogged windows. To Anna's astonishment, he opened the driver's side door of her car with no difficulty at all. He turned off the motor and removed the keys, handing these to Anna.

She took them, speechless with shock.

"One of the things you got to watch out for is snow in the exhaust pipe," he stated matter-of-factly. "When that happens, it's easy for your car to fill up with carbon monoxide."

At that moment, to Anna's further dismay, René opened the door all by himself and scampered out. Anna's brain was seared from the insanity of it all. This kid, who for thirty minutes resisted her pleas, was suddenly all perky and child-like again. It didn't make sense.

Chuck almost jogged as he worked to attach a winch to her car. Anna stood well back, keeping a firm grip on René. As the chain pulled and groaned, the car lifted. In two minutes, it was back on flat land. Chuck unhooked the car and turned his tow truck around. He called to Anna above the roar of the motor: "I'd write you up an invoice but I really need to get to this other job."

She tried to hand the tow truck driver a hundred-dollar bill but he would have none of it.

"You take care—and be more careful," he admonished. "Winter ain't for wimps."

CHAPTER TWENTY-ONE

Doctor's Opinion

René took in a deep breath and then exhaled, just as Dr. Rocha requested. The petite red-haired paediatrician smiled at her patient.

"Good boy. Now let me have a look in your eyes."

Rocha flashed a light and peered into his pupils. "Everything looks great."

"What about the bruise on his chest?" asked Anna, hovering at his side. She had taken René in that afternoon for a special check-up. She had nagging worries about her son's health, and of course, his behavioural changes.

"Hmmm," Rocha touched the dark irregular spot. "Does this hurt, René?"

"No," the little boy answered, sitting quietly and politely.

"Well, I don't think we have anything to worry about." Rocha gave Anna a reassuring look. "He seems to be doing really well."

"But where did the bruise come from? Why is it getting bigger and not shrinking?" Anna said, her voice testy. She didn't like that Rocha was making light of the weird mark on her son's body.

Rocha hesitated, glancing at the boy. "René, why don't you hang out in the waiting room while your mommy and I have a chat?"

René mumbled in agreement. Anna took his shirt, a turtleneck with dinosaurs, and slid it over his head, and down over his torso where it covered the mysterious pattern on his chest. She led him to the adjacent room, to a corner where children's toys and books were stacked on bright shelves.

A moment later, when she had returned to Dr. Rocha's office, Anna let her pent-up anxieties spill forth. Like an overfull bag of groceries ripping apart, her stories rolled like spinning cans in every direction.

"The hypothermia, the coma—what did that really do to him?"

Dr. Rocha tilted her head and gave Anna a sympathetic look. "I had a chance to chat with the St. Boniface team and they said your son suffered no ill effects."

"But Groves said he coded twice. He was clinically dead twice, and there's no brain damage. Nothing?" Anna voice was demanding, insistent.

Rocha frowned as she flipped through the file some more. "He scored well on all the aptitude tests. All the brain scans were normal."

"But he's different," Anna insisted.

"Children grow up," Rocha stated. "They evolve."

"His personality, too?"

"Of course." Rocha said. "Especially his personality."

Anna swallowed. "I feel like something has happened to him—"

"I can lend you some reading material on child development."

Anna tried not to show her irritation at the doctor's condescending response. She knew her own child, for Pete's sake. "This is not another stage of childhood," she said. "Why is he suddenly left-handed?" Anna heard her voice rising and fought to stay calm. "Isn't that unusual?"

"That, I don't know," said Rocha. "Are you sure?" she continued. "I mean maybe he was ambidextrous. Is that the only change in René?"

"He eats more!"

"A growth spurt, perhaps."

"He eats a lot, lot more."

The doctor nodded, still unconvinced.

"He snoops around," said Anna.

"What child doesn't? They're very inquisitive."

"He eavesdrops on conversation," Anna added.

"Adults are fascinating for his age group. He sounds very normal. I wouldn't worry about it." Rocha said.

Anna sighed, feeling the doctor was just not getting it. "He knows stuff no six-year-old should know."

"Like what?" Rocha asked.

Anna hesitated about revealing more. "He can drive a car," she said in a low, urgent voice. "He tried to reverse it over me!"

Rocha took a deep breath in. Then looked away.

"He seems so different. I don't recognize my son, anymore!"

"Maybe it just seems that way. Perhaps it's you who has changed."

*   *   *

The next day, at work, Anna's cell phone rang. A general number for St. Boniface Hospital popped up on the screen. She answered, expecting it to be a referral to a child specialist following René's visit to Dr. Rocha.

"Ms. Docstedder?

"Speaking."

"It's Megan Shannon from Outpatient Services."

"Uhuh."

"I was just calling to see when you might be available to come in for a counselling session."

Anna was silent for a second. "Excuse me?"

"This would be in regard to the recommendations from the hospital following the incident—"

"Right," Anna interrupted, testy. She had almost forgotten about the agreement that she had signed—under duress—after flipping out at the hospital.

"We have some openings next week."

There was just no way to fit counselling sessions into her already crazy schedule. She had so much going on: work piling up; trials around the corner; a baby arriving soon; no reliable childcare for René; and worst of all—a very sick aunt. Moreover, Anna did not have the patience or energy to explain to some newbie psych grad the very strange history of her life. Nor did she expect anyone would understand—anyone but her aunt.

Though she had no intention of following through, Anna assured Megan, that she would get back to her soon.

CHAPTER TWENTY-TWO

Death Rattle

Steam rose up from a large pot of boiling soup. Anna threw in a spoon of seasoning and stirred it into the thin broth. She fished out the chicken carcass and set it aside on a plate. It reminded her of whalebones bleaching in the sun.

Flo's jarring coughs cut through the silence. They came in prolonged and painful bouts. Anna's heart sank with each episode, knowing her aunt was worsening.

Anna ladled up some soup, the vapours sending up a savoury hint of the rich ingredients. She placed the bowl of broth on a tray and made her way to Flo's bedroom, navigating the household clutter with caution.

"Here you go," said Anna setting down the tray, praying that Flo would let her spoon some liquid therapy into her. But Flo was so weak she only took a few sips. Bitty jumped onto the bed and sniffed the bowl. "Scram," Anna ordered the cat. When Bitty would not move she lifted it to the floor. "You have your own food," she scolded.

Anna turned back to her aunt. "Is that why Bitty is so big? She eats her food and yours too?"

Flo was not in the mood for humour. She gripped Anna's arm. She shook her head, gesturing for Anna to lean in. "Stay here. With me," she whispered.

Anna would have liked to stay with her aunt, but home and work were waiting. She hated that Flo had to be alone when she was so sick, but Flo was stubborn and wouldn't let anyone take her to the hospital where they could at least do something for her. For all they knew she might have pneumonia.

Anna couldn't leave her aunt by herself, but she also couldn't face dropping her off at a hospital emergency department either. Based on experience, they would have the old woman languish on a bed, midst the noise and the glare of the fluorescent lights of the waiting room, while they took their time triaging her and getting her admitted, only to have her escape by cab the next day. Anna gave in to her best instincts. She took her cell phone and punched in Xavier's number.

"I'm going to sleep over at Flo's tonight, keep an eye on her," Anna told her husband.

"Oh, yeah," he said with irritation, "Well, it's too late to say good night to René. The kid's asleep."

Anna bit her lip, resisting the impulse to get into an argument with her husband, only to deepen the estrangement between them.

When Anna did not reply, he added grumpily, "So what's the plan for tomorrow?"

"Can you stay home with the boy?"

Xavier exhaled loudly.

"Why is it only up to me to arrange childcare?" Anna complained.

"You have a responsibility to your family, to me, to René. Why are you giving in to her?"

"She's very, very sick, Xavier."

"Of course she's sick. She never listens to what any doctor says. You go through the trouble of getting an appointment somewhere, take time off work to drive her, and then she doesn't take her meds. And to top it off, she expects you to be her nursemaid."

"I know, I know," Anna replied, agreeing with everything Xavier said. She paused, a lump catching in her throat, and then continued, "This time it feels different. She's never been so bad."

Xavier sniffed. "You do what you have to do."

They hung up without saying goodbye.

* * *

It was around 1 a.m. when Xavier woke up. He had to take a leak. Feeling sorry for himself, he'd helped himself to several beers the night before. He might still have been a little drunk when he rose from the bed and stumbled to his feet. Seeing Anna's side of the bed was empty, he was reminded that she was in town that night.

He staggered to the bathroom, relieved himself and then made his way back. He stared briefly out of the bedroom window onto the snowy yard, gazing at the flat surface of the lake and the distant tree-filled shoreline. It was a moonless light, but there was a wintry glow in the atmosphere, as though a distant light refracted onto everything.

A small tapping noise drew Xavier's attention away from the window. He paused to listen. It was unusual enough that he decided

114

to investigate. He padded down the hallway following the faint sounds.

Tap, tap, tap.

It seemed the noise was coming from René's bedroom. A light shone out from underneath the door to the boy's room. Xavier tiptoed toward the doorway and paused. By this time the sounds had stopped.

The door was slightly ajar and Xavier peered into the room, noticing the bedside lamp was on. His son sat up in bed, holding the carving of the woodsman. René repeatedly lifted the miniature arm with the axe and let it drop on the wooden log.

Tap, tap, tap.

For whatever reason René chose that moment to look up at the doorway. His father instinctively shifted back, keeping out of view. Something about the boy's intense expression gave Xavier pause. After a moment René reached for the bedside lamp and shut it off. He slid under the covers, but his eyes remained wide open and fixed on the doorway as though sensing the presence of an observer.

He was still awake and watching as Xavier retreated.

* * *

Anna slept fitfully. The thin mattress and the wire frame of the pull-out couch were worse than a medieval torture rack. Her back ached and her legs went numb by turns. In this wakeful state, she became aware of a light rhythmic sound.

Tap, tap, tap.

Anna sat up and listened for a few seconds waiting for it to return. Now fully awake she eased herself to a standing position, feeling pins and needles in her feet and back. She shuffled gingerly toward the kitchenette and poked around looking for a clean glass, trying not to make any noise. Finding one, at last, she turned on the tap and let the cool water run over her fingers. Then she filled her glass with water and sipped it slowly, enjoying the cold taste. She realized how refreshing it was in contrast to her aunt's well-heated house. How strange to feel warm at last, Anna marvelled.

After the drink, Anna headed to Flo's bedroom, tiptoeing softly as she inched toward the sleeping form under the quilted coverlet. Bitty was curled up alongside Flo. The cat raised its head, acknowledging Anna's presence.

Anna stared down at her aunt and thought how frail she looked. Her salt and pepper hair lay scattered across the pillow. She slept with her mouth open, her parchment skin stretched over her cheekbones. If it were not for the old woman's ragged and raspy breaths, and the shallow expansions of her upper chest, Anna might have made the mistake of thinking Flo were dead. *Dear old lady, please get better. Don't leave me*, Anna prayed.

Reluctantly she left her aunt's bedside. She reasoned that at least the old lady was sleeping and hopefully the rest would help her recover. Tomorrow, Anna might try again to convince Flo to see a doctor. Anna returned to the couch and attempted to get comfortable. She needed her sleep too. So, when the strange sounds returned she tried to ignore them, attributing them to the settling of the old house or the wind rattling loose objects.

There was indeed a wind. An ill wind that whooshed in and lifted René's finger painting off the counter and set it aflutter, carrying it toward Flo's room as though conveyed on the back of an invisible beast, up and down it travelled, but always more or less waist high, through the doorway and toward Flo's bed. The cat reacted to it immediately. She arched her back, her fur sticking straight up. She delivered a low hiss toward the floating form.

Then the paper dropped suddenly and heavily, almost like a corner of an iceberg shearing off. At that moment, all of the paint particles loosened from it, pulled upward in white wispy strands, floating and forming into an ominous spectral shape that spun over Flo's bed in a swirl of glassy particles. The mass shifted, cutting across Flo's face like a raw wind, then gliding knifelike through her parted lips, funnelling into her chest, down her lungs, filling all of her veins and airways with crystalline death.

Flo woke briefly, only enough time to let the terror and excruciating pain register on her face. She struggled against the blockage of her air passages, the strange suffocation from within. Like a fish pulled from the sea, Flo's mouth opened wide, attempting to take in a breath, but unable to draw in any air. No suction was possible because the freezing was immediate and spread throughout her body. She stiffened before being able to emit much of a cry for help, anyway certainly not loud enough for Anna to hear in the next room.

Flo brought her hands toward her chest. Trying to free herself from the grip of the congealing blood. Death came to her with her arms locked midway above her waist. When Anna found her in the morning she assumed rigor mortis had already set in. If she had not been so completely consumed by grief she might have remembered that rigor mortis takes much longer.

Anna threw herself on Flo, wailing and sobbing as she had never done before. It can't be, she thought. Flo was a strong person. She was going to get better. Flo of all people had a cure for every ailment. It was like her mother had died all over again. Flo had been her anchor, her guiding light, the one who had looked after them all. They would be lost now, thought Anna. They were all doomed.

*　*　*

There was no funeral in the traditional sense. A mass or church service of any kind was out of the question. Instead they held a memorial event for her at the Finnish Hall in town. Anna had considered and then dismissed the idea of holding it at the Legion. That place held too many bad memories.

The room was packed with many of Flo's friends, some of whom came from her bingo gang, and her craft clubs: the basket weavers and beading groups. Several of Anna's colleagues and clients also attended, as well as a few of Perry's protégés, distinguishable by their hardened appearances, and by the way they headed straight for the sweets and coffee. Anna was reacquainted with various cousins and second cousins, some of whom she had not seen since her mother's funeral. Perry knew them better than Anna did. In the family, Perry was now the last remaining member of his generation.

When Flo was cremated she was wearing her beaded dance regalia with a cluster of eagle feathers in her hands. Anna put her ashes in a simple unglazed clay urn, decorated with the imprint of strands of grass. At first she thought that she might take Flo's ashes and scatter them in the lake in the spring, but then she remembered how much her aunt had hated Lake Mikwam.

That afternoon, the question "What did she die of?" came up frequently. Diabetes, heart attack, pneumonia, old age, take your pick, thought Anna to herself. But however many health issues had plagued Flo, Anna could not help thinking that she had somehow hastened her aunt's death with the pressures she had put upon her. Flo's complexion had gone from a rosy glow to waxen and grey following the ritual in the hospital. How much of Flo's longevity was sacrificed so that René might live again?

After the memorial, Anna and Xavier packed up the many gifts that were left as offerings to Flo: pickles, jams, knitted blankets, soap, and figurines. Anna assembled them, along with the cards and placed them in a box on a table by the door. While she waited for Xavier to pull up with the car, Anna studied the bulletin board. Amongst the announcements for polka dances and country and western concerts, was a missing person's poster for Tamryn.

With a pang she remembered the day the girl went missing. Anna had helped distribute some of these same posters and might have even tacked this one onto the board. She felt guilty for not helping more. The search had slowed down in the last while, or at least Anna had not been as aware of it, being so preoccupied with her aunt's illness.

The door flew open just then and Xavier marched in with René in tow. The air shifted suddenly. A gust of wind rattled the notices, pulling one loose from the thumbtack holding it in place. Tamryn's smiling face slid to the floor and landed at René's feet. Anna stooped heavily and attempted to retrieve the poster. Sodden, it clung to the floor making it difficult to peel up, and then René stepped on it. To Anna it had seemed deliberate.

"Sweetie, move to the side," she said. But he did not budge. Finally, she had to wrench the poster from under his boot. By the time it was in her hands, it was wet and torn.

"I think that's a goner," said Xavier, oblivious to the subject of the poster. Anna crumpled it before he could have a look at it. She vowed to return soon with a replacement for the bulletin board.

Anna took Flo's urn out to the car herself, not trusting anyone with her dear aunt's remains. She hugged the earthen vase close to her bosom, and felt its rough surface, like the calloused, timeworn hands of her late guardian. Inexplicably, the clay vessel felt warm pressed up against her, like one last hug from Flo.

When they got home, Anna placed the urn on the fireplace mantel, and there it would remain undisturbed for several weeks. For Anna, the sadness was deep, the grief unrelenting, and the guilt, ever present.

After that, Xavier and Anna decided that it was okay for René to go back to school. From then on Xavier would make sure to be home to meet René's school bus.

The return to school seemed to go smoothly at first. There had been a small welcome-back party, with cupcakes and hand-drawn pictures from René's classmates. Anna went through the cards and drawings, marvelling at the endearing innocence of those first-graders. But soon the honeymoon was over. It started with a message from René's teacher, Claire Humber. Anna put off phoning her back, guessing that there had been a problem.

"He's having some issues," Claire began hesitantly.

"Like what?" Anna swallowed, tension filling her chest.

"I think he's having a tough time settling back in."

"Oh, how so?"

"I was really hoping we could discuss this face to face," the teacher pleaded.

Anna sighed inwardly. In her head, she calculated the drive from town to the school. Wondering how and when she could possibly fit in a conference with René's teacher. She had already missed work for Flo's illness and memorial, and now this. She had so much to catch up on, and it all had to get done before her maternity leave began just weeks away.

"I work in Glace Bay," explained Anna. "It's not impossible, but it would be difficult to get to the school—I mean if you could give me a better idea of what's going on with him."

There was an audible sigh on the other end of the line. Anna waited.

"Maybe it was a mistake to make too much of his return. He seems to like being the centre of attention."

"The party was a nice gesture. He really enjoyed it."

"I hope you don't mind me saying this but I'm wondering if he's given more latitude following his accident?"

"More latitude?" asked Anna.

"Do you finding it difficult to discipline him?"

"We're treating him the same as before," said Anna, somewhat huffily. Although, she realized seconds after she made the statement, that it was simply not true. She and Xavier had been indulging René like nobody's business. Was the kid taking advantage of their fear, their guilt? More than likely.

"I will speak to my husband about this and see if we can—uh—address the situation."

"Alright," said Claire with an air of resignation. The meeting she so badly wanted was not going to happen.

"I appreciate your calling," Anna said before hanging up. She guessed this would not be the last of messages from the school.

CHAPTER TWENTY-THREE

Where Tamryn Was

She had already been home for several minutes, sitting on a kitchen chair, trying to remove her long boots from her swollen legs. She was frustrated and on the verge of tears when Xavier suddenly appeared and kneeled before her. He took over and pulled off the clinging boots, surprising Anna with this unexpected gesture of kindness.

"Thank you," she breathed, her voice laden with exhaustion. She bit her lip, afraid to give her emotions free rein. She realized how much she missed being in love with him. The war between them was wearing her down. Xavier watched her for a few seconds and then he spoke almost robotically, his voice flat and even.

"They located Tamryn."

Anna sat up, suddenly revived. "Well, that's great!" she said, assuming the student had returned from a spur of the moment trip, her unexplained absence just a miscommunication with her parents. "Where was she?"

"No, Anna," Xavier said heavily, staring at the floor. After a moment, he added, almost in a whisper: "They found her body." He leaned toward Anna, offering her an embrace. But she pulled back.

"Oh, God, no." Anna stood up, stepping away from Xavier. "What happened?"

"It was an accident. Just down the road. Not five miles from here."

"Nooo!" Anna's knees buckled. She reached for the back of a chair.

"They say she was texting and driving. Seat belt not done up."

"Ohhh, God!"

"They figure the car hit an icy patch and just went over the guard rail. And flipped."

"Ohhhh," Anna wailed. "How awful! Poor Janice."

"What college grad doesn't wear a seat belt?"

"I don't get it," moaned Anna, shaking her head. Xavier took Anna in his arms. "Are we cursed?" she sobbed.

"That's crazy talk," he said soothingly.

The word crazy didn't sit well with her. She didn't like that people kept thinking she was just imagining things. Flo would have understood. Her warnings still rang in Anna's ears, but she knew it wouldn't help to explain that to Xavier. He wasn't a believer like she was. And besides he had never been told about the ritual at the hospital. The one performed on René. She pulled away from her husband, avoiding his gaze.

After a moment, Anna murmured, "I should call Janice," though she dreaded it. What comfort could she possibly offer her friend?

The only relief was that Tamryn's body had been located and that it was determined to be a road accident—nothing unseemly like a kidnapping or murder. Just an error in judgement on Tamryn's part, thought Anna.

Although she had no reason to feel guilty, she still did. There was no connection to the Durand-Docstedder house, other than Tamryn being in such a hurry to leave here that she forgot to put on her seatbelt. So, why should Anna have any reason to feel guilty about that?

CHAPTER TWENTY-FOUR

Ghosts

She was drawn forward, floating as though a mechanism outside of her controlled her, not wanting to see but compelled to know. There was an odd clinking sound. And the usually burbling motor of the aquarium was somehow different, strained and wheezing as though the pump were struggling before an imminent mechanical breakdown.

It was so bizarre. Before she saw him, she heard him humming the familiar strains of a country and western tune, popular decades ago. A song she wouldn't have expected her son to know, much less repeat with such lusty confidence.

What was even more stunning to her was what she saw as she peered in her son's room. She could not immediately reconcile what her eyes took in—it defied all logic.

René's small hands were lifting fish from the aquarium and then dropping them back in—*frozen*. Their stiff bodies tinkled against the walls of the glass tank, like ice cubes in a drink tumbler. More astonishing than the rapid freezing was that the fish would come to life again, seconds later, swimming away in panic, terrified now more than ever of the small hand—albeit gigantic to them— plunging down, hunting them for the sheer cruel pleasure of it.

Finally, sensing he was being watched, the little boy slowly turned and gazed at his mother. Anna, gripped by fear, dared not breathe. Part of her wanted to step forward and scold her son for playing with the fish but another part was unsure. It was as though she did not know this child anymore. She had never before seen him display this type of cruel behaviour. René narrowed his eyes at her. He sniffed as though detecting her lack of courage. He waited, revelling in her timidity, letting his newfound power take firmer hold.

"Baby," she said, immediately realising the irony of her choice of words. He was no baby anymore. All innocence was definitely gone from him, washed into the lake and settled down with the muck and sediment deep below.

122

"Baby, aren't you hurting the fish?" It was an unnecessary question. Of course, she knew he was fully aware of the damage he was doing. She had a small hope that he would give her an explanation that would restore her belief in him, but she got nothing at all. She gazed at him now, as though seeing him reflected from a sheet of ice, distorted and barely recognizable.

He paused, letting his hands rest against the tank. A tiny golden fish bobbed on the surface like a plastic toy, faded and out of place. Ice formed in a thin film where René's fingertips touched the surface of the water. Anna stared hard at the formations. Could it just be her eyes playing tricks on her? Momentarily, René lifted his hands and rubbed them on his flannel pajamas. They were the baby blue ones with cartoon penguins and polar bears, a gift from Flo last Christmas.

René leapt onto his bed and pulled the covers up, turning his back away from his mother. Anna felt stunned by his cool aloofness and realized that to try to kiss him or hug him goodnight would have been difficult and awkward. A feeling of vast and terrifying loneliness overtook her.

Anna retreated from her son's bedroom as though entering his room had just been a mistake, like accidentally trying a key in the wrong door at a hotel.

*　*　*

Xavier and René went to town the following Saturday. Movers were coming to take some of Flo's heavy furniture out of her house for donation to charity. Anna had already cleared out Flo's personal items but did not have the emotional strength to visit her aunt's old place again. It was too painful. Besides Anna was glad for a day at home alone.

She wanted to cheer herself up with a bit of 'nesting.' Putting the finishing touches on the baby's room: decorating and stocking it with both new items and belongings kept from René's infancy. Anna had stored a lot of his things that were both sentimental and still functional.

She folded onesies and sleepers and tucked them in the drawers of a tall white dresser. She washed the old change table and vacuumed the colourful rug that was laid out in the centre of the room. She laundered new flannel sheets and made up the crib, attaching a bright bumper pad to the inside of the railings. On the wall she hung prints of vintage children's storybooks and artwork created by René.

She had been so wrapped up in her work that she had not noticed how much time had passed. When she went downstairs for lunch, she realized it was late afternoon and starting to get dark. As she waited for water to boil for tea, she sliced bread and layered it with cheese and cold cuts.

Suddenly there was a roar behind her. The knife slipped from her hand and clattered to the floor. She spun around, glancing out at the lake. A caravan of snowmobiles whipped by only a few hundred feet from the backyard. Anna felt vulnerable standing near the exposed window. She wondered if the snowmobilers could see into the house and tell she was alone.

Anna listened as the deep rumble reverberated and then faded away. With her nerves on edge, she checked the lock on the side door and fastened the deadbolt. Meanwhile, she had lost her appetite and left the sandwich untouched. She retreated upstairs with only the mug of tea.

She went into René's room to check for any remaining storage boxes. Crouching beside the bed, she lifted the duvet out of the way and reached underneath. She found a wide thin box, labelled 'baby stuff.' She lifted it up and carried it to the nursery.

She set the box down on the floor and opened it. Just as she lifted the lid, she felt a gust of cold air travel through the room. Above her the mobile stirred and tinkled.

The top layer of the box was exactly as she had remembered it, layered with an embroidered blanket and knitted hats, but then below that Anna was startled to uncover a stack of yellowed news clippings and a worn scrapbook stuffed with papers and more newspaper articles carefully cut out.

As she perused the clippings, all from northern Ontario newspapers dating back almost two decades, she realized they all dealt with murders and mysterious deaths. It was baffling and terrifying. It sickened her even more to think that the gruesome catalogue was nestled between her precious keepsakes of René's infancy.

She suspected it tied back to Munson somehow. More than likely it was he who had stashed the memorabilia here. But why had he chosen to bring it into their house, and leave it beneath her son's bed of all places?

For several moments she could only sit stunned midst the records of all those destroyed lives. At last she made up her mind. With a burst of energy, she gathered up the papers and ran downstairs, heading for the fireplace. She pulled back the screen and threw the whole bundle onto the flames, then watched incredulously as the fire sputtered, and with a puff, was snuffed out almost instantly. The only trace of the flames that had burned only seconds before was a single wisp of smoke. It now curled up lazily and then vanished.

Puzzled, Anna touched the top of the scrapbook but could feel no heat from it. And when her fingers probed below, she found the carbon chunks and ash were stone cold. She pulled back and stood staring at the fireplace, uncomprehending. It was as though she expected that simply by looking at it, she would be able to make sense of what had just happened.

A sound from behind drew her out of her trance. She turned around, spotting her purse. Her cell phone was vibrating, likely receiving a text. She pulled out her mobile and found a message from Xavier.

Me and the kid are staying with Perry tonight, the text read.

Had things been different between them she might have called Xavier and shared with him her discovery, confiding in him about the baffling occurrence of the fire going out just now, and how she was sorry he was staying in town—not so much because she could not bear one night without him, but more so because she was terrified to the bone.

Phooot!

Anna screamed. Just then the entire pile of papers slid forward, bursting through the chain metal screen and scattering across the floor.

Trembling with fear, Anna tried to tell herself that the papers had moved as a result of the force of gravity, and nothing more. She chose to ignore the fact that not one single scrap of the macabre documents had remained in the fireplace.

It was as though the ghosts of the dead were forcing her to take note. They would not allow her to turn their memories into ashes. Reluctantly, Anna picked up each clipping and restored them to the scrapbook, shaking off the soot as she did so. Afterwards she took a pail of soapy water and washed up the grey powdery mess, then shoved the scrapbook into a large clear plastic bag that she left by the back door.

By the time she was finished, several hours had elapsed. She trudged upstairs, feeling grimy and exhausted. Her bones ached for a hot shower.

* * *

She shivered as she got undressed, bracing against the frigid air around her. She slid the shower door open and turned on the tap, stepping in as hot water gushed down. She showered quickly, scrubbing the dust from her skin. Behind her steam on the glass turned to frost, and a ghostly face began to take shape. Had Anna turned the other way she might have seen it, but for now she held herself forward, under the healing spray.

Suddenly the water turned cold. Anna yelped and switched off the tap, bringing her arms close to her sides for warmth. Just as she turned around, the image melted into an unrecognizable shape.

Anna was angry now and making a mental note to call about the water heater first thing in the morning. Perhaps this was why she did not notice the frost on the glass and the remaining traces of a ghostly visage etched upon it.

CHAPTER TWENTY-FIVE

Cat and Mouse

When Anna dropped the scrapbook on Dale Corbeau's desk, he looked up sharply.

"What's this?" he said.

"Papers Munson stashed at our house." She was like a cat relinquishing a dead mouse to her master. There was a mix of regret but also pride in this gift.

The detective grasped the yellowed pages tentatively at first. But as he read more of them, he began to lean in.

"I came across them last weekend," Anna said, taking a seat.

"What makes you think it was Munson's?"

Anna shrugged. "Just a guess—see for yourself. I mean those are cases you thought he was good for—and a few others."

"Kind of coincidental that you should find this now."

Anna shook her head. "I was cleaning and just came across it. I swear."

He seemed to regret his remark. He thought he could detect tears in Anna's eyes.

"It doesn't matter anymore. I mean, the guy's dead, right," he said softly.

For a time, there was silence, save for the rustling of the brittle newsprint and Corbeau's occasional exhalations as he reacted to the content of the scrapbook.

"He is dead?" Anna shifted in her seat. On his quizzical look, she repeated her question. "You're sure it was Lance's body you pulled out of the lake?"

Corbeau stared at Anna. "Oh, yeah. No doubt about it. I mean we tested him. His fingerprints were a match. His DNA. The tattoos. It was definitely Munson."

"Sometimes I wonder if he has a twin out there," Anna said.

"That would be everybody's worst nightmare," he said, "But no. We're pretty sure it was just him and the two sisters."

"Do you mind if I have that carving back?"

He gave her a puzzled look.

"You know, after the trial I gave you that wooden thing Munson made."

Anna showed Corbeau the photocopy he had once given her and then he remembered. "Right. Lemme see. Might be over in evidence," he said, pulling a file folder from a stack on his desk. He ran his finger down a long list. Midway through he turned to Anna and said, "By the way, we did like you said. Had that workshop equipment tested, the knives and what not."

"And?"

Corbeau shook his head. "Nothing," he said. "Excuse me for a minute."

Anna watched as Corbeau exited. As soon as he left the room, she leaned over his desk. She scanned the assortment of files and loose papers. She saw a folder, marked Munson with a case number she knew by heart. Opening it, she quickly perused the contents. Her eyes flitted up occasionally to check on Corbeau's whereabouts on the floor.

Her hands riffled through the sheaf of notes and photographs. The mug shots of Munson shirtless, showing his various tattoos. Her heart stopped to see the photographs of her one-time client. The cocky, defiant expression that so reminded her of someone else—*who was that?* Yes, she knew it now—*her own son, René.*

"See anything interesting?" Corbeau asked, as he handed her a small plastic bag with the ornament.

He was surprised by Anna's frightened expression. He might have expected embarrassment, contrition maybe—though Anna was not the apologetic type—but the one thing he did not expect was her look of sheer terror.

CHAPTER TWENTY-SIX
Sixty Percent Water

The steam rolled up and coated the bathroom mirrors. It hung in a thick layer like the air on a particularly foggy day.

Hot water gushed into the tub. Towels bunched around Anna's knees. Her hands threaded the racing flow, testing the temperature. It was perfect, she thought. So much so she herself was tempted to strip off her clothes and get in for a good soak, though she had run the bath for René. It was definitely his turn.

It had been days since the water heater had been repaired—again. René had suddenly become averse to baths so Anna knew she would have to coax him into the water.

She went looking for him now and found him in his bedroom, lying next to his bed, almost hidden by a comforter he was using as a makeshift tent.

"Are you camping?"

No answer.

"Guess what?"

He scowled, noticing her wet knees and damp arms. He knew about the bath. He had likely heard the water running. He was having none of it. "I'm not gonna!" he said.

Anna braced herself. This was where she tried to don a Teflon coating. She wouldn't take no for an answer. "The water is nice and hot—I promise." Although by the time she got him into the bathroom who knows whether it would still be comfortable."

"No," he pronounced firmly.

She found it puzzling. René used to love baths.

"Come on, you don't want to smell like stinky socks."

Was he frightened of being immersed in water? The bath was so shallow. "Let's pick out some special toys." Anna went to his toy chest and found a plastic wind-up crocodile.

"Let's see if this guy can swim." She waved the croc in front of René but he ignored both her and the toy. As she reached for him, he dug his heels into the carpet and flopped low to the ground. Still she managed to peel him off the floor. When she lifted him, he grabbed onto the bedding and clung, making it harder to move him.

Damn it, she thought, *he is not getting away with this. I am not giving in*. And so, she half-carried him out the bedroom door, the bed linens dragging along, like the train of a reluctant bride.

"Nooo!" he wailed.

"Come on, it's not that bad," said Anna, huffing from the exertion.

By the time they reached the bathroom, he had released the sheets, and then dug his hands into her instead. Kicking the bathroom door shut behind her, she plopped him on the mat in front of the tub and pulled down his fleecy pants and underwear, then without even removing his shirt she just plopped him in the water. He screamed bloody murder but she persisted. Teflon, she told herself. Keep to the plan. You're the boss of him.

Trying to ignore the cacophony of screams and splashes, the little hands pummelling her and the water splashing her face, she gripped his shirt and pulled upwards, sliding it over his head in one fell swoop. She flung the shirt onto the floor behind her. There, Victory, she thought. Naked boy in bath. Finally! Her heart was racing, her head throbbing from the strain.

"Was that so bad?" she asked him, breathlessly, panting so hard from the efforts of the last few minutes, she could barely speak. Yes, she thought to herself, it was bad.

When she turned to look at him, she saw his inflamed cheeks, his defiant eyes, rigid jaw, and angry quivering lips. But then her eyes were drawn to his chest. There it was, the bruise. Poor thing, she thought at first until she looked again, across the paddling arms, the fists hitting the water, splashing and thrashing. The bruise was not a bruise at all but a drawing. A finely detailed etching of a thunderbird. *Someone had given her son a tattoo*! It made no sense. Who would have done that? When could this have happened?

It was like a train thundering through her mind, the sound of it so loud she could not think. The rattling, the vibration.

"Stop splashing!" Anna screamed at René. He was a fury, pulsing and churning the water. There was no keeping it in the tub. Anna spun around, mopping up the floor with all the towels at hand but to no avail. In a tsunami of anger, he jetted out water faster than she could contain it.

Rather than prolong the bath she scooped her son out and set him on the floor rather roughly, then grabbed the last dry towel and enclosed him in it. The eye of the thunderbird seemed to mock her.

"Where did you get that?" she had to ask, although she feared what his answer might be.

All she got was an insolent stare. She found herself opening the towel to study the markings on his chest. Who could have done that to her son? Was that why he was so angry? Who? Flo had been dead for a while now and had avoided René. Perry had rarely been alone with her son. Tamryn had only spent one day with René. It had to be Xavier. But really, *Xavier*?

"How did you get this? Did Daddy take you somewhere?"

"No!"

Who could have done this to her baby? Even though she posed it as a question, she still couldn't imagine it. It could only have been her husband, as only he had access to René. Oh, how she hated him at this moment. Xavier could be so careless. But…he had never been deliberately unkind. Besides what tattoo parlour would allow this to happen to a child?

If it wasn't Xavier, then who? Could she have done this without realizing? Was it a Munchausen by Proxy act—in her sleep? In a half-waking state? Or did she suffer amnesia? A memory block? Because she did remember seeing this bird before, this same design now traced by her hands. Where?

René pulled the towel over his chest. She knew she shouldn't stare at him, make him feel bad for something that he had no control over. He was clearly uncomfortable with her reaction. She must remain calm. Not let on that she was horrified.

But who could she speak to about this? They would think her either mad—or abusive for letting this happen to her son. She was trapped. They would not only take René away, but the baby too! She couldn't say anything about this.

But then she remembered the bruise, the steadily changing bruise coming up from under the surface of his pale skin that instead of getting smaller and fainter only increased in depth and intensity. She had shown the bruise to the doctor. It had started weeks ago as a subtle blue-black smudge. And then became a welt and then a tattoo. Was this a freak phenomenon? An inexplicable occurrence like the outline of Jesus on the wall of a donut shop, or the messiah's face on a piece of toast? Was it miraculous—or diabolical?

Was someone sending her a message from the afterlife— through René? It would have to be Flo. But what was her dead aunt trying to say? Using her mind, Anna channelled this question to Flo's spirit, appealing for some insight.

Impulsively, Anna's fingers reached out to touch René's chest once more, pressing into the skin, following the blue lines. The ink went deep. Yes, it was definitely a tattoo. A real tattoo.

"Ow!" she screamed.

René had grabbed her hand and was squeezing it hard. She wrenched it back, astonished at the force that came from such a small person. It was like a surprise bee sting during a barefoot walk on grass, a misstep in the clover. The insect lashing out, surprisingly powerful for its size.

"Get dressed," she ordered a little sharply, handing him some clothes from a safe distance. He grabbed them from her, anger in his gestures. While he slipped on his underwear and pants, she found herself staring once more at the lines that someone had etched into her child. René noticed her watching and deliberately turned his back on her.

"Put these clean ones on instead," she said suddenly remembering the purpose of bathing today, trying to keep up hygiene standards in their chaotic world, but he was having none of it. He paused and sighed, then kept going, ignoring the offer of the newly-laundered garments.

"René," she pressed wearily, "those clothes are dirty."

She shuffled closer to him holding out the alternate clothes, and seeing him proceed to don his soiled shirt, she pulled it out of his hands, and tried to slide the clean one over his tousled black hair. At this, he erupted in anger. He pounced on her, enclosing her in a vise grip. His little arms wrapped tightly around her neck, prompting her to cough. She tried to pry his hands away, but he clenched her in an unusually powerful hug. As he squeezed, he exerted the strength of a man, with the technique and skill of a wrestler, shifting around her and bracing against the floor. Through a blur, she saw her little boy, the waifish child she had been breast-feeding up until three years ago. She looked into his face, and marvelled at his porcelain skin, his raven-black eyelashes that swept down like Chinese brush strokes on a scroll. He was—had been, she corrected herself—such a beautiful boy.

In her detached self, Anna marvelled at René's brute strength. The strong thumps that his feet delivered to the hardwood floor as they shifted, moving strategically to take advantage of her weaknesses.

As René deprived Anna of her breath, he also deprived the baby. The seven-month-old fetus inside her protested, panicking at the attack, flopping about as though it too were part of this battle, the oxygen, its life force cut off with every constriction, every compression by his older brother. *We haven't met, but you want to kill me? Why?*

With the attack came a deep cold, a chill that reached her bones. Inside of her, she sensed the amniotic fluid congealing and slowing. René was fast-freezing her and the baby. Anna realized that she had to get away, not just to save herself, but more importantly to save her unborn child.

With René still clinging to her she crawled out of the bathroom toward the staircase. She flung her arms out and stretched her fingers, grasping for the railing. Grabbing hold of the spindles, she pulled herself forward. Then she threw her body against the bannister, trying to use the impact to dislodge René, which it did—but only briefly. In those few seconds he lay stunned, she scurried to the top of the stairs.

Then with a crushing thud, René was back on top of her, pressing down on her with the weight of an avalanche. Again, she tried to free herself, shuffling sideways, down the first step, and then the second, whereupon she lost control. Flailing, trying to grab the handrail, but unable to reach far enough, she tumbled backwards. Before she fell, René finally released his hold on her.

Dizzy and faint, she catapulted forward, each tread knocking the wind from her. As she went down, her limbs flopped about, awkward and heavy. In fleeting glimpses, she caught his gaze from the top of the stairs, where he watched her, his black reptilian eyes, dark and unblinking.

She landed hard, like a broken doll. A guttural wail arose from deep within her and echoed through the house. As she lay on the frigid floor, her lips chattering, her fingers numb with cold, she cried for her unborn child, knowing it was dying within her. The kicking slowed and stopped, like the abrupt end of a drum roll. Where her belly had once been warm and full, she now felt nothing but a frozen lump, the life draining away like melting ice. She stared bewildered at the cold dark blood oozing from between her legs. It was incomprehensible.

She prayed, she chanted, beckoning the spirit of Flo to fight with her but it was like trying to hold onto a straw in a hurricane. She was overwhelmed, weakened to a state of submission. The roaring in her ears had long since stopped, and all she heard now was her own laboured breathing, the chattering of her teeth. The floor dug into her back like a blade of steel. She smelled the iron from the blood, the wet embers of the fire in the hearth, dying down, giving in. After a time, there was no sound but her intermittent gasps. And then silence, as she languished in a wet pool of near-frozen blood.

She saw him watching from the railing above, his face framed between the vertical spindles that reminded Anna of prison bars.

"Call Daddy," she gasped, using her last reserves of strength. Somewhere in there, in the little boy's body, behind those dark eyes, was perhaps some vestige of her son. "Please."

But he simply stood above her like a statue, unfeeling, unmoveable, staring at her as she faded, the life blood oozing out of her in sludge-like pulses, a river slowing down as it froze over, the essence of her being becoming locked in ice. He gazed blankly, as though he had been still like this for an eternity, like a carved rock facing the sea.

CHAPTER TWENTY-SEVEN

Undone

"Pulse 70 over 40."

Anna felt herself being lifted, her head cradled in big generous hands. Floppy like a ragged doll, unusually light, she let herself be shuffled and moved and poked. She felt the loving bursts of warmth, the flow of life return to her.

"Annie, hang in there!"

She heard her father's voice and let herself relax. She was safe again. There was hope. She had been given another chance, but then flashes of the struggle came to her. She felt the absence of movement. The unusual stillness within her.

"Did I give birth?" she asked, the question strangling in her throat. "Where's the baby?"

Her father's voice came to her through a fog.

"You lost the baby." The words were wrung from him. Regret in every syllable. He choked as he repeated the thing he knew she didn't want to hear.

"The baby didn't make it. I'm sorry, Annie."

A blast of cold air ran over her. Goose bumps formed on her skin. She rubbed her arm. She sunk back on the bed. Free-falling into an abyss. Slipping into a chasm between glaciers, between coldness and cruelty. Why did they bring her back only to suffer like this? Why didn't they just let her die?

An overdose of painkillers. It would be so easy. If only they could read her mind, make a mistake with the dosage. "Let me go," she tried to tell them.

* * *

Perry shook his head. He had never seen Anna this bad. He would gladly go back to the days of her drunken rages, to the wild teenager who defied him. He would do it all again not to be here now with rabid and crazy Anna. The one who thought her kid had pushed her down the stairs and killed her baby.

What had they done to anger the spirits like this? Was he not a good man? He had cared for his alcoholic wife and seen his daughter through recovery. He had suffered the death of his son, his wife, his sister. He had hung on while René remained in a coma. And now this. *I can't take much more,* Perry thought. *I don't know if I can always be the strong one.*

Most disturbing was her talk about Munson. The strange questions about his habits, his carvings, even his tattoos. Why did that matter anymore? The man was dead.

He had been so proud of her, his daughter, the lawyer. It gave him hope that they could overcome anything. Perhaps he had been too proud, too full of himself. Had conceit gotten in the way of common-sense thinking? Had it made him blind to the facts?

He found himself remembering the ceremony, performed at this same hospital, months earlier. What had they unleashed by going against nature? Was this some demonic punishment, he wondered. Remembering that awful night, he felt a chill run through his body.

*　　*　　*

She thought about how the pattern of her thoughts had changed, going in circles, spinning, spiralling downward. She used to be a logical, practical thinker, forward-oriented, with straight line clarity, but lately she'd lost her way. Her mind had become muddled. It wallowed in a quagmire of self-doubt, layered with secrecy and a desire to explain the inexplicable in a socially acceptable way. The stories she made up in her head, refashioning reality to cover up her flaws, her husband's mistakes and the truth about the ritual at the hospital weeks earlier, and at the core, the strangeness of their son, and his possible guilt.

If I told them about the freezing, the little boy who came back to life as a dangerous con man, a lethal wrestler, how in his shape-shifting form as her beloved son René, he killed the baby—if I told them all this, they wouldn't believe me. Moreover, if I did reveal my true thoughts, they would take him away from us. But then, isn't that what I want? But what if I am crazy? What if I did throw myself down the stairs like they believe? Like René told them I did. But what if he does it again? What if Lance Munson were guilty? What if he killed those other women? What if Lance Munson is acquitted?

And then Anna remembered that Lance Munson was dead.

"Anna," the disembodied voice jolted her from her foggy state, "Anna, I'm giving you something for the pain. You're going to feel a small sharp stab."

"Killer," she murmured, as the needle went in, her voice slurred and hoarse.

136

"Oh, it's not that bad," came the reply.

* * *

A thin metal grille embedded in the glass did nothing to diminish the intensity of the sun. It felt like laser beams piercing her eyes. The room was overheated. That and the drugs made her so thirsty. She took a sip of water from the plastic cup with the straw. The crushed ice had long melted. Her hands were shaking as she set the cup down on the wood grain side table bolted to the wall.

She turned to her guest. His face was in shadow. He sat on the plastic chair, his hands folded together, almost prayer-like. He was uncomfortable about something but that was just tough, she thought. He really needed to step up his game.

"His fingerprints," she murmured. "Do they match Munson's?"

Corbeau did not reply right away. He glanced to the side, avoiding her gaze. His expression gave away his confusion. She guessed that he was having trouble with her claim that Munson had come back as her six-year-old son.

His glances toward the left side were an indication he was lying and so Anna kept that in mind when he replied.

"We haven't got the results back yet from the lab."

Bullshit, she thought. Either he hadn't sent the prints in, or he had, and they were a match. But that didn't prove anything because it was an established fact that Munson had been in the Durand-Docstedder home.

"It's kind of crazy, isn't it?"

Corbeau shook his head.

"I mean, how do you ask for print comparisons on a dead guy, without raising concerns?" Anna said.

"It happens all the time. It's the part about matching them with…" Corbeau exhaled.

A face peered into the window portion of the door. A fellow officer made eye contact with Corbeau. He nodded in reply, signalling that he was okay.

Anna smiled to herself. *They think I'm the dangerous one.*

"I'm mostly concerned about the survivor," Anna said, changing tack.

Corbeau frowned.

"There was a woman he left for dead—Gloria Nagel."

* * *

Corbeau narrowed his eyes. What was she planning, he wondered. He made a mental note to have the survivor watched or

137

warned at the very least. But he knew from talking to the medical director on the ward that Anna wasn't going anywhere soon. She was deemed psychotic and a danger to herself and her family.

"For Munson, it's an ego thing. She got away. She's unfinished business and he likely won't let it rest."

Corbeau screwed up his face. One half of him was genuinely interested in her theory, but the other half battled with the notion that he was swallowing her crazy ideas.

"Hadn't Munson been trying to find her for years?"

"Yeah."

"He was keeping in touch with her friends."

"They grew up together," Corbeau said. "Grew up in the same town. But they really had separate lives."

"She's unfinished business," she repeated.

Corbeau shook his head. "Munson is finished business."

It was Anna's turn to cast her head from side to side in disagreement.

"Gloria was so relieved when she learned that Munson had died." Corbeau stated emphatically. "I'd really hate to have to tell her that she should start worrying about him again. She's got some peace now."

"The damage is done, Dale. Either way, her life is never going to be the same." Anna stared hard at him. "Besides, there's lots more like him out there, and she knows that."

Corbeau could not deny that was true. Once victimized, these women would never feel safe again. He returned Anna's gaze. For a brief moment they understood each other.

"I mean you didn't suddenly stop working when Munson's body was pulled up from the lake." Anna swept her hands up for dramatic effect. "Like, hey, look at me, I can retire now. Job's all done."

He gave a small nod, but inside, he felt uneasy. Munson's own lawyer was ragging on him and worse she was trying to say her son and Munson were somehow connected.

"If it's not Munson himself, it's his double. Someone very, very much like him, with the same goals. In fact, *exactly* the same."

"I suppose I could get in touch with Gloria," Corbeau offered, although in his heart he knew he would likely not get around to it. He could just imagine Gloria's face when she saw him on her front porch. She was in no more imminent danger than the next person.

"Leave the door open for other possibilities," Anna said enigmatically.

Corbeau stood up to go. He felt that her fog had crept into his brain, and scrambled the circuits.

"And submit those fingerprints." Anna added. "They'll be the same, only smaller."

Corbeau sighed. *She has come undone*, he thought to himself. It was sad. He would miss her as an adversary. She had given him a lot of grief over the years, but he had always respected her. Now he felt only pity for her.

He carried out the paper cup, careful not to spill the cold liquid inside. There was just one thing worse than station coffee, boiled, overcooked and stale—that was hospital coffee, it had all of the same negatives but with one extra—the taint of disinfectant.

*   *   *

Anna sounded subdued. Xavier guessed they were pumping her full of drugs.

There was not much news. Anna told him he could expect a visit from Dale Corbeau, the detective she had often locked horns with.

"Why, what does he want from us?"

"He's going to come by and pick up some things."

"What?"

"He'll call you first."

"You want me to just let this cop go through our stuff?"

"Yeah, he knows what to get."

"I dunno," said Xavier shrugging. "What's this for?"

Anna didn't answer, so Xavier pressed her further. "Are we being investigated? Does he have a search warrant?"

Anna did not reply.

"I'm not sure why you would help them."

Anna's lack of information was disquieting but Xavier decided to let it go for the time being. If the police showed up, he would deal with it then.

"I'm not sure when we can come up and see you," said Xavier, hesitating. "Right now I am waiting on the furnace repair guy. Can you believe it, we're without heat again."

Anna clucked sympathetically. She was not surprised. Not anymore. She came to realize there was nothing they could do against the deep cold invading their home. It was not a mechanical problem, nor a construction problem, but a spirit problem.

"It's like the north pole here. I got the fireplace going, all the space heaters plugged in. I'm wearing a coat—*indoors*," he grumbled. "So that's why we can't come see you."

"That's alright," she said, secretly glad not to have to face René. She was not sure she would be able to restrain herself. "Are you okay?" she asked Xavier, which threw him off after all she was the one in the hospital.

He let the question hang for a moment, then replied. "I'm alright," he lied. Truth was he felt like death warmed over. He felt gutted and raw. Tears welled up in his eyes, and his chest got tight thinking again about their lost baby, remembering the scene that greeted him when Perry called to tell him to come home.

Xavier also worried about how the miscarriage might have damaged Anna's sanity. He didn't need to ask how she was. He already knew. He'd had a report from the hospital team. She was relatively calm after a few difficult days. The searing rage was no longer ever present, but had been dulled with medication. What the pills could do nothing about, of course, was her persistent belief that René had caused her miscarriage.

It was all Xavier could do to keep his head above water. René, for his part, seemed calm and unperturbed by the events of the last few days. He padded around the house in his stocking feet, rebuffing Xavier's attempts to place slippers on them.

Xavier recalled with a sick feeling an incident from the day before. He had been flipping through the calendar, pen in hand to mark down an appointment for a quote on a job when he happened to see the baby's due date. Months before Anna had scribbled it down. "Peanut arrives today!" it said in red ink, a squiggly star surrounding the note. And then he just lost it. Suddenly he had no control over the pent-up emotions, the choking sobs, the tears falling from his eyes like warm rain. When he looked up he saw René watching him, showing no sign of distress or concern at his father's breakdown, but rather the child stared coolly, with what Xavier detected was a small smirk, as though he found the whole display somewhat amusing.

Xavier wondered later if he could have misinterpreted his son's reaction. Was the boy simply embarrassed or uncomfortable at his father's emotional breakdown? Whatever it was, Xavier felt deeply alone. Whenever Xavier probed René about his feelings, the boy would break away and make himself scarce for a while, as though unwilling to get into it.

When Xavier ended the call with Anna he took refuge near the fireplace, and pulled out his guitar. But the soothing strumming would not come today. When his fingertips made contact with the strings they burned in pain, stinging from the cold. And the sounds emitted rang hollow and tinny. Finally, he leaned the guitar back against the wall in frustration.

Xavier made another cup of coffee, this time pouring it into an insulated mug. The rising steam vanished almost immediately, snuffed out as soon as it met the cold air.

He thought about working on the addition, but he worried he would not hear the furnace repair people if he were there. The thought of unscrewing the boards blocking that area was also a deterrent. It could wait till they had heat or better weather.

Xavier glanced at the stove clock. The neon green block numerals read 11:40 am, and still no word from Heat Pros, the company that had first installed their new furnace only a year before, assuring the Durand-Docstedders they would never feel chilled again. But how could the Heat Pros have known about the curse that plagued the icy house by the lake. There was only so much the Smartaire 3000 Forty HP furnace could do against evil spirits and the cold that swept up from the lake and scattered their happiness like the dry leaves of fall.

Xavier put together lunch for him and the kid. Grilled cheese sandwiches and tomato soup. They ate together in near silence, the only sounds were the spoons tinkling against the white Corelle bowls.

It was half past three when the white van with the bold red and black Heat Pros logo showed up. Xavier eagerly welcomed Ivan, a tall stick of a man, with steel blue eyes, and hair yellow like the wheat fields of his homeland. A thick Eastern European accent flavoured the many excuses for his late arrival. "It vos difficult this location," he waved his arms, recreating the winding pattern of the road that led him here.

Xavier showed Ivan into the basement where the furnace sat quietly waiting his magic touch. Within moments the machine was humming again.

"Machine is good," declared Ivan. "Only pilot light should not go out."

"Of course, it should not go out, but it does! I don't know how many times I've relit the damn thing."

"In one hour, all heat should return."

"What was wrong with it?"

"Pilot light was out."

"That's it?"

"I find nothing else."

Ivan held up a temperature gauge and walked about the house. Xavier followed him, his pride somewhat offended by the grunts of dismay from the Russian.

"Look at this, cold here, very cold here," Ivan exclaimed. "Wow," the 'w' taking on an extra vibration. "It is like wind coming down from there. Right through building." Ivan pressed on, walking toward the addition, clutching the thermometer like a priest holding up a cross as part of an exorcism. "Oh, my God, Siberia is warmer," the repairman said, whistling. "Temperatures go down below freezing."

He pointed, in front of him, to a gaping chasm. Xavier was dumbfounded at what he saw. It was not possible. There it was, the entrance to the addition, wide open.

"You should close door or insulate in this area," said Ivan, pronouncing insulate *'eeensoolate'*.

Ivan must have thought it was odd that Xavier stood staring at the opening. Xavier could not comprehend that the plywood boards he had only seen the day before, tightly screwed across the doorframe, were now leaning against the wall.

"What the hell," he muttered. "Who did this?" Had Perry been here, he wondered. Had Anna hired someone to come by and continue work while Xavier was out? No, that can't be. Only yesterday he had checked for leaks and had seen the boards up.

Curious, Ivan took himself on a self-guided tour of the addition. Rather presumptuous, Xavier felt. His neck muscles tightened as he stood back listening to the Russian talking to himself. He didn't understand the man's words but could hear the contempt in his tone. "What is this?" Ivan asked.

Xavier strode in and saw Ivan pointing to the Boberge light fixture.

"Okay, are we about done here?" Xavier growled, his lips thinning with anger.

The Russki shrugged and lumbered out of the addition, giving a few sideway looks to show he was still inspecting Xavier's work. When the two men returned to the kitchen, Xavier cleared a spot on the table for Ivan to write up his invoice.

In the background, Xavier could hear the television—*Ice Truckers of Alaska* was on again. The roar of the motors and the C.B. crackle failed to drown out Ivan's irritating humming.

"I vill check feeelter."

"No, it's good," asserted Xavier. No matter that Xavier had long waited for the repairman to arrive, now he was even more eager to see him go. His smug attitude was barely tolerable.

*   *   *

After settling René to bed that night, Xavier went to secure the addition once more. A feeling of dread came over him seeing the plywood boards once again unscrewed and leaning to the side of the hallway. Xavier forced himself to re-enter the cavernous addition, the space they had so longed to occupy. The great room.

As he stepped around the debris he noticed the repairman's footprints and then was taken aback to see smaller footprints as well. Had René been there that afternoon? Presumably he had explored the area while Xavier was otherwise occupied with Ivan and the furnace. As Xavier moved about, the plastic dust sheets crackled and fluttered. They were like the shrouds of the dead, thin and brittle with age.

Xavier mentally calculated the remaining hours of work. Inspecting the idle tools and stacks of building supplies, he pressed his fingers into the bundles of insulation, recalling another time, a playful scamp around the room, a game of tag. The echo of a child's laugh caught in a time warp. He was remembering it or hearing the ghost of happy play. It was not so long ago, yet seemed as though from another era.

Xavier had not noticed the dripping tears off his cheeks. The catch in his throat. Here he was bawling again. He clenched his teeth together to stifle the cries. He did not want René to hear him.

CHAPTER TWENTY-EIGHT

Daddy Knows

Despite Ivan's criticism, Xavier had decided against closing off the addition the previous night. He had been unable to locate all his tools as well as the extension cord. He had been afraid the pounding of the hammer and the pulse of the screwdriver would awaken René. So here he was the next morning, with bright sun streaming in, back at it.

For a few minutes, he stood admiring his handiwork, the giant windows positioned to capture the glorious view, and debated leaving the space unlocked so he could have ready access to it. But in the end, he went ahead to board it up again.

He took the electric drill and bore down on a long wood screw, burying it in the sheet of plywood that he braced with one knee. He grabbed another screw from between his lips and popped it in place. The board was the last in a row of three, and once it was fastened, the addition would be secure once more.

He became aware of muffled sounds behind him: a thumping followed by the scraping of something against wood. He pivoted, his back to the plywood boards. A chill ran up Xavier's spine. There was René, standing at the end of the hall staring at him. Or at least—a person of René's height. But his face was in shadow. His stance had none of the light and boyish quality he had come to associate with René. This person before him had a bulkier frame, a more powerful bearing like a seasoned martial arts player or wrestler. In the two seconds these impressions whipped through Xavier's brain, his subconscious concluded he was facing some sort of killer dwarf. But the real clincher, something he not just felt but could see was that René held a nail gun at his side.

When René raised it in the air, Xavier gulped. "That's not a toy," he said automatically. This was an expression Anna would use frequently. He regretted her not being there. She would have handled it with more confidence. "It's very dangerous to be swinging that around so let's just put it down, on the floor."

Xavier fought a growing unease as René ignored his command to lower the nail gun.

"What did I say?" Xavier hoped he sounded more authoritarian, trying to suppress the panic that began to overtake him. *He's just a kid being stupid*, thought Xavier. *Why do I feel so afraid?* It was irrational.

Something compelled Xavier to suddenly duck to the side.

Phhht!

In that second, the nail gun went off, shooting into the wall directly above Xavier's head. He bolted forward and before René could blink Xavier unhanded the kid of the nail gun, whipping it as far as the attached cable would allow. Then Xavier bounded around the corner, stumbling over the large red compressor tank on the way, and yanked the cord from the outlet, as though it were the lifeline to a raft.

Afterwards, Xavier sat up on his knees, breathless, chest heaving, and still adrenaline-charged, when he caught sight of René's expression. He was certain he saw a mischievous smile play across on his son's lips. But as René turned and faced him full on there was no sign of any humour, only earnest concern and the sweetest of countenances.

"I'm sorry, Daddy," the little boy said.

Xavier gazed on his son, dumbfounded. A jumble of conflicting emotions raced through Xavier. He was dizzy from the effort of securing the nail gun, from the turmoil of his feelings, and from fighting the numbing cold.

* * *

In the austere surroundings of the basement, Xavier rubbed his hands together, trying to agitate the flow of blood to his deadened fingers. He tried again to ignite the furnace, pulling a match from the small cardboard box and striking it against the abrasive rectangle. There was a briefing rasping sound preceding the flare of light. It flickered and glowed giving the poor man a beacon of hope. He brought the match in range of the pilot light, where it caught and began to glow. Xavier watched for a while, taking in the warming energy, drawing in its curative essence as though imagining a holy spirit enveloping him in a protective shield.

Above him small footsteps padded. Xavier became alert to their advance, his body tensing as the noise stopped exactly above him. He arched his neck, staring up, as though if he focussed long and hard enough his eyes might gain the power to see through the floorboards. For a few seconds, he held his breath and then he became alarmed, perceiving a change in the direction of the steps. They were now approaching the basement door. It shouldn't have come as a shock to Xavier that there soon followed the sound of the creaking door as it swung open, yet the whining hinges, the protest of metal still surprised him. A glacial wind swept down just then, heralding the approach of an unwelcome presence. The icy onslaught wended its way below as though seeking out every warm-bodied creature, intent on extracting whatever remained of one's living heat.

Xavier cowered near the defunct furnace, quivering. He paused for a moment in his efforts to bring the machine back to life. He waited for a long while, anticipating that René would come down the stairs and actually face him. But after several minutes he felt as though he had lost track of the child. Xavier heard nothing more and even wondered if the boy had gone away.

With trembling fingers Xavier resumed his attempts to create heat. He shook open the box of matches and tried once more to light the furnace. And again. And again, until the box was empty. He knew there must be other boxes of matches in the house somewhere. He had no desire, however, to go in search of them. He was deliberately slowing down, moving with the knowledge that he must conserve his strength, and save the calories for survival. But deep down he knew the real reason he was not rushing back upstairs to look for matches, was quite simply because he dreaded facing the boy.

*　*　*

Like the futile messages of prehistoric cavemen to their future ancestors, Xavier wanted to tell Anna the story of how he finally came to believe her, especially about the unnatural cold. He wanted to tell her he had badly misjudged the situation, that his arrogance had let them all down. When he called her he already knew that there was nothing she could do, nothing that anyone could do to save them.

"Are they listening to us?" Anna wondered out loud.

"I don't think so," whispered Xavier. It had not occurred to him that the hospital might record their conversations.

"But *he's* listening," said Anna.

"He? Oh, I suppose so," admitted Xavier. He could sense the small boy, the evil imp, around the corner.

"It's not really him, you know."

"I know."

Sadly, Xavier had come to this realization too late. When he coughed, Anna cringed, listening to the deep rumble that accompanied each draw of his raspy breath. Xavier's voice had become

146

thick and rough, his thoughts muddled and incoherent as his brain began to shut down.

Ironically, locked up and far away, Anna was no longer in danger, and had never been a real threat to anyone. The menace was still on the loose, residing side by side with her husband, slowly tormenting the man with what would be surely a long and painful death, as deep and prolonged as the ice age advancing on a continent, grinding down the fleeing mammals, encasing all living forms in glittering and shattering frost.

* * *

The wisdom was already evaporating with the last of his warm breaths. Teeth chattering and body shaking, delirium wrapping its way like a muzzle on his mind, he lay curled unto himself, burrowed under a useless duvet.

The little boy placed his cold bare feet against his father's back, chilling him, sending frigid daggers into Xavier's core. "Tell me a story, Daddy," he asked almost innocently.

"Story?—You want a what?—What kind?" his father asked, his words slurring, like the last survivor pulled from a failed arctic voyage, his reasoning floundering somewhere on the shoals.

"Tell me how she died." There was a lightness to René's words. A giddy lilting tone that belied the gut-wrenching subject.

"Who?—Who died?"

"My baby sister."

It was calculated. Like a well-aimed ice pick. As though the physical pain were not enough, the toes and fingertips blackening with frostbite, the words, the memories, would kill the spark of life where sheer cold, plummeting temperatures had not yet reached. Xavier wondered how René knew that the child Anna had miscarried was female.

Xavier's teeth rattled like empty milk bottles in a horse drawn cart, clattering as the wheels bumped over rough roads, a frightened animal running blind.

* * *

Corbeau was still pondering a strange phone call from Anna from a few days earlier when she called him again. This time there was no polite preamble. She got right to the point.

"Xavier's in danger," the words came out breathlessly.

"Oh, yeah?" Corbeau hedged, not wanting to make it easy on her.

"I'm afraid for him."

"So, what's going on?"

"Someone's trying to kill him."

"Who?"

"A relative."

"Is that right?" I can't be dealing with this, thought Corbeau. Why weren't the shrinks talking to her, instead of him? He sighed. "Look, if you really think it's an emergency, dial 911." It was all he could suggest.

"Like I haven't tried! Think about it, I've been calling them from inside a psych ward. They're not taking me seriously. Go figure!"

Corbeau shook his head. It was true. A dispatcher would likely dismiss any complaints simply based on where the call was coming from. While Anna had been saying some crazy things, the bottom line was he couldn't dismiss her outright. There was the tiniest hint that there was something suspicious going on. He wondered if they had missed something, a partner or relative of Munson's who had it in for Anna and her family, someone who was coming back to avenge Munson.

Around the small lake community, there had been numerous complaints about the snowmobile traffic, the noise from the machines, and the trespassing. Then there was the proximity of Munson's trailer to the lake and Anna's home. Was there a person in Munson's life who would pick up where he had left off?

He could send a patrol car out to check on Anna's husband and the boy. In the end, he decided he might as well go out there himself. He would stop by the Pines trailer park and have another look around. Talk to some of Munson's old neighbours.

He had been waiting on a search warrant for the Durand-Docstedder home but with Anna's permission to go ahead and look around he could enter the dwelling and at the same time do a welfare check. He could always come back later once he got the search warrant—or so he thought.

CHAPTER TWENTY-NINE

Last Chance

He was teaching a couple of young men how to install a door hinge. It was tricky. A common mistake was to cut straight across to the edge of the door rather than make a rectangular indentation that was just large enough for the hinge plate. He liked to slow this part down and get the men to measure once, and then measure again. There was no sense hurrying things only to have to correct a problem.

While they were working, he felt the phone humming in his pocket. He pulled it out to glance at it. Perry recognized the number for St. Boniface Hospital. He let the call go to voice mail. Then there was another call and he put the phone on silent.

He had been to see Anna just the night before and spent quite a bit of time with her. In a way, he was relieved his daughter was in the hospital. At least she was getting the help she needed. She was better off there than being in that icebox of a house with Xavier and the kid.

There was a lot of Anna that reminded him of his late wife, Louise. For sure, the feistiness. Louise wouldn't put up with bull from nobody. She was courageous like Anna. Always thought she was right, but that had led to problems. He had grown tired of being the one to always compromise.

There was also a fragility that Louise sometimes displayed. The way she would finally crumple from all the disappointments. The sadness would just creep up on her and no amount of cheery talk or sweet gestures could bump her out of that deep rut. Poor Louise. He had let her down, assumed she would make it through one more bout of sadness like she had so many times before.

Anna was different. Or so he hoped. This is what he had convinced himself of, anyway.

Perry cursed. The new kid had taken a router right across the side of the door. Just like he had told him not to. Did they ever listen? A young punk with tattoos all up the side of his neck. How much had that cost?

No woman in her right mind would let someone with "FUCK U" inked up his throat anywhere near her house let alone to come in and fix a broken door.

Damn it. His own attention was wandering. He couldn't focus on his students when he knew his daughter was spiralling out of control.

"Let's take a break, guys."

Perry watched as the group of them filed out the side door, reaching for their cigarettes as soon as the word "break" left Perry's lips. They were hungry for the tobacco, aching for the burn on their fingers, and the smoke in their airways. Perry would have liked to have joined them on the cracked cement stoop, shooting the breeze, swapping prison stories and keeping things light-hearted. Some things never changed. There were some that would invariably miss the black cone ashtray and grind out their butts under their feet or simply toss them toward the snow banks.

Teaching them good habits. Being tidy. Taking the time to measure carefully. Cleaning and oiling tools, putting them away in their correct spot. Some of the guys would never learn. They didn't have it in them to be master tradesmen. They didn't care enough about the craft. They didn't have a feel for wood, didn't notice the texture, the grain, the smell of pine of oak or ash or maple. They had no patience. And yet he had to take them through the paces.

It was like tree planting. Carrying a load of seedlings in a sack down rough ground, the thin soil over igneous rock. Scrape a little hole, stuff the puny stalk into the earth. Tamp it down and move on. Some would grow, and some wouldn't make it.

He'd had such high hopes for Munson. He had been a craftsman, but perhaps it was his skill with wood that had dazzled Perry and had fooled him. It was one thing to learn to work with tools and another to learn to walk among the free, back in society, to quit the life for good. Perry realized too late that Munson had accomplished one but failed at the other. The rings grew around him, in thin fine layers, but at the core he was just rotten.

Perry sighed, pulling his phone out of his pocket. There had been nearly twenty missed calls from Anna. He braced himself as he punched in the number for voice mail. He listened to each of her messages, noting her panic and worry escalating, until he too was sufficiently disturbed. He swallowed the lump in his throat, his mouth dry from the anxiety.

"Dad, I can't get through to anyone at the house," Anna had said on several of her messages. He looked out to the yard, at the men and knew he would have to send them back early today. He could no longer ignore his daughter's warnings.

* * *

The route to St. Boniface Hospital was so familiar he could probably have driven it with his eyes closed. As Perry pulled up, he opted for the short-term parking, thinking he would only stay as long as needed to reassure his daughter that all was under control.

"Dad, remember the ceremony that we had, when René was in a coma."

"Of course, how could I forget."

"Well, we're paying for the consequences."

"I don't think anything happened 'cept I got a sore back from sleeping in a chair."

"It did work—but not how we wanted it to."

Perry was making a face, as though trying to tell what strange food he had just tasted.

"It brought a soul back—just not René's."

Anna studied her father's expression. Perry looked at his hands, picked at a sliver on his thumb.

"Auntie Flo didn't want you to know."

Perry thought back on the months before Flo's death. Her strange behaviour, her low depressed mood, in such contrast to her usual light-hearted self. Tears flooded his eyes. He had always been so hard on her.

"I don't think Flo really had the power to do—"

"Daddy, please you never gave her credit—"

"She was a self-taught witch doctor—"

"Flo had a gift!" said Anna, her voice rising in defense of her late aunt. "She knew stuff. She predicted so many things—"

"Annie, Flo is gone. We got to worry about you now. You're the one in the hospital here."

"Dad, I don't want to stay. I'm being forced to stay. I want to get back to the house. I'm worried about Xav and, and—" She wouldn't say her son's name, the person whose body had been taken over by a dead spirit.

"He's fine. I talked to him just now."

"You did?"

"Before I came here."

There was a pause.

"I tried calling but he wouldn't pick up. The hospital is limiting my calls to home."

151

Perry pulled out his cell phone and punched in a number. They both listened to the ringing sound.

*   *   *

At the Durand-Docstedder house, the phone in the kitchen rang, and rang, and then all of a sudden, a chair was pushed against the wall and a small person hopped onto the counter and grabbed the receiver. His face was hidden. He cradled the phone under his ear.

"Hello?"

"René—it's grandpa. How you doing, little fella?"

"I'm okay."

"Say, is your dad there? Your mom wants to say hello."

"Dad's sleeping."

"Well, you mind waking him up?"

There was a pause. Then Perry continued, pressing his grandson. "He's not sick is he?"

"No."

"Well, then can you get him?"

"Okay, grandpa."

René set the receiver down and jumped off the counter. He ran across the room and then down the hallway toward the staircase. He started to ascend the stairs but then stopped abruptly and very deliberately sat down. He stretched out his legs and then folded them back up again. He hummed something and then became interested in a fly hovering about the stairs and fixed his eyes on it. His gaze intensified until he was completely focussed on the insect's flight path. Then as the fly came close, he blew on it, a frosty exhalation. The fly crystalized and then dropped heavily to the floor, shattering in many small icy fragments.

Finally, René got up again and returned to the kitchen, taking his time and dawdling. Then using exaggerated thumping steps, he approached the phone and picked it up.

"Hey," came the greeting—*in Xavier's voice.*

"You okay, man?"

"Sure, just a little under the weather."

"Anna's been trying to call you all day."

"Oh, yeah, gotta juice up my phone. Battery must have died."

Anna listened on speaker, as Perry conversed with her husband.

"You coming up to the hospital?" Perry asked.

"I would have but I had to wait all day for the furnace guy."

152

"Is it fixed?"

"Yeah but the place is just getting heated up. Cold kinda slows you down you know."

Anna frowned.

"Xavier, you okay?" said Perry.

"Sure, why?" came Xavier's response.

"You sound a little off."

René smiled to himself.

"How's that?"

"Are you alone?" continued Perry.

"Uhhh. Yeah. Other than your grandson."

Anna signalled something to Perry. Her father shook his head. Not getting her drift. She waggled her ring finger.

Anna took over the call from her father. She leaned into the phone and said, "When did we get married?"

"Huh?"

"When did we get married?" she repeated.

There was a clicking sound on the line. Elsewhere in the Durand-Docstedder house, another extension picked up.

* * *

The little boy leapt off the counter and ran out of the kitchen. He bounded toward the staircase and climbed it at lightening speed.

He soon arrived at his parents' bedroom. He stood in the doorway for a brief second, gazing upon a shivering form. Xavier, delirious, his arm outreached, barely hung onto the receiver, struggling to speak into the bedside phone.

"Panama!" was all he was able to gasp, before the receiver was snatched from him—by René. The boy slammed the phone down. He turned to his father, glaring at the trembling man. Xavier tried to still his shaking hands by clasping them together.

It was then René noticed the wedding band. He grabbed his father's hand and pulled on his frostbitten finger, snapping it off, and extracting the ring. Xavier moaned and fell back onto the bed, writhing from pain.

René turned the gold band around in his hand and studied the date inscribed on the inside.

He ran back downstairs, and once more picked up the phone.

"May 16, 2006. I had to check my wedding ring."

* * *

Anna stood rigid, staring at the phone.

Perry was about to speak, when she leaned over and hung up the phone.

"Why did you do that?"

"Did you hear that?"

"So, he had to check his ring," Perry shrugged.

"No, no. Before that. Another voice. Did you hear it?"

Parry was sceptical. "I'm not sure."

"There was a second voice. Kind of low."

Perry frowned, unconvinced.

"It's hard to tell but I think it was Xavier. He said 'Panama.' That's our safe word."

"Panama?"

"Yeah. Did you hear it?"

"You know with all the shop machines, my hearing's pretty well shot."

"I know I heard it."

"Well, there's one way of finding out. I'll play it back." Perry fiddled with the phone and then hit play and the conversation with Xavier was repeated.

They both listened intently as the odd recording echoed in the small hospital room.

"It's weird," said Anna. "'Juice up' was an expression that I remember Munson using. Xavier would never say something like that."

Perry shrugged. "You don't know that for sure. Maybe he picked it up from him."

"They didn't spend that much time together." Anna stood up and paced about the small room, becoming increasingly agitated. "Play the recording again and turn up the volume."

"One more time, but I think you're making a mountain out of a mole hill."

They listened again to the disembodied voices and sounds, and this time at the word 'Panama,' Perry nodded, gazing at Anna.

"You heard it, right? 'Panama.' That's Xavier trying to tell me he's in danger."

"But it all sounded like Xavier."

Anna stopped in the centre of the room.

"Something's not right, Dad."

"I think you're over-reacting."

"Lance Munson has got a hold of him."

Perry went quiet. He studied his daughter. He wanted to remind her that Munson was dead but decided against it.

"You got to help me get out of here," Anna pleaded, rubbing her arms as though chilled.

Perry sputtered, "I don't know if that's a good idea, Anna."

"Oh, Dad, come on! Get them to release me into your care."

Perry sighed. "I am in a position of trust. You know, I can't just bust you out of here."

Anna huffed. "You think I'm going to do something crazy?"

You're damn right, Perry thought, his eyes carefully averting her gaze. He said nothing in response.

"Please, Dad. Munson is back!" Anna gripped her father's arm and made him face her, and in a serious voice uttered the unbelievable: "He hitched a ride on my kid's body."

Perry gulped. He deliberated over what to say, but in the end thought better of it, and remained silent, bowing his head instead, eyes to the floor. His brilliant lawyer daughter had gone nutso.

"I better head out now, if I want to get to the lake house before dark," he said, his throat catching.

"Dad!"

Perry held his hand up defensively. "I can't, Anna," he watched her face colour in anger. "You're safe here." He leaned toward her and gave her a long embrace. "As long as you're here I don't have to worry about you."

"Please, get me out!"

"Don't worry, I'm gonna check on Xavier and René."

Anna's hands flew up in exasperation. "Fuck, René!"

Perry bit his lip. He strode past his daughter and exited the room. He rushed past the nurse's station, avoiding making eye contact with any of the staff. The glaring fluorescent lights, the antiseptic smells, the odours reminded him of other crises, other dark moments in hospitals. Why had he been cursed like this?

Down the hall, he stood at the exit, pressed a button to request the door be unlocked. An orderly appeared and using his card key, released the lock and let Perry out.

*   *   *

Anna sat on her bed, stewing. After a moment, she stood up and exited the room. She strode to the nurse's station with its plexiglass wall.

"I'd like to see my Form One paperwork."

"Uhh—One moment."

*   *   *

A conference was hastily arranged in the Tamarack Boardroom. Anna was brought in and provided a seat at the far end. She felt exposed in the thin blue cotton gown, held together by thin ties. Deprived of her usual courtroom accoutrements: the pointer, the

155

power suit, the technology, she was at a psychological disadvantage. Nevertheless, she could tell the hospital team was not prepared for her arguments.

"The Form One has expired, and legally you have no grounds to hold me any longer," Anna insisted.

"The commitment has been extended." This statement came from the hospital patient liaison person, a sleek silver-haired woman.

Anna was stunned. She blinked, "Excuse me?"

"We spoke to your husband just now and he feels that you are a danger to yourself and your son."

"You spoke to him?"

"Yes."

"Can you confirm that you spoke to Xavier Durand, and not someone impersonating him?"

This took the silver-haired woman aback. "Dr. Hannan recognized his voice, his accent."

"Legally, that's not enough. You can't hold me here because of a he-said, she-said situation. Especially in a contentious divorce—"

"Divorce?"

"If you don't release me and return my clothing and personal effects immediately, I will sue this hospital—"

"Just a moment, please," said the grey-haired woman. The white coats leaned their heads together and began an agitated discussion. Finally, the silver fox led them outside the room, out of earshot of Anna. She watched their palaver through the glass windows of the conference room. She saw one of them respond to a phone call. A moment later, a young man in a suit joined the discussion. Anna guessed he was a hospital legal advisor. From time to time, they glanced in her direction as they huddled in animated debate. Then they signalled for the doctor still remaining in the conference room to join them. Anna was left alone, but remained in view, behind the glass wall as though she were a museum specimen. She strained to hear what they were saying, tried to read their lips, and gauge their expressions, a skill picked up from years of studying the body language of jurors. She could only be certain of two things: that they were talking about her and—they were not on her side.

The forces against her seemed to increase as another woman joined the group of white coats. The slender red-head held out a sheet of paper for the others to read. This seemed to be the holy

grail, as immediately the new document raised the level of anima-
tion of the group. Anna was instantly curious, and also almost as
quickly, disheartened. By their expressions, she sensed she would
not be given permission to be released.

It was then she noticed the jacket on the chair next to her. A
security pass clipped to an inside pocket. She swivelled her chair
closer and snatched the pass. The stealthy moves of her teenage
shoplifting days had returned to her in this time of desperation.

And then the medical militia was back, the gaggle of doctors,
now fortified with reinforcements, two additional experts. They
seemed smug, having armed themselves with new paperwork. An
ace up their sleeve.

This was a different kind of battle than Anna was used to.
She knew she was at a disadvantage, with the woozy, unsettling
effect of the anti-psychotic drugs. Her bearings were off. And she
was facing them in a gown and paper slippers, exposed and chilled,
and above all, misunderstood. All that was missing from her many
disadvantages was a straitjacket. How could she convince them she
was not crazy? But did she even need to?

"Ms. Docstedder, we have made a decision to extend your
commitment for another 72 hours, uh, based on new information."

"New information?"

The perky one with the red hair, and the gold nursing school
grad ring flashing on her left hand, passed the mystery document to
Anna.

She scanned it quickly. The damning words swirled in front
of her eyes: "delusional"; "a danger to her son"; "worried about
her." They hit her hard, wounding her pride.

But the signature at the bottom was what really killed her—*it
was her father's*.

CHAPTER THIRTY
Mikwam

Corbeau tapped his dress shoes against the bottom of the car door, knocking off a clump of snow. He had come from a court appearance and was dressed in a suit and tie, visible through his unbuttoned overcoat.

His tour of Munson's mobile home and the surrounding trailer park had yielded nothing. The Munson home was one of the more decrepit units, the once-white aluminum siding was now tinged a yellowish hue, and brownish stains dripped where rust had leached. A plain landing in pressure treated lumber flanked the single-wide dwelling. A brown and white awning leaned over toppled flowerpots. Donut shapes hinted at tires hidden just beneath the surface. Behind the house, was a small aluminum shed, inaccessible now due to the snow heaped in front.

The state of neglect seemed to indicate that no one had been around for a while. The house appeared unoccupied. Across the road, an elderly man was shovelling his walk. He paused, leaning over his shovel to stare at the visitor.

Corbeau took the opportunity to cross the small road to speak with the man, trying not to look foolish as he slipped from side to side in his loafers. The neighbour didn't look familiar. The old man was likely one of the residents who had been absent during the police department's first door-to-door enquiry.

"Killer winter," said Corbeau.

"Thought we'd be done with the snow by now. We just come back from Florida."

"Snowbirds, eh?"

"Uh-huh. Every winter for twenty years now."

"Where'd you go?"

"Florida."

"Yeah, what part? "

"A little place called Cedar Key, on the Gulf side."

"Nice."

"Don't know how much longer we can keep doing it. With gas prices the way they are and medical insurance and all."

Corbeau nodded sympathetically. His own folks headed to Miami every November. He spent many a holiday golfing near their condo.

"Say, Mr.?"

"Roman Buzniki." The senior extended a gloved hand to the investigator.

"Nice to meet you, I'm Detective Corbeau. I'm wondering how well you knew the folks across the way."

"Oh, see, to be honest, we never cared for them much."

"Them?"

"Well, the people who actually owned the place were alright. But he—" Buzniki paused trying to remember the name of his loathed neighbour. "Uh, Len, was it?"

"Lance," Corbeau offered.

"Uhuh, Lance, that's right. So he would just stay there once in a while. Now, he was an odd one. You know, he would get it in his head to fix something. He'd get started, pull the thing apart, and then just stop and leave all his junk lying around. And then we heard he was a thief. Afterwards we put two and two together and figured out why stuff had gone missing."

"Hmm."

"Skidoos, go-carts—we got back from Florida and we found out he was in the pen and didn't see him for the longest time."

Corbeau was nodding.

"Next our daughter calls us about the thing at the lake. We were away at the time. She said he'd been skidooing, you know."

"Did Lance have many friends?"

Buzniki shook his head. "A few, like him. Heavy into the booze. They'd come riding up on their machines, and park all over the place. We were glad not to have to put up with that but the neighbours hated it. Summer time it was ATVs."

"Thank you," Corbeau said, pulling out his card and giving it to the old man. "If you think of anything else. Give me a shout."

"Will do, "Buzniki grunted, and he resumed shovelling, a weariness to his movements.

* * *

Perry found the drive long. He ruminated over his decision to ensure Anna remain in the psych ward, convinced it was for her own good.

When he arrived at the house by the lake, he felt oddly chilled, like the property had a sub-zero microclimate all of its own. He felt the tires of his truck spin in protest upon hitting the

159

driveway as though the vehicle wanted to forewarn him. He tried to shake his apprehension.

The afternoon light was fading. A grey gloom had settled over the house. There were no lights on inside. It was the in-between hour, not yet dark enough for interior lighting, but the beginning of the hiding time. As he approached the entrance off the kitchen, he heard the muted sound of the television. Someone must be home.

Rather than use his key, he rapped on the door. And then after getting no response, he knocked again. This time the door swung open and René appeared, solemn and distant.

Perry remembered how the little boy used to jump for joy upon seeing his grand pops. So much had changed. His mother and grandmother gone. Now he was such a sad little tyke.

"Hey kiddo," Perry said, trying to be cheery. He glanced past the child, catching the flicker of the television screen. Grim music and dramatic narration accompanied a criminal investigation show.

"Where's your dad?"

"He went on the lake, to get a fish."

Perry frowned. That's strange, he thought. Xavier wasn't known to be big on ice fishing, and after the incident involving René, he would have expected the lake would have been even less appealing. Moreover, wasn't all that done for the season? Most of the fishermen would have removed their ice huts by now. But sure enough, as Perry gazed out, he spotted a single hut on the lake.

"I'm gonna go talk to him. I'll be right back." Perry gazed into the dark eyes of his grandson. They were strangely hollow and emotionless.

"Now, you stay here, okay?" Perry gripped the kid's shoulders and made sure he had absorbed the message. "You got that?"

"Yeah. I'm no dummy."

Was it just his impression, Perry wondered, or was this kid sounding more and more like a sulky teenager every day.

"You got something to eat?"

"Uh-huh. Bugles and corn nuts—and beer." For effect, the kid even emitted a loud burp.

The smart-ass attitude gave Perry pause. He dropped to his knees and grabbed René by the arms and stared him directly into the eyes. *Who are you?* Perry thought as he studied his grandson. The kid only tolerated a second of scrutiny before he pulled away and ran to the den, bouncing off the sofa and landing like an Olympian gymnast in front of the TV.

Perry suddenly noticed several crumpled beer cans scattered about. He sighed at how things had gone downhill since Anna's hospitalization. It was apparent Xavier had started back on the sauce. Couldn't really blame him, given all that had gone on. Perry made a mental note to speak to Xavier about René's attitude, the importance of being a good role model, and the too-easy access to booze in the house.

"See ya," Perry called out to the child. René glanced up at him with a smirk.

"Catch ya later," René replied, gesturing irreverently at his grandfather, his small hand shaped like a pistol.

Perry furrowed his brows and gave the boy a stern look. Then he exited into the frosty pre-dusk, banging the door shut behind him.

He set off, skirting the safety fence and then descending toward the shore. He reached the edge of the lake and hesitated. What had possessed his son-in-law to go fishing, leaving René alone? Perry began the trajectory toward the ice hut, intent on having stern words with Xavier about his responsibilities. But within a few feet, Perry stopped, becoming worried about the stability of the ice. Against his better judgement he continued however, following Xavier's path, marked by the recent footsteps in the fresh snow. Startlingly, Perry discerned smaller prints as well. Had Xavier been foolish enough to take René out here too? Had he been tanked enough to do something so idiotic? The lack of common sense of his son-in-law never ceased to amaze Perry.

When he was within reach of the small hut he called: "Xavier!" and then "Halloooo?" but his greetings were met with silence.

When Perry got to the outside of the hut he was surprised to find it dark and cold. The door was jammed shut. He pushed and it gave way with a groan. He entered the room, so eerily still. As his eyes adjusted to the lack of light, the hair stood up on the back of his neck. A dark shape perched on an old stool.

"Xavier! What's going on?" But Perry got no answer from the immobile man seated nearby, so Perry moved in for a closer look.

He gasped to see his son-in-law hunched over, his clothing covered in hoar frost. "What the—!" When Perry touched Xavier's shoulder it did not budge. He was frozen solid, his whole body rigid, as though he were an ancient human, discovered on a frozen mountain top. Even more horrific were the blackened stumps on

Xavier's hands, the damage from frostbite. Most of his fingers were gone—*Xavier was gone*.

The shock blew through Perry like a blast of arctic air. The whole thing didn't make sense to him. Hadn't he just spoken to his son-in-law only a few hours ago? What had possessed him to drag himself to this shack halfway across the lake? Clearly, he had not come to fish, as there was no rod or bucket or other gear in sight. Perry's thoughts raced, although he knew it was too late for Xavier, he realized he needed to alert the authorities right away. Poor René. His family was disintegrating all around him. Perry wondered how he would break the news to the dear little boy—and, of course, to Anna—*poor Anna*.

He felt a hot wave of shame just then thinking about how he had betrayed her at the hospital. He had not believed her, but she had been right to be concerned about Xavier.

* * *

Just at the moment his grandfather was worrying about him, René was thinking of his grandfather too.

The child perched on a chair by the windowsill, looking out into the silky swirl of snow, the meringue-covered lake, his dark black eyes zeroing in on the small grey fishing hut, barely visible now in the encroaching gloom of night. But there was nothing sad or worried in the child's expression, only the gleam of something evil in those dark eyes.

* * *

PHLAMMM!

The door banged shut behind him. Perry wheeled about. The hut was suddenly cast in darkness. He fumbled around and found the handle, turning it forcefully, but it would not budge. He tried again, twisting with all his might. No luck. He put his shoulder against the door and slammed against it, but again the door resisted, as though somehow it had been locked and reinforced from the outside. Perry was both puzzled and frightened. He pondered his next move, his heavy breathing the only sound against the eerie quiet.

The hut creaked softly, as though settling from a change in temperature. A soft wind whistled through the cracks in the walls.

Suddenly a calamity of shrieks and crashes broke the near silence. The wood frame of the hut strained as the ice below shifted, suddenly disintegrating, breaking up with a burst of cataclysmic force. A joist splintered and fragments of wood shot out and scattered around the room. Then the entire shack began to tilt to one side, throwing Perry off balance.

He yelped as the chair with the frozen body catapulted against him, pinning him to one corner. He thrashed in revulsion and pushed off the leaden weight, tossing the corpse to the side, the sound of brittle limbs cracking from the impact.

Midst the shifting and collapse of the hut, Perry pawed the insides of his coat, looking for his phone. With one hand he braced himself, while the other searched his pockets, finally locating the device. With shaky fingers, he hit 911 on the speed dial. The screen cast a green glow on the structure falling around him. It was a death trap.

"911. What is your emergency? Police, Fire or Ambulance?"

Perry grunted and gasped, barely getting out the basics. "Ambulance, I'm sinking."

"Ambulance?"

"I'm on Lake Mikwam! Ice breaking—fishing hut's falling!"

"Could you repeat that? Wigwam?"

"MIKWAM! Near the Durand house! I'm gonna drown—"

"What's your name?"

The shack fell over, and Perry slid toward the open water. In his scramble to grab onto something, he let his phone drop. It tumbled into that dark abyss: the hole in the lake. In the last seconds before the phone's power shut off, he saw the bright screen, a message with a red backdrop and the letters S.O.S. His lifeline was disappearing below the surface.

*   *   *

Anna pressed the key card on the security pad next to the exit. She heard the click as the lock was released. She pushed outward, her arm against the glass doors, directing her gaze forward, trying to keep her gait steady.

There was a strange buzzing in her brain, like a thousand hornets butting up against the receptors, bouncing on her synapses. She was wired to the point of being overloaded like a circuit box ready to arc. And all the while she told herself to move calmly. She made straight for the elevators but rather than hitting the button for the main floor and making a run for it, she hit the 4th instead—a floor where she was familiar with every nook and cranny. First, she would pick up some essentials like clothing and footwear.

She knew she had to get back to the house before Munson killed off the rest of her family. She had to get there before her dad arrived, but there was no way she could make it on time if she drove. Not to mention the difficulty of finding and stealing a car. It would be much easier and faster to fly.

CHAPTER THIRTY-ONE

Above and Below

It was a marvellous thing this card key—from a doctor no less. She was a lawyer and a doctor, thought Anna wryly. Dr. Walter's card key hidden in her waistband was the only thing that prevented her anger from escalating into a nuclear rage when she learned of her father's condemnation of her. How could he have done that?

Anna, now sporting scrubs and a coat, rose to Level 8, the rooftop, with a medical cooler and a clipboard in hand.

From the glassed-in control centre, Anna could see there was a chopper idling on the tarmac. She could tell it had been out recently. The rotors were clear of ice, and condensation appeared on the port windows.

The desk was occupied with a couple of E.M.T.s chatting with the dispatcher. Anna exited onto the tarmac. She spotted someone she thought might be the pilot, and jogged toward him.

"For a heart transplant patient. At the General."

He paused, caught off guard, and Anna guessed this was not how they usually did this.

"I don't have it on my manifest," he said.

"There's some computer glitch. It has to get there, a.s.a.p.," Anna said, holding up the cooler. "They've got a patient waiting on this!" The wind buffeted the grey parka she wore unzipped. She had grabbed it from the back of a chair in a waiting room, the thin green scrubs had been scooped from a laundry hamper. Her skin crawled thinking about the dark burgundy stains, but realized it gave her the look of a genuine surgeon or medic, and gave the impression of a situation too urgent for her to have changed out of operating room garb.

"Give me a second," he said.

"Please hurry," she urged.

The pilot took the clipboard from Anna and strode past her back into the command centre.

She did not accompany him but instead turned and darted toward the helicopter. She hopped in and closed the door behind her. She dumped the cooler on the floor and slid into the pilot's seat, immediately lighting up the controls, bringing the engines up with a whirring and wheezing commotion.

It was coming back to her now, the months of training in Portage La Prairie. The pilot's license she had just missed out on. Another life opportunity she had blown.

She kept the cabin lights low until she was ready to take off. The rotors picked up speed. The engines reverberated with energy. The bird was ready to fly. Out of the corner of her eye she saw the pilot emerge from the rooftop control centre.

The throttle trembled as she burst upward. The confused pilot began gesturing to her, jogging around the contours of the landing pad. Anna saw him wave the clipboard, the falsified documents fluttering in the draft created by the plane's lift-off. And then she was aloft, the real pilot gone from her sightline, and soon out of her mind as well.

She was flying high now—in all senses of the word. Exhilarated to be piloting this beast. Glad to be free of the confines of the hospital. And buzzed by the powerful drug cocktail she had been fed these last few days. Nobody was going to keep her down, try to tell her what she could or couldn't do.

Getting her bearings from the hospital was not too difficult but once she was away from the city lights, she realized the trajectory toward Lake Mikwam would be challenging as the illuminated landmarks were fewer and farther between. Everything looked so different from above.

Thankfully there was a little bit of moonlight that reflected off the ponds and exposed water, rivers breaking free in the spring thaw. It was a stunning vista. For a second, no longer aware of the thundering vibration of the chopper, she could imagine she was a dark beautiful bird, a hawk gliding home.

The last ice age had scraped and gouged this rocky surface, leaving pockets of glittering water, and rugged thatches of spruce and pine, often solitary, scraggly trees that leaned from the force of the wind, their roots barely hanging onto the thin layer of soil.

The radio crackled, and a stern voice ordered her back to the landing pad at SBH but she ignored the request, trying to tune out the authoritarian command, but the voice returned again, each time more urgent and threatening. Her own self-doubt crept in mixed in with the verbal assaults from the radio.

As the power of the psychotropic meds faded, she was able to reflect with dizzying insight on her actions. She gasped inwardly at how in a few short days she had set into motion the destruction of all she had worked for in her life. All her achievements, her reputation, the pillars of her social standing, all were in shambles. This latest folly—stealing a helicopter—a hospital transport vehicle of all things—was an insane attempt to get back to the house. But her gut told her it was the right thing to do.

When she arrived, she was not sure what she hoped to accomplish exactly. How do you fight a monster who is the embodiment of a six-year-old? Yet fight him she would, to shield her father, and Xavier, and the next person—for there would certainly be other victims, as there had been many in the past.

She was certain Munson's list was long, and still growing.

* * *

Anna missed the turn-off from the highway onto Lake View Road, the speed at which she was travelling now, compared with her usual driving distances, messed with her sense of timing. She realized she had overshot but simply corrected herself and headed further north and east.

She was coming up on Lake Mikwam. She recognized the cabins and cottages that straddled the skinny section of land between the road and the water at the south end. She mouthed a silent thank you to all the neighbours who had porch lights or pole lights that cast golden swatches on the otherwise dark terrain. They guided her way, counting down until she got to the Durand-Docstedder home.

And now she was there. She hovered nearby, noticing four vehicles: their two, and a truck that was probably her Dad's and another… they had company. Yet strangely no one emerged to see what the noise was about.

Anna let the chopper edge eastward as she considered where to land, finally opting for the road.

As she let the beast down, there was a uniform spray of snow all around. When she shut off the motor, she could still hear the echo of the chopper's whirring and whining in her head. But no wait, that was not it—those were sirens—distant sirens. Could it mean that they were after her, already? Or was there an emergency elsewhere?

Anna rushed out of the chopper and raced down the driveway.

* * *

Minutes earlier, Corbeau had rounded the lake and turned onto the Durand-Docstedder property, skidding to a stop in the driveway. He pointed the car toward the lake, and directed his high beams forward. It would help other first responders whom he expected would arrive soon.

The dispatcher had been vague about the exact emergency, something near Lake Mikwam, someone sinking in water near the Durand house, she said, but didn't have more than that. The call was cut off yet she felt the request was genuine and that someone should check it out. Corbeau was nearby so he volunteered to look into the mystery. Then Corbeau got another call.

It was his supervisor. "Anna Docstedder's gone missing from St. Boniface Hospital."

"Seriously? How long ago?"

"Less than an hour. They didn't call it in right away because they weren't sure she had left the hospital. Then not fifteen minutes ago the hospital reported a chopper stolen. A woman matching Docstedder's description took off with it."

"No shit!" Corbeau shook his head. "If it's her, I bet she's heading this way. She wants to get to her son. She's bonkers."

"See what you can find. Back-up is on the way."

Corbeau approached the house on foot. He regretted not having his service revolver with him. His other regret being his unfortunate choice of footwear.

The stoop was icy and had not been cleared. Corbeau tried the front door but it was dark, and there was no response. Then he saw a light in the back area and proceeded there.

He found the side door unlocked and he let himself in, calling for Mr. Durand. He had seen Anna's husband on the news following the accident on the lake but had never met him. At that moment, he couldn't recall his first name.

"Hello! Police!"

The house was frigid almost as though the furnace was off. The fireplace was burnt out. It was dead quiet. No sign of anyone. Suddenly, a blast of deafening sound hit Corbeau. His heart stopped for a beat and he ducked instinctively. The television was turned to maximum volume, broadcasting a crime show. Corbeau found the remote and shut off the offensive noise. Suddenly it was quiet again.

"Hey, Dale," came a child's voice from behind him. Corbeau nearly jumped out of his skin. *What the fuck!*

He veered around. Staring at him was a small boy, black eyes glistening with mischievous delight. This presumably was

Anna's son—the miracle boy—the kid Anna wanted to kill. Corbeau was of the same mind right now. *What a brat*, he thought.

He tried to steady his voice. "Is your Dad home?"

René paused for a long while. There was something snakelike and cunning in his delayed response. "Upstairs," he said at last.

Corbeau scanned the main floor and spotted the stairs off to the right. "Is he sleeping?" Corbeau looked for a response from the child but only got a blank stare. Tired of getting no answer, the detective decided to see for himself. He was uneasy about René's presence. He had this insane urge to cuff him and put him in the back of the car while he looked around. But that would not likely sit well with his bosses. He could only imagine their reaction to such a decision.

There was something so insolent and defiant about René's bearing, Corbeau could not help but feel that the boy was up to something, not an innocent prank but an act of real malevolence. He exuded such a feeling of evil. The detective could not shake it. It was illogical. It was only a vibe, and vibes were something detectives were trained to ignore. And usually Corbeau would do just that, dismiss it or tuck it away on a shelf as something interesting but he could not today.

Corbeau tentatively walked toward the staircase. But as he started to take a few steps up, a voice came into his head. *"Get out, now!"* it urged.

Rather than proceed up the stairs, Corbeau swung over the railing, bounded to the floor, landing on his feet. He pivoted and turned briefly to glance at the boy. Corbeau was chilled to see the kid was smirking, as though amused by the detective's fear or perhaps from the knowledge that Corbeau didn't stand a chance.

The cop ran for the front door and burst out, his first step on the unprotected porch sending him into a tailspin. The surface was so slippery with ice that Corbeau's courtroom dress shoes had no traction. Corbeau flipped, landed on his back, and rotated painfully on his spine. He then thudded down the concrete steps and stopped at last, terminating at an odd angle. His head back, his body strangely limp. His arms and legs floppy, twisted in an awkward pose. Yet his eyes were open, just enough to see the dagger point of a long heavy icicle clinging to the eavestrough directly above. Refracted in the frozen layers, were multiple images of René, who now stood in the doorway.

Corbeau no longer wanted to watch but was surprised to find he could not shut his eyes. The realization came to him as he stared at the manifold faces of evil, his thoughts travelling just as quickly as ever, even though all his physical movements were frozen. He suddenly grasped that he was paralyzed. *I am at the mercy of this monster!*

A cold draft came from the inside of the house and settled over the detective. If he could have shivered he would have. The organ that is the skin still sensed temperature, however. And nerves could still feel pain. And the brain could comprehend dread. Corbeau picked up on a familiar *whoop whoop* sound. A helicopter was approaching. And also sirens, faintly, nearing where he lay helpless. *Back-up was on its way!*

He was starting to think he would be alright, hope was replacing dread, when a drop of water landed on his face. A cold, icy drip that ran from the bridge of his nose to the corner of his right eye, pooling there like a tear, as though he were already mourning the sad outcome of his life.

Above, some force was working to loosen the icicle, freeing it from its base, until it was not attached by much at all, and gravity took over, sending the heavy ice weapon with the razor-like point downwards, dropping like a guillotine—into Corbeau.

*   *   *

Where was everybody? Anna wanted to know. How could she show up in a chopper and have no one come running to find out what was going on? Seeing the vehicles in the yard, there had to be at least four persons somewhere on the property: Xavier, her dad, René, and—guessing from the black Crown Vic parked out front— a detective. Presumably someone recently arrived, based on the still-warm hood. But most importantly, where was Munson?

She ran toward her home. Her stolen boots were ill-fitting and she had to take care not to let them slide off her bare feet. Rather than go directly into the house she circled it, trying to get a sense of where everyone was. There were a few lights on in the house, yet she could see no one through the uncovered windows. Treading across the front lawn, between the pine trees and bare maples, she spotted a shape on the front steps. A figure sprawled at the foot of the landing. Upon closer inspection, she saw that it was a man, his face familiar.

"Oh, God!" she gasped. Corbeau! What had happened to him? A glittering spear of ice protruded from his eye socket. Blood spilled from the wound. She recoiled at first, then stepped forward to feel for a pulse. Miraculously he was still alive.

"Hang in there, man. I'll be back," she promised.

* * *

The ice hut teetered and wobbled. It took in water from all sides. It leaned treacherously over the widening chasm of open water. Perry was caught in a corner. There was no exit, it seemed, except through the bottom of the hut that hung over the lake.

"Help! Somebody!" he shouted. He repeated his cries. He could only hope the emergency dispatcher had taken his call seriously and could decipher his appeal. He shouted for help repeatedly, until his throat was raw. Then he paused, sensing a vibration in the air. Bat wings. Echolocation. A helicopter!

"Thank, God!" They were coming for him. He listened and waited, thinking it was no use shouting until the bird had landed. It would be no time now, before they found him. He hoped there was still enough light to see the hut on the lake.

* * *

Anna pushed a stepladder up against the back wall of the garage and retrieved the long box. Opening it she withdrew a shotgun. Holding the weapon to her side, she grabbed some cartridges and loaded the gun.

She descended the ladder and exited the garage, making her way quietly toward the side door. It was as though someone had been waiting for her arrival. The door was ajar. She saw wet footprints on the floor but otherwise there was no sign of a disturbance. The room seemed unoccupied.

She tiptoed toward the den, eyeing René's favourite hiding spots, the couch cushions, behind the chair and inside the storage ottoman that sometimes served as a coffee table. She poked around, lifting blankets and opening doors. There was no sign of him.

She found Flo's serpentine beads and instinctively grabbed them and threw them around her neck. The string of cool polished stones calmed her a little. She was about to move upstairs when his voice came at her like crushed ice thrown at her face.

"Hi, Mommy," he said in a little boy timbre, all saccharine and lovable. "I missed you, Mommy."

She felt a damp fog invade her brain. She was at war with her heart. The part that implored her to *drop the gun and hug her boy*, fought with the part of her that insisted this presence before her was just a mirage. Lies, lies, and deception, she repeated to herself.

A chill air unfurled from René's aura and slunk toward her like a slothful mist, lumbering, yet steady. She quivered as the mass came upon her and began to take hold, like an icy blade held to her throat.

"Don't hurt me, Mommy," the child whimpered.

But almost as an echo, she also heard Munson's voice, *"Put the gun down, bitch."*

The order made her brace the weapon even tighter. She raised it slightly and aimed the barrel at her kid's chest as he inched forward slightly. She gulped as she suddenly noticed the tiny indentation above his left eyebrow. A scar from falling off a swing set. She remembered that accident. *That was real, wasn't it? That made him real, didn't it? He's not a ghost. Not a shapeshifter.*

"Mommy, you're making me scared!" René whimpered as tears ran down his cheeks and his bottom lip quivered. He looked so pitiful.

She found herself crying as well, yet she tried to stand tall, and stay firm.

The sweet frightened pleas from René were at odds with the way he inched ever closer. The contradiction was what finally compelled her to pull the trigger. The bullet blasted forth but when it hit, it had no impact. It was like a small stone tossed at a block of ice. The bullet pinged and fell to the ground. She shot at him again but with the same result.

She saw him snicker, just before he lunged for her. He arrived within a second, clutching her, the small hands so powerful, his grip so strong, like that of a man, a seasoned killer.

"René, stop it!"

He yanked at her legs and toppled her. She kicked at him and broke free, but he was quickly upon her once more. In the scuffle, René pulled the stone necklace from her neck and the string broke and the beads scattered. His hands encircled her throat. He hung on, pressing against her trachea. These small hands had killed before. She floundered, feeling the deep cold grip her, her breaths becoming shallower.

She glimpsed Flo's clay urn on the mantle. In a last desperate move, Anna bucked free and bolted for the mantle, grabbing the vase. She held it between her hands, and then with the greatest force she could muster, smashed it on top of his head. The pottery shards flew outward and the boy dropped with a thud, a cloud of gray powder misting him like volcanic ash.

A scream erupted from Anna, echoing through the empty house. The force of the vibrations hit the panes of glass and made them quiver.

CHAPTER THIRTY-TWO
Baptism of Ice

It was an automatic impulse. Like an instinctual homing device inscribed in her DNA. She was going with the Flo. The guiding spirit her aunt had left with her. Auntie was drawing her toward the water. It was telling her to go toward the primeval gap, the hole into which evil must be thrown back, like an ancient Mayan offering.

Pumped with adrenaline, Anna lifted her child to her chest. It felt like he weighed nothing at all. But she knew she was carrying a man—two hundred and forty pounds of pure deadly anger. Tattooed and scarred, bitter and vengeful, muscles primed to kill.

The boy-man, the killer-kid, the Munson-like child, was quiet. His lips half-parted as though he were asleep. His soft silky skin was soot-covered. Like a papal dusting, ashes to ashes, Anna thought. As she studied her baby, her first-born, she was surprised to see splotches of wet in the gray powder. Surprised to realize that she was crying. Rivulets of tears were flowing down her cheeks and landing on her little René, muddying the waters.

She paused and caught herself. *What the hell am I doing!*

As she headed down the slope and onto the ice, looking in the darkness for the hollow where weeks earlier her boy had lain, she heard sirens approaching and then the *whoop whoop* of a helicopter, getting stronger. For a second her mind went back in time, to the other terrible night, not so long ago, when all had fallen apart. How to undo the past? It was too late, she knew, but she had to try.

The light from the helicopter was jumping around her, like the searchlight from a watchtower.

She picked up the pace, stumbling with the dead weight of her child. *So heavy, for such a little boy.*

Her eyes scanned the bumpy surface of the lake. She saw ahead of her, a dark area, likely open water, and she made for it.

"Put the boy down," came a voice from a loudspeaker. "Stop, or we will shoot!"

Out of her peripheral vision, she saw them, armed officers surging toward her. Strangely, it made her think back to their game of tag, she, Xavier and René. The zig-zagging around the unfinished great room. It would have made her smile had she not been so terrified.

She saw them kneel on the shoreline and saw others navigate the patches of unstable ice. They were all on thin ice, physically and metaphorically. The melting lake surface was like a dangerous lace doily.

"Stop! Stop Now! Drop him!" They shouted.

"Three! Two!"

It occurred to her that she had often used that very same countdown technique to warn René and it had generally worked well. She had found it effective to slow down between the two and the one, to give René more time to reconsider. However, the police did not follow that same approach to timing.

"One!"

"Freeze!" How ironic Anna thought, that is all she had been doing for a while now. *Freezing—freezing her butt off.*

But time was running out and she could not stop. Instead she pushed her body forward in another burst. She sped like a deer fleeing a wolf. She flew in spite of her feet being dragged down by slush and melting ice.

Phhtff! Something stung her arm. Out of the corner of her eye she saw fairy-like plumes spilling from her jacket sleeve. Odd, she mused. She was snowing.

Crack! Anna's steps faltered. The ice was failing, collapsing, the surface shifting like tectonic plates. She balanced on ice floes that reminded her of surfboards, dipping and arching unsteadily. She leapt forward into an area where there was less and less ice and more open water. Knowing she was doomed, she nevertheless hoped others could be saved and so plunged headlong into the water, holding the boy to her.

Aaagh! She was hit with a numbing full-body assault. The bracing purity of it! There was no more of this wondering if she was cold. She was finally certain of it.

She gasped as René's eyes opened and bubbles spilled from his mouth and nose. He looked at her with alarm, suddenly trying to wrestle free. She clamped down on him as he struggled and struggled. She was not letting him go—no more chances for the killer.

CHAPTER THIRTY-THREE
Come-uppance

Snow fell on the windshield of the green Ford. Tires spun on the icy road and exhaust billowed out in the cold air.

Brent McKay, dark hair, bespectacled, glanced at his cell phone while waiting for the light to change. He rummaged around for a charger and plugged it in. As the car idled, he fidgeted. He switched on the radio and upon hearing the first few words of the news story, turned up the volume, his body tensing as he listened.

Some very tragic events at Lake Mikwam on Thursday. Police still don't know what the motive was, whether there was a domestic dispute or one of the parties had a mental breakdown. The main suspect, a woman from Glace Bay, has been recovering in hospital but will be appearing in court this morning. Here's more on that story from Jennifer Hawkins.

Yes, that's right Marilee. A thirty-eight-year-old woman is appearing in court today in relation to an attempted murder of a child at Lake Mikwam on Thursday. Police are still examining the circumstances surrounding two other deaths and a serious injury to a member of law enforcement also around the same property at the lake. Police spokesperson Jaime Bala says the authorities may still press additional charges pending the outcome of their investigation, but there is still a lot of work to be done to sort out what happened this past March 11.

Prior to the attack on the child, a seventy-three-year-old Point Walker man drowned when his ice hut sank and forced him into the lake. Police are neither confirming nor denying a relationship to the others involved.

As the details of the report were relayed, McKay leaned his head back and sighed heavily. He was lost in a dream space when the

174

sound of a horn brought him back to reality. He lifted his foot off the brakes and let the car glide forward. Only partially aware of his surroundings, he piloted the vehicle as though in a trance. The strange news story so preoccupied him.

> *The 45-year-old veteran detective received paralyzing injuries. He had been called to the rural dwelling to do a welfare check on a local resident who was ice fishing. It was not certain whether the detective's injuries were as a result of accident or foul play.*

McKay slowed until he came to a large parking garage. It was directly opposite his destination, the Lavin County Court House. He pulled through a gate for the parkade and rolled down his window, reaching with his long arms—those limbs, that were once the ticket to a free education thanks to a basketball scholarship, were now used to tap the electronic parking pass. The gate lifted and McKay drove in.

The gates of hell, he thought. The garage was one of those gloomy decaying structures, with black mould and water stains streaking the cement walls. The gloom permeated the interior of his car.

It was a busy morning and there were no spots available on the main level. McKay pulled his car around the corner to the next floor and paused behind someone in a small compact car who appeared to be leaving.

McKay tapped out a number on his phone. A woman's voice uttered a tentative hello.

"Maggie, it's Brent."

"Thank, God."

"Why?"

"I didn't want it to be another reporter."

"Seriously?"

"Yes, they seem to know. They're fishing. I've been getting calls all morning."

Honk!

McKay glanced in the rear-view mirror at the driver behind him and noted the line up of cars around the bend in the ramp. He made a move to go past the vehicle with the rear lights lit up but just then it made a move to reverse.

"Come on!" Brent growled.

"What?" Maggie said, taken aback by McKay's outburst.

"Sorry, Maggie, I'm trying to get into a parking spot."

"At the courthouse?"

"Yeah. I'll call you back."

"Call my cell."

That reporters were calling the law office, meant they had likely gotten hold of details about the incident at Lake Mikwam—details that were supposed to have been suppressed under a publication ban. If reporters had ferreted out all this, McKay could only imagine what was on the internet. It was probably going to go viral, further hurting Anna's chances for a fair hearing.

As the honking behind him continued, McKay felt blood pounding in his temples. The driver in his rear-view mirror had no idea how close he was to being pummelled by someone pushed too far. McKay considered just driving on. There were likely other spots on the upper floors but he needed to get into the courthouse.

He was worn out after a sleepless night of mulling over the things that Anna had told him. She hadn't made much sense in their last few meetings at the hospital and McKay wanted to try to speak to her again before the hearing. There were things he wanted to better understand. Not so much for today's court appearance but to get it straight in his mind.

How did one explain the catastrophe at the lake? The tragedy of epic proportions: the deaths of Perry and Xavier, the attempted murder of René, and the horrible injuries suffered by Corbeau. That couldn't all be on Anna.

The whole thing was incomprehensible. But one thing was clear and that was that Anna had gone off her rocker. The only way out was to get her to plead guilty by insanity.

Beautiful, brilliant Anna, he thought. *What a shame.*

McKay wondered if he would get a chance to talk to the kid. René Durand was already released from hospital. He had apparently suffered no ill effects from being dumped in freezing water for the second time this winter. McKay idly wondered if the boy had possibly built up some resilience to icy temperatures much like polar bear swimmers.

At last the car in front was backing out, but ever so slowly. McKay reversed a few more inches to make room, prompting more honking from behind.

"Fuck me!" sputtered McKay. He'd had enough. He threw open his door, burst out and raced to the car behind him. Despite the haze of his own anger and the smeared and salt streaked windows, he thought he noticed the driver shrink back a little.

McKay pounded on the dusty window until finally, the glass was lowered a couple of inches.

"McKay?"

Anna's lawyer was gobsmacked. He froze, slowly dropping his arm.

"Your honour," he offered by way of a greeting.

The driver of the antiquated and slightly rusty Volvo was none other than Justice Felix Mallard, a normally pleasant man who now seemed both frightened and irritated at the same time.

"Are you going to take that spot, McKay?"

The lawyer felt his face redden. He stammered. "No, why don't you go ahead and grab it."

"You sure?" asked the judge curtly.

"Yes," blurted McKay, before hurrying back to his vehicle and speeding off, trying to create as much distance between himself and the magistrate, knowing full well it would be futile—they would face each other in court that morning.

CHAPTER THIRTY-FOUR

She Talk Crazy Talk

Anna's hands were shaking. They had pumped her so full of Thorazine, the go-to anti-psychotic, that her senses were dulled. The previous night the chemicals had effectively shut her up so the rest of the jailhouse occupants could get some sleep. But this morning the drug was not anywhere strong enough to suppress her mad ramblings, her conviction that a killer was on the loose.

McKay felt a heaviness in his heart as he looked at Anna's neglected appearance. Her fingers rested on his arm as her body leaned heavily into him, the grogginess depriving her of control over her posture. She whispered into his ear, her breath reeking. White film coated the edges of her mouth.

McKay was repelled both by her statement and her condition. "Excuse me?" he said weakly. He had heard her clearly but could not fully comprehend her words.

"You got to stop him," she repeated. "He has Lance's tattoos. Where does a kid get tattoos? Explain that to me, Brent."

Still reeling from the parking lot encounter, and on borrowed energy after his sleepless night, McKay tried to remain calm. But the outlandish statements coming from Anna—his respected colleague—were so disturbing it was impossible to remain immune to them.

"He killed them, he froze the baby, he killed Auntie Flo."

"Anna, please. We'll talk about this after the hearing. I just need you to plead 'not guilty' and we'll take it from there."

"Now they're telling me I can't speak to Xav." Her face crumpled with grief. Tears welling in her eyes. "Is he dead too?" Brent caught his breath as he studied her devastation. How could anyone say she was responsible?

"How did it happen, Brent?"

McKay worried she was on the verge of hysteria. The realization of all she had lost was building in her and she was near bursting.

"Anna, I'm sorry," McKay sighed. He hadn't wanted Anna to know just yet but, somehow, she had found out that her husband had passed away too.

"How?"

The lawyer shook his head. "I don't know, Anna. I'm sorry." He grabbed her hand and looked at her in the eyes. "Anna, all you need to remember is 'not guilty,' okay?"

* * *

The deputy called out "Oyez, oyez." The courtroom attendees were roused and moved to stand. McKay helped Anna to her feet as Judge Mallard entered, his robes giving him an air of seriousness that was missing when McKay had seen him earlier that morning.

"My father too."

"Shhh!"

But Anna could not help herself. She blurted out "He killed Dad. He killed all of them."

Judge Mallard fixed his gaze on the attorney and his unkempt client. McKay felt the sweat bead around his forehead.

"The man in my son's body is the real murderer. He's going to kill someone else!"

Judge Mallard slammed the gavel down.

"Dale knows about the other rapes and murders."

"Quiet!" McKay hissed.

Anna was silent at last. It was as though she suddenly realized where she was and remembered the sanctity of the courtroom. The rules of respect and order returned to her.

"Your honour, if I may, I'd like to approach the bench," said McKay, flushed with embarrassment.

"You may come forward."

Before McKay stepped away, Anna grabbed his arm, "Brent, you got to stop the kid because he will kill again. Don't let him get away with it!"

* * *

"She was with it enough to steal a helicopter and fly it to her house," interjected Bjorn Samuelsohn, the sandy-haired crown prosecutor. "Besides, she's not denying she tried to kill her son."

"In her mind, it was not her son."

"She's an intelligent woman who is abusing her knowledge of the law—"

"Anna," interrupted McKay, "Ms. Docstedder, has been through a great deal. She suffered a miscarriage, the loss of her

179

husband, her father, her aunt, not to mention the trauma of her son's accidental hypothermia a few months ago. In my opinion, she's having a mental breakdown."

"Besides, we don't know exactly what happened," McKay explained. "The crime scene extends over a large area, including the lake. It involves some very unusual circumstances. The investigators can't make sense of what really occurred out there. Anna could have been fleeing a violent situation in the home."

"She wasn't fleeing," Samuelsohn exclaimed in exasperation. "She showed up in a helicopter!"

"She was concerned for the safety of her husband and tried to get help from 911 before she left Glace Bay."

"Your honour, reports are that she battered her husband."

"Anna's not fit to stand trial," insisted McKay.

Mallard cleared his throat. "At this moment, I would have to agree with Brent. But the charges are very serious. I suggest we put this matter over until the police investigation is complete."

CHAPTER THIRTY-FIVE
Second Chances

Sharla watched the little boy with her own two children, four-year-old Bevan and seven-year-old Kyle. René's dark eyes revealed neither joy nor sadness and that was puzzling to her. He had lost everything, including—for a while—life itself, yet he showed no outward signs of disturbance. Could it be that he was in a state of shock, and his emotions were suppressed?

The three kids played harmoniously ensconced in a debris field of Lego that stretched from one end of the den to the other. Half-formed structures and vehicles jutted from the uneven expanse of plastic blocks. Small fingers picked and sorted through the collection, searching for the right piece. The child's play continued peacefully for the better part of the afternoon, with little conversation, other than "Hey, that's mine" or the simulated sound of motors revving.

Sharla's mind wandered to the news stories and the crazy rumours. She tried to reconcile them with the picture of peace and serenity on outward display. This little guy seemed so calm. How much tragedy could a kid take before buckling under? His father, his grandfather and great-aunt were gone. His mother locked away in a mental hospital. Yet there was no hint of any suffering in the child's demeanour. Was he hiding it, keeping it all bottled up?

Sharla thought about the woman who tried to kill her own child. What had scrambled her mind so badly that she would think to do that? Especially in a way that mirrored her son's near-death a few months earlier?

From her own experience as a social worker, Sharla knew not to make assumptions. But she would have to work hard to stay neutral toward this person that she instinctively wanted to hate, and who was reviled by anyone and everyone who had heard about the case. She hoped to speak to Anna Docstedder at some point, to hear her version of events, but that would wait. For now, Sharla was focussed on giving their new foster child a stable and supportive home.

Rather than split the kids up in different bedrooms, Sharla and her husband, Matt, decided to put all three boys together in one room. The idea of having René sleep all on his own seemed too harsh for the newly arrived visitor. What if he had nightmares? The boys' room would be crowded but at least it would be cosy.

With only a day's notice they borrowed a bed and squeezed it in alongside the two other singles. She outfitted it with fresh sheets—albeit a mismatched set—cartoon monsters on the bottom and colourful stripes on top. The pillowcase was a faded purple shade. Sharla cleared out some of Bevan and Kyle's toys to make space for the few things that René had brought with him.

As she unpacked the personal items that came along with René, she arranged some in a couple of empty dresser drawers. For the rest, she found two clear plastic bins into which she placed René's toys and knick-knacks.

Whoever had put together the boy's suitcase must have been distracted based on the odd collection of items contained within. There were well-thumbed junior reader books, stuffed animals and toy vehicles, but also some carpentry magazines, construction tools and bits of wood. As she sorted through the things, her fingers caught on a sharp edge. She pulled out a carving—a woodsman holding an axe. Seeing red droplets smearing it, she realized it was from a cut on her hand. *How annoying.*

She left the statue and went off in search of a bandage. As she rummaged through the medicine cabinet, blood splashed in elongated streaks into the white porcelain sink. With her left hand, she unpeeled a bandage, awkwardly applying it to the oozing cut. *Why hadn't someone come up with an easier way to dress small wounds?*

After cleaning up the bloodstains in the washroom, Sharla returned to the bedroom intent on resuming the business of unpacking. Concerned about not having any sharp objects around, she decided to store the woodsman elsewhere, out of reach of small fingers. But when she returned, the woodsman had vanished. She searched briefly under the beds and in the corners of the room thinking it might have rolled away somewhere. But she had no luck in locating it.

Finally, she had to break off the search to get ready for dinner.

*   *   *

"What happened to your finger Mom?"

"It's nothing, Kyle."

"It's bleeding."

That was just like Kyle, so sensitive and always concerned for others. His green eyes took in the bulging red bandage and the smears of dried blood caked in the folds of Sharla's knuckles.

"You're right." Sharla looked helplessly at her husband, Matt. The tiny bandages were just not suitable for this gash. She held up her hand and his eyes widened.

"You giving me the finger?" he joked.

"That I am, Doc."

He was laughing as he walked toward a hall closet, where he extracted a rugged professional grade first-aid kit. Sharla readily admitted to all her girlfriends that the fact that Matt was a paramedic, was one of the reasons she had married him. She felt safer knowing that Matt could patch up any 'boo-boo.' In fact, over the years, Matt had saved their little family from several trips to the doctor's for minor scrapes and bruises, and even more importantly had helped deliver Bevan four years earlier when Sharla's labour had come on quickly and suddenly. From time to time, at parties, the gory details of how it all happened would be the subject of shocked amusement. Friends who had heard the tale several times before came to recognize small discrepancies and variations in the story but one thing stayed the same, that Bevan was born on the living room floor and he slipped into the world right into the arms of his father.

Sharla joined Matt at the kitchen counter where the efficient emergency medical technician unsnapped the plastic case and dove into the treasure of life-saving paraphernalia. In view of the curious gazes of their children and the visitor, Matt staunched the bleeding and dressed the cut. He was done in three minutes flat.

"That should do it," he said.

"Thanks sweetie," said Sharla, planting a kiss on her husband's cheek.

Sharla could swear that when she returned to the dinner table, René's expression had changed from one of bland disinterest to a sly smile. She felt it was not a smile that reflected shared amusement from Matt and Sharla's banter and their fun approach to problem solving. But the look was something else, something almost sinister, chilling even. She couldn't be sure. She felt it was odd but then the truth was she really didn't know the boy. Perhaps she was just imagining things.

*   *   *

Sharla and Matt Trager's Greek Revival home at 103 Hill Hurst Avenue was nestled in a pretty pocket of Glace Bay's historic Warren Park area, a neighbourhood dating back to the 18th century when prospectors had flocked to the region, discovering rich deposits of gold, zinc, iron and copper. The town soon became a supply point for the mines in the surrounding territory.

The wealthier founding families settled on the elevated area above the river flood plains. The city thrived for many years until the 1960s when key mining deposits had become depleted. Then the population waned and houses were abandoned.

But in recent years, the town had experienced an economic resurgence. Some of the statelier homes, like the Tragers' place, were restored while others remained rather neglected, their exteriors still marred by ugly additions and aluminum siding thoughtlessly slapped on, covering up worn but beautiful architectural details.

There was so much history here that the Warren Park area was sometimes referred to as War-P, for time warp. Preservationists and heritage home advocates fervently sought to prevent the destruction of old and storied properties. Not only were buildings protected under this umbrella, but also those phantoms of residents past.

That the War-P area was more haunted than anywhere else in Glace Bay was a given. The tumultuous gold rush days and frontier attitudes had led to plenty of premature and violent deaths, with many troubled spirits seeking to sort out justice for centuries afterwards.

But there was a brand new presence roaming about tonight, colliding with the more established spirits. It stirred up the ether and disturbed the air. It drew the rotten smell of sulphur from the boreholes and abandoned mining pits that lay all around.

There was a new ghost in town.

*　*　*

Kyle and Bevan were already in their p.js but René had been dawdling, likely because he was uncertain of the bedtime routine in his new home.

"Come on," Sharla said to him cheerfully. "Let's get you out of those duds." She wasn't going to bother with baths tonight, not until her cut finger had healed a little.

René stepped forward solemnly. He was compliant, raising his arms up to let her lift off his t-shirt, revealing a smooth boyish chest, unblemished by any markings of any sort. She studied his skin, unable to restrain the look of surprise that came over her face.

184

René seemed to notice it and quickly turned away. He slid his pajama top over his head. "I can do the rest myself," he said quietly.

Sharla nodded, forcing a smile. "You're an independent guy, I guess."

"I don't need help."

"No problemo." Sharla stood up unsteadily and walked toward a tallboy dresser painted fire truck red.

"We'll stash your stuff in these two drawers for now. The top two are for Kyle, and the bottom ones are for Bevan."

When René was done changing, he grabbed his dirty clothes and bunched them in his arms. "Where do I put these?"

"Oh, wow. You're well trained. My guys just toss everything on the floor." Sharla laughed. "But hey, maybe you'll teach Kyle and Bevan how to use that laundry hamper over there."

She pointed to a grey mesh tube decorated like an elephant. René tossed his clothes inside and closed the lid. It was almost like he had been trained at a military camp, thought Sharla.

* * *

It was a half hour later, after stories and bedtime kisses, that Sharla left the boys' room. She entered the master bedroom noiselessly. Her husband was reading something on his i-pad. When he saw her come in, he closed the cover and gave her a probing look.

"So?" he asked.

Sharla reached for a shawl and slid it over her shoulders. She exhaled as she plopped onto the bed.

"What do you think of our guest?"

Sharla thought for a moment, not wanting to jump right in with her misgivings. It was not in her character to present the glass as half-empty. "He's awfully quiet," was all she would offer as an assessment.

"That's cuz Bev and Kyle can't shut up."

"Not really." Sharla said as she drew closer to her husband. "They were kind of quiet tonight too. I think they're feeling out the new guy. Not wanting to overwhelm him, I suppose. Or maybe they're shy of him."

"Is something the matter?" Matt asked.

Sharla hesitated. "Wasn't he supposed to have something across his chest?

"Huh?"

"A tattoo? They made such a fuss about it."

"Really?"

"Well, there ain't nothing there, now."

"Oh."

"No marks, no scars. Nothing."

Matt eyes were fluttering. He was trying to stay awake. He yawned. "Maybe it was just a rumour," he said.

"I guess so."

Matt slid his reading glasses off, setting them on the bedside table. He turned off the lamp near him and settled lower into bed, pulling the duvet up over his shoulders. In a moment, he was fast asleep.

Although Sharla was exhausted she knew she would not be able to fall asleep as easily. She sat, staring ahead, deep in thought. A small furrow appeared across her forehead. In her mind's eye she could see him now. The small silent child with the strange smile and the dark unreadable eyes.

She became aware of the tension in her spine, her body's alert stance as though anticipating danger, the churning in the pit of her stomach. She tried to use logic and reason to explain away her apprehension. She was tired, of course. The boy's traumatizing history no doubt affected her mood. But all of that was behind him now, hopefully. He would not be returned to his mother. They would take care of him now and protect him from harm.

She knew it was irrational to be fearful, yet she could not help but feel uneasy. A flicker of panic raced through her.

What the hell had they done by letting this child into their home?

Sharla shivered involuntarily.

Acknowledgements

Polar bear hugs of appreciation go out to the many people who helped me get my book out: to all the writers group members in Toronto and Victoria: Bill Glassman, Brenda Craig, Carol Howard, Helmuth Mueller, Caroline Mufford, David Axelrad, Brigitte Talevski, et al.; to those who read the early drafts and gave me feedback: Gail Heaslip; Brian Bogaert; Jody Kinsey; Laura Elliott; Susana Albuquerque, Tony Golea, and Vicki Badger; to Danny Santos for inspiration, advice, and for creating a terrific book cover; and especially to my husband, Christo who assisted with formatting, proofing, editing, financial and moral support, and most of all—assembling my kneeling chair.

About the Author

Grace Bogaert is an award-winning screenwriter. Her first novel, *The Girl from Mena Creek*, has sold thousands of copies in Australia and has been translated into Chinese. She is currently researching a true-crime TV series. She divides her time between Vancouver Island and Toronto.